BULLET WORK

BULLET WORK

STEVE O'BRIEN

A & N Publishing

Washington, D.C.

First printing 2011

ISBN 978-0-9820735-9-9
LCCN 2010913972

**ATTENTION CORPORATIONS, UNIVERSITIES, COLLEGES,
AND PROFESSIONAL ORGANIZATIONS:** Quantity discounts are
available on bulk purchases of this book for educational, gift purposes,
or as premiums for increasing magazine subscriptions or renewals.
Special books or book excerpts can also be created to fit specific needs.
For information, please contact A & N Publishing,
3150 South Street, NW Suite 2F, Washington, D.C. 20007.

www.AandNpublishing.com

To Nick and Alex

PART ONE

OUT OF
THE GATE

◆　　◆　　◆

ONE SECOND CHANGED EVERYTHING.

One second altered fate for a lifetime.

The winner zigged; the loser zagged.

*One glance spotted true love, the next was
blocked by a city bus. The victor reacted; the
vanquished hesitated. Some called it luck. Some
called it a gift. But it was just the second.*

The second didn't care.

The second was relentless.

*The second was waiting. It always waited, like a
street mugger on a drizzly night. It waited in the
shadows, emotionless.*

The second was coming.

A series of seconds made a lifetime,
two billion or more. Five, maybe six of those
seconds altered one's life forevermore. Would
they come in the beginning or at the end?

The second wasn't fair; it wasn't orderly.
It would come on its own schedule, never
revealed until it was too late.

Who would be wealthy, who would be poor?
Who would have fame, who obscurity?
Who would be loved, who scorned?

One moment a man cruised along a
sun-drenched highway in a sporty convertible.
The second appeared, and the car careened
down the canyon wall, end over end,
awaiting the explosion.

The second was unpredictable.

The second was unforgiving.

There was no bargaining with the second. It
tested the strong and the weak alike.

Into each life the second would come, without
warning, without hint. It could not be avoided.
It could only be endured.

Life became the response to the second.

In hindsight the second could be seen, dissected,
and analyzed. Being in the second was like being
in the eye of the hurricane: eerily quiet and
completely beyond control. Only after the wind
subsided could the story be told.

This is that story.

Chapter 1

THE BOY was a ghostlike creature—just a child. He and the mare circled the shedrow. Dan spotted him for an instant as he crossed the end of the barn and disappeared around the far side.

He'd be back around in about two minutes.

Dan swirled the stale coffee in his Styrofoam cup, then splashed it on the ground. He yawned and stretched his arms.

The boy wasn't that different from most backside help. All lacked a certain degree of cleanliness. But there was something memorable about the boy. His limp wasn't like others. He'd rotate on one side and swing his leg on the off stride. The right side was near normal; the left, a carnival ride. Nothing too striking, Dan thought—if you spent enough time around 1,200-pound thoroughbreds, one way or another, you wound up with a limp.

His was different, though. Something caught Dan's attention. The boy wore a tattered T-shirt with ripped jeans, just a shade lighter. The cardboard edge of his baseball cap was peeking its way out between the red fabric. Maybe it was his size, so small in comparison to the mare. Perhaps it was that someone so tiny in comparison to the horse could possibly be in control of the relationship.

Walking hots was the lowest level of the food chain on the racetrack backside. Hotwalkers were just that, walkers. They stretched and paraded race horses either as the day's regimen of exercise or to cool out after returning from a workout or race.

A good hotwalker allowed the horse to take the walk, but he'd also pause when the horse wanted, let the horse graze when it wanted, and generally kept it from harm's way.

Hotwalking included talking, too. The best talked constantly. It calmed and reassured the horse. It also provided someone who would listen to the hotwalker.

Hotwalking was a safe harbor between dreams and reality. The steps didn't take either participant closer to anything; they were just steps.

The boy came around again. Fourteen, maybe fifteen, he was quickly obscured by the massive mare as he crossed the end of the shedrow again. Always walk on the inside. That way, the horse can see the hotwalker while being led into the turns.

Another odd thing—he held the shank in his left hand and had his right hand on the horse's neck, patting, stroking, sometimes just still. Certainly this wasn't the most comfortable way to walk a hot. A bond or closeness was apparent between the two, also not uncommon on the backside.

Dan watched as the boy went by again, then turned to walk toward the backside kitchen.

Jake Gilmore came out of his stable office and fell in step alongside Dan.

"Who's the kid?"

"Where?" Jake muttered while staring at something on his boots. He scrubbed the stubble on his neck and surveyed the area.

Gilmore stood just a shade over six feet. In the last decade of his fifty years, the once powerful upper body had melted around his waist, now supported by a sturdy leather belt and oversized rodeo buckle. Guy could give himself an appendectomy just sitting down wrong. Jake's eyes betrayed recent sleepless nights. For those like Jake who rose well before the sun each day, it wasn't out of the ordinary.

"The kid hotwalking the mare." Dan nodded toward the adjacent barn.

Jake looked over. "Don't know." Two or three steps later: "Just some kid." More silence. "Dick Latimer's barn."

"Recognize the mare?"

He looked over, turned back, and spat on the ground. "Nope. Latimer don't have nothing in his barn. Bunch a loose-legged claimers and two-year-olds he'll tear up 'fore the meet's over."

It didn't matter whether it was true or not. Trainers had to protect their relationships with owners and feed them information that prevented the owners from even thinking of moving their stock to a competitor's barn. It was all part of the game. Dan had learned the game.

Dan ran his fingers back through his short, dark hair and scratched the back of his neck. He was a good five inches shorter than Gilmore but significantly more athletic in tone. In contrast to the customary wardrobe on the backside, Dan's blue pinstriped suit pants and crisp, open-collared dress shirt said "owner." His well-groomed, youthful appearance said "new money." On the latter count conventional wisdom would be wrong.

A frenzy of activity dominated the backside from 5 A.M. to 11 A.M.; then, just as quickly, it became a sleepy little village. There was a system and rhythm to the chaos of the backside. Some horses going to the training track, jockeys and trainers discussed the latest workout. Jock agents hustled the latest Willie Shoemaker, just trying to get their boy a decent ride.

Vet vans parked in the roadway, with their doors hanging open, displaying the meds and appliances necessary to keep the warriors in the game. Wraps hung on a makeshift clothesline. Stable hands mucked out stalls. The dull smell of manure and urine mixed with pungent hot salve.

The ever-present sound of water running provided the soundtrack. Stable hands washed down horses, filled tubs, or simply knocked down dust in the shedrow. The clip-clop of hooves on the narrow asphalt roads signaled horses crossing to and from the track. Pickups hummed as they crept along slowly enough to hear the gravel pop and churn as it was spit out by worn tires. The breeze carried a joke, laughter, and shouts of instruction. In many corners it was reunion time.

Today was Tuesday. But it was not just any Tuesday. It was Tuesday before opening day. The backside had been empty thirty days ago. Now a vibrant community had sprung up. Three hundred small businesses occupied the backside, complete with bosses, employees, payroll, and equipment. The most important assets of the businesses rolled in on fifth-wheeled trailers.

For the past three weeks the assets had been rolling in, some coming from campaigns at other racetracks, some from training farms, some returning from injury, and, this time of year, late summer, some were babies. These were the two-year-olds who would soon learn about their new environment and routine, far from the calm, consistent life of the training farm. For them, this was the equine version of culture shock.

Dan and Jake stepped onto the wooden landing. Jake pulled open the screen door to Crok's Kitchen. It resembled many other backside kitchens. The décor was totally utilitarian, filled with metal folding chairs and laminate-topped tables, none of which stood level to the ground. Each wobbled the direction of the newest elbow that rested on it. All random and disordered atop an uneven concrete floor.

Time stood still in backside kitchens. Revelations about cholesterol hadn't arrived yet. A remarkable place where the taste served as the only discriminator and fat grams were ubiquitous.

Crok was a seventy-something short order cook, by choice, and kitchen manager by default. She hovered like some relic left behind in an unexplained time warp. Barely five feet on her best day, Crok graced the kitchen like a blocking dummy on legs. Her gravelly voice bounced off the walls as she barked at customers. A black net pressed her gray locks down onto her head. Smiling wasn't her strength. All paid full fare, but she made sure those who were down on their luck had a meal. It might involve time served at a sink full of dishes, but no one was turned away if they were sincere.

The kid came in as Dan and Jake sipped coffee, surrounded by tables of similar groups, all talking about the meet, the stakes schedule, but mostly about how they were going to make money.

The boy limped through the line, filling his tray with biscuits, gravy, and grits. A large glass of milk finished the meal. Crok smiled and whispered something to him as he completed his journey through the stainless steel line. The kid didn't spill a drop of milk as he counteracted his limp across the room to one of the only empty tables near the door.

Jake continued his explanation about the outcome of throat surgery for Dan's three-year-old, Hero's Echo. A release of the trapped epiglottis required six weeks of rest. That meant six weeks of vet and boarding bills with no opportunity to recover costs. The surgery was needed and would hopefully move him to the next level. Jake was mapping out the recovery process as the noise level elevated in Crok's.

Three wiry grooms in muddy boots and weathered T-shirts had surrounded the kid as he sat alone at the table.

"Hey, retard," the tallest one spouted. "How's breakfast?"

The kid didn't look up. He just stared down at his plate.

Another of the three, the shortest of the group, scraggly blonde hair and overly tight blue jeans, reached forward and slapped the kid in the back of the head with an upward movement.

"Stupid, what's for breakfast?"

The shot wasn't meant to inflict pain, but merely to knock the kid's baseball cap into his plate of food. The three laughed heartily and high-fived one another. The kid still didn't look up.

He was used to this treatment, Dan thought. It was a battle he couldn't conceivably win, so he sat motionless, enduring the verbal and physical onslaught.

Crok flew from behind the serving counter, wielding a large metal spoon.

"You leave that boy alone." She took a swing at the nearest boy, but he leaned backward, like Cassius Clay taunting Sonny Liston. She missed. The boy stared at his plate. The trio scoffed at Crok but continued out the door.

"See ya, retard," the short one shouted.

"Have a nice day," said the tallest one.

Crok swept away the kid's plate, dusted off his ball cap, and in a matter of seconds returned with a clean, even larger plate of food. The kid said, "Thank you, ma'am"—still without looking up.

Dan watched the entire scene, glued to his chair. He just sat there. He didn't help. He didn't do anything. Finally, he looked down into his coffee cup.

"God, I hate myself."

Chapter 2

MANY WATERING holes and taverns served the race-track crowd. Business was good during the times the track was dark, but when the twelve-week summer meet was on at Fairfax Park, in Manassas, Virginia, these places rolled in the cash. The backside traffic was like having an entire new town spring up in the area. Local businesses had more patrons and needs to satisfy.

Plenty of options existed for quenching the adult thirst of this transient community.

Clancy's wasn't one of them.

Clancy's was a biker bar in Dumfries, Virginia, tucked between a tattoo parlor and a wholesale tire store in a dingy strip mall on the far side of Interstate 95. It was sixteen miles from the racetrack.

The man pulled up, parked, and turned off his headlights. He noticed the white pickup truck he'd been looking for, got out of his rusted Jeep Wrangler, and slipped on his black cowboy hat. Several motorcycles stood at ease nearest the door.

Cowboy Hat walked in and surveyed the crowd. Several men occupied prime seats at the bar, and two men stood sentry around a pool table while a third slammed home a shot and backed up the cue ball. A solitary figure in a baseball cap sat in the far booth facing him. The man from the booth nodded to Cowboy Hat. In response, Cowboy Hat poked his chin toward him and continued to the bar. After a brief discussion with the bartender, two longnecks were produced. Cowboy Hat put down some bills, grabbed the necks of the beers with one hand, and walked to the far booth.

Baseball Cap slid his empty bottle aside, took the offered beer, and poured a good portion of the new one into his mouth, then looked out the window.

"All set?" asked Cowboy Hat.

"Yep."

"When?"

"Tonight." Baseball Cap appeared preoccupied with tearing the paper label off the neck of his beer. To make their operation a bit more covert, the two had adopted code names. Baseball Cap was known as "Falcon." Cowboy Hat was "Raven." They joked that they were birds of prey—might as well carry the titles.

"Who you think will give us problems?"

Falcon shrugged. "Lot of 'em. At least at first."

"That's why we need to hit hard right away. Fear is a powerful motivator." Raven stared at the man in the baseball cap. *Had he picked the wrong guy?* Falcon had the access and the knowledge to pull this off. He also had the need. Raven was sure of that. Only question was whether the man had the stomach for it.

Falcon wadded up the label in his fingers and flicked it onto the floor. He looked at Raven for the first time and nodded in agreement.

Raven continued, "How many we hit in the first week?"

"Two tonight, then more after the note goes out."

"Note's ready. Twenty bucks a head. Damn reasonable, then we'll move it up when we have their attention."

Baseball Hat nodded and turned his label-stripping action to the larger one. "We'll have to focus on the larger stables. If we get them, the smaller ones will go along."

"Which ones do you need to get on board?" Raven asked.

"Probably Gilmore, Dellingham, and McDonough," said Falcon. "They're all tough pricks. If they go, we'll get most of the rest."

"We have to show them they have no options. Twenty a head is chump change for those guys." Raven hunched forward, leaning on his elbows. He needed to get Falcon's head in the game. Punk was way too sedate for this gig.

"It's not about the money for them," said Falcon. "It's a control thing. This will piss them off."

"We have to show them we're more pissed off than they are," said Raven, raising his voice. "You mess with a guy's meal ticket, they wise up fast," he said, pointing a finger at Falcon. Feeling that he made all the emotional progress he was going to make, Raven leaned back and relaxed. "Who you gonna hit tonight?"

Baseball Hat sat for a long time. An AC/DC tune cranked over the speaker system, and pool balls clicked in the distance. Light flickered from the juke box and cut blue and red shapes into the shadows blanketing the bare dry-wall. Laughter drifted from the pool table as the cue ball fell into a side pocket. Falcon's ball cap finally rose, and he said, "Emerald Stone."

"Hhmmm. Gelding?"

"Yep."

"Cashed a bet or two on him over the years," said Raven.

"Me, too."

"Who's the trainer?"

"Daniels."

"He's got better stock. Won't miss him that much," Raven said, smiling. "Hell, we're doin' the guy a favor."

Falcon killed his beer, got up, and walked out of the bar.

Raven sat focused on the label-less beer bottle left behind. Even though he owned the guy, Raven couldn't help feeling less confident than when he had walked in.

Tonight, Falcon gets blood on his hands. A smile spread across Raven's face as he held his cowboy hat steady, dipping his head down and back up. Then he'll be locked in. There will be no turning back.

Chapter 3

THE MAN slipped along the side of the shedrow, staying in the shadows. He stopped, listened, and looked up and down the darkened gravel road that separated the barns. Many barns housed stable hands in empty tack rooms, so he had to remain quiet and aware.

The barns were uniform with a dozen horse stalls on each side, back to back. The inhabitants were confined by webbing clipped to either side of the stall door. The webbing was two feet high and positioned optimally to prevent the horse from sidling under or jumping over. A contraption of psychology, as a 1,200-pound animal with determination, could barrel through the chain and plastic device in a flash, but its presence somehow kept them in place.

A large sloped roof ran down either side of the shedrow, providing a walking ring around the stalls that was covered. On one end of the barn were two rooms, one a tack room and the other the trainer's office. The best barns had small grassy areas on one side where horses could graze and be washed down—green space in a world of dirt and gravel.

Silence and darkness were the man's friends. At three in the morning he had plenty of both.

He crossed through the fence opening beyond the barn and walked onto the gravel road, stepping lightly to minimize the crunching sound. He took three large steps to the other side of the road and eased onto the grassy area behind the adjoining barn. The stall he wanted was the fifth one on the backside of the shedrow.

Horses murmured and shuffled around when they sensed his presence. He reached the fifth stall and looked inside. A horse whinnied quietly and stared back at him. The man clucked to the animal and quickly slipped under the webbing into the stall. The horse shifted uneasily as the man reached out and stroked the horse along the neck. He scratched along the neck and continued clucking quietly to the horse.

With his left hand he reached into his pocket and drew out a hypodermic needle. The man stroked the horse and made quiet kissing sounds to soothe the animal. When the horse was standing calmly, he jammed the needle into the horse just below the withers. The horse shivered and cried out. Horses in nearby stalls whinnied and moved about nervously. He quickly pushed the plunger to the base, withdrew the needle, and replaced it in his jacket pocket.

The man patted the horse's neck and stroked upward behind the ears. In an instant he ducked back under the webbing and disappeared into the darkness.

◆　◆　◆

OR AT least the man thought he had escaped into the night. Across the road a pair of eyes had watched him enter the stall. He recognized the fright in the horse's reaction. When the man moved to the right toward the main gate, the eyes followed.

Apparently feeling that his mission had been perfectly executed, the man didn't move as stealthily as he had just minutes previously. He walked down the middle of the gravel road back toward Crok's kitchen and the main gate. The eyes kept to the shadows.

When the man reached the road's dead end at Crok's kitchen, he tossed something into a trash can. Then, rather than moving left toward the main gate, he went right. The eyes followed.

Thick woods of Manassas State Park framed the backside area away from the racetrack. The man passed four sets of barns and continued on to the fence, which divided the backside from the U.S. Forest Service Park. Without stopping, he slid through a separation in the fence and moved out of sight through the heavy underbrush.

The eyes waited and listened—silence but for the sound emitted by his own breathing. He backtracked to the garbage can outside Crok's kitchen. Light coming off the soda dispenser outside the front door of the diner gave him enough light to see what he needed. He used a discarded overnight sheet to lift the object. He wrapped the sheet around what he had found, put it in his pocket, and moved back toward his tack room.

He stopped briefly in front of stall five. A snort and one blinking eye greeted him. The horse moved forward, and the new visitor patted and scratched the side of the animal's head. He turned and returned to his makeshift apartment. Eyes didn't recognize the man. He didn't know what the man was doing, but he knew it was not good.

◆ ◆ ◆

THE HORSE in the fifth stall snorted and took several bellowing breaths. He shook his head and blinked. After several seconds he leaned and stumbled to his left. The stall's wooden planks prevented him from falling. He looked out over the webbing, and lights flickered among the darkness. No movement, no activity. He snorted again, rocking his head up and down. His head dipped slightly, then he lost his balance, crashing onto the matted straw.

The sound caused shuffling in the compartments of his neighbors, but only the equine variety. They were in no position to help.

The horse tucked his head and lunged upward, trying to get his feet under him. One leg propped him momentarily, then it slid away, and he collapsed back onto the stall floor. His chest heaved as he tried to get air into his lungs. Sweat poured off the once glistening coat. He lunged again but wasn't able to generate as much motion as the first effort. He lifted his head and whinnied, but the sound was hardly noticeable beyond the stall door. Finally, unable to hold his head off the ground, it, too, succumbed to gravity. He nuzzled the straw as if nodding in agreement with the inevitable.

He blinked twice, then his final breath left him.

Chapter 4

MORNING CAME early to the backside.
Falcon was even earlier.

In about thirty minutes the first of the grooms and ho-twalkers would start to fill the shedrows. Only "morning people" need apply to work in this world. Several would yawn and spit, trying to manage the hangovers from the night before. Others would be sharp and alert. For now, there was just silence.

Falcon picked the horse based upon the escape route. Bad luck for the horse. The end of Juan Camillo's shedrow backed up to one of the three restrooms on the backside. He would be quick, and he would get away.

He carried the two-and-a-half-foot section of lead pipe alongside his leg. In daylight it would've looked suspicious, even criminal. At this time of night he was just being care-ful. A few horses were shuffling in their stalls, but the world was asleep. He had to move quickly.

The gelding stuck his head over the webbing, and Falcon scratched him behind the ears, keeping a furtive watch down the shedrow for any visitors. He held a slice of apple up to the animal with an open palm.

A few licks and slurps preceded the crunching bite. The apple was quickly smashed and chomped, much to the animal's pleasure. With the expectation of a puppy, the horse nuzzled forward, knowing there was more.

Falcon stayed with the plan. He tossed the apple into the back of the stall. The gelding quickly turned around to find the prize in the straw.

So predictable.

The back legs of the horse came toward the webbing. Falcon knew this gave him a better angle, but he also liked the idea so he wouldn't have to look the animal in the eyes.

He stepped back and gripped the pipe like a baseball bat. The horse had found the apple and was devouring it happily. Falcon spotted the cannon bone. It was the part of the horse's lower leg that connected the fetlock to the hock, the equine equivalent of the shin bone. It was the piston of these warriors' engines.

Falcon lifted the pipe above his right shoulder and swung fiercely toward the animal's leg. The pipe whooshed through the air, accelerating as it descended. Falcon felt the bone snap and crumble as he followed through. The horse shrieked out, stumbled, and hopped on the good hind leg.

Falcon stood for a split second holding the pipe, then realized he needed to move. He zipped around the corner of the barn, tossed the pipe toward the shedrow, and ran into the men's room. More horses joined in the commotion.

Fear was a virus, and several barns were now infected. Over the din he recognized the animal with which he had shared the apple. The horse cried out. The sound pierced him, haunted him. Falcon covered his ears. It didn't help.

Soon voices appeared and the sound of people running. Falcon went into one of the stalls and locked the door. He would wait out the storm. He wiped the cold sweat from his face.

What the hell am I doing?

He held his face in his hands. This was all wrong. He had no options. It was a trap, but now he had to ride it out.

Falcon took some deep breaths to steady himself. It didn't work. He turned, leaned forward, and vomited.

Chapter 5

A RACETRACK BACKSIDE quickly became its own community with neighborhoods, gossip, and jealousy. Each barn was a small business, and each small business lived right next door and out in the open with its competitor.

The backside had a chapel, a security force, a café with dining hall, and mock community center. There were restrooms with camp-quality showers, basketball rims, and makeshift soccer fields.

And there were laws. Don't poach other people's help, don't steal other people's equipment, and don't brag too much when things went well. Other than that, life was fair game. And as games go, this one was wickedly cruel.

Winning was everything. Trainers got ten percent of any purse money, plus day money for each horse in their stables. For trainers, day money just kept them afloat; they needed to win races.

In this town winning was everything. If trainers don't win, owners don't buy new horses and don't pay their bills on time. If trainers don't win, they develop a reputation that they can never outrun. If trainers don't win, they can't pay their staff, feed bills, vet bills, or their own rent. If trainers don't win, they're dead.

They become victims of the unforgiving fate known as inadequate cash flow.

So, trainers thought about winning all the time. Where can I place this horse to get a check? Can I drop him down in the claiming ranks and not lose him? Can she run out her conditions at this track, or do I need to look at a softer spot? I need to win so I can approach that owner about that horse we can claim for a quarter.

The average field was nine horses. Purses paid through five spots, though third, fourth, and fifth paid diddley. So in every race nearly half the businesses walked away with nothing. They fired a shot and got bubkiss. They had to get checks, they had to get good checks, and they had to get a lot of checks.

Many things played into winning: jockeys, vets, condition books, training regimen, feed, and meds. All invested in a 1,200-pound animal with ankles like a teenage ballerina.

There are ten million ways to lose a race, and sometimes trainers couldn't find a way to win.

As trainers liked to say, there's a reason jockeys were known as pinheads. Trainers brought their horses up perfectly for a race, training like a monster, sitting on a huge race, on his feed, kicking down the stall, and the pinhead gets behind a wall of horses or moves too early like he's suddenly riding Man o' War rather than a quarter claimer.

It was so hard to win, and sometimes a trainer had to have a horse that could win despite the jockey. Fact was, he could train his horses perfectly, could make every decision perfectly, could plan and strategize perfectly, but events conspired, and he still lost.

It wasn't a game for timid souls. Trainers had to scrap like hell to win and, if they didn't win, have the courage and confidence to lift their heads up and truly believe they would win the next one.

If a trainer had the big horse, the dominant animal in the division, he was the alpha male. He was the mayor of this community. Everything worked. The world was easy. Owners thought he was Gandhi. His horses were first call for the top jockeys at the track. The barn took down purses for the fun of it. Life was champagne and roses. That trainer was the belle of the ball.

For trainers without the big horse, life was an endless series of back alley knife fights. The small businesses in this community came and went. Trainers that didn't win on a consistent basis went.

And they went fast.

Two other things made up this community. A newspaper, commonly known as the overnight, which was a sheet of coming day's entries with ads for nightclubs, steak houses, and accounting services printed on the back. The community also had a post office. Unlike the real post office, this series of 4-inch by 5-inch boxes sat outside the racing secretary's office in the administrative office of the track.

Aside from serving as a mailbox with official business between the track and a trainer, this post office was a source of contact that ranged from messages from a stable hand to his employer, notes from track administrators to trainers, media inquiries, and occasionally notes from one trainer to another.

The post office was one place left behind in the digital world. Although trainers had migrated to email and text, the post office was still a main form of communication.

The boxes were stacked sixteen rows high and twenty rows across. The names of the trainers were marked with masking tape at the bottom of each box. At the start of the meet, they were in alphabetical order based on stall requests. By the end of the meet, new names were pasted over the old names, and for all but cryptographers there was no semblance of alphabetical order.

The post office was a high traffic area, with most trainers dropping by after morning workouts, between races or at end of day. The racing secretary's office hummed most hours of the day with new condition books being formed, trainer complaints being registered, and an endless happy dance being done when any media types bothered to poke their heads around.

There was one time when the hallway by the racing secretary's office was vacant. That was post time.

When horses were called to the post, the staff, secretaries, and officials all stopped what they were doing and walked to the balcony to watch the race. People only worked in this industry if they loved horses. It made no sense otherwise.

And those who loved horses wanted one thing—to watch them run. So when horses were called to the post, everyone from the racing office went to the balcony.

That's exactly what Raven knew and exactly what he counted on. He had seen them just walk away from their desks, hang up the phones, and move to the balcony.

Raven waited until they were all gone, then he slipped in through the stairwell entrance and walked to the post office. In each mail slot he inserted the same letter. He did it quickly, like a blackjack dealer firing out cards.

A blackjack dealer wearing latex gloves, that is.

Then he disappeared.

Chapter 6

OPENING DAY—there was nothing like it in the world.

Dan jogged from the parking lot toward the turnstiles. The deposition ran just over five hours. Dan would have stayed all night. He owed that to his clients, and his work always came first. But since he was defending the depo, he just needed the testimony to bear out and hold his case together. Mission accomplished—and now he was free to catch the last half of the opening day card.

He quickly traded bills with the program vendor and ripped open his treasure map. For a short twelve weeks, the circus was in his backyard, and he wasn't going to miss it.

Dreams took flight on opening day—renewal, opportunity, and the chance to be a winner. Today was a fresh start. He took a deep breath as he strode toward the paddock on the backside of the grandstand. Memories of long shots hit and photo finishes won filled his senses.

Dan was seven years old when Uncle Van brought him to the track for the first time. He sat in the car while Van went inside the grandstand to bet; then, they would stand near the rail and watch the races. When he'd gotten the hang of it, Dan started making his own selections. He told Van to bet the purple one.

The silks were his singular means to tell one contestant from another. Numbers weren't a challenge for him, but the beauty of the jockey's silks and the majesty of the horses captured his imagination.

"Did you bet the purple one, Uncle Van? You bet the purple one?" Dan pleaded. Van was a proud handicapper. The purple one was 25-1.

"You got the purple one, Dan-o." Of course, he didn't bet it. It was Dan's first lesson in "booking" bets.

Dan screamed at the top of his lungs as they came rushing through the stretch. The purple one was going to the lead and pulling away. Dan jumped up and down, pumping his fists in the air. Some other railbirds congratulated the boy on his big winner. Van gave the railbirds a sheepish smile and muttered something about beginner's luck.

They shuffled back toward the car. Van turned, checked the tote board, and confirmed that none of his tickets could be cashed. He tussled Dan's hair, then handed his program and losing tickets to him. "We'll get 'em next time, Dan-o."

Uncle Van and Dan were late getting back home for dinner. The two had gone out to pick up some mulch from the gardening center and had been gone nearly three hours.

Aunt Frannie pulled Uncle Van into the dining room and lectured him in a stern whisper. "What were you thinking? Taking the boy to the racetrack? Sakes almighty, if Jean knew you'd done that, she'd never let Danny come back."

Dan scrambled up the back stairway to his room with the worthless pari-mutuel tickets and the day's racing program. At that age he didn't care about the business side of racing. He didn't understand gambling or the economics. He didn't know the roles of the people involved. The only thing Dan knew for sure was when those animals ran past, his heart nearly came out of his chest. It took his breath away.

Uncle Van filled a huge gap in the boy's life. Dan had been five when his dad died. Heart attack—he just dropped on his way to the parking lot from his office in Clarendon.

Dan didn't understand what happened at the time. He just knew he never saw him again. Dan had to wear fancy clothes a lot, and everyone was sad. The life insurance kept his mom and him in good shape for a year or so, but eventually she had to get a job.

She was able to get a position in the secretarial pool at the Central Intelligence Agency. It sounded cooler than it was. "The Firm," as it was known in the D.C. area, had prestige and allure as a place of intrigue and mystery. For his mom it was just a job. She worked hard and made plenty of friends, but being a single mom and working full-time was a constant drain on her.

Fortunately, his mom's sister, Frannie, bought a house in the same neighborhood. They used to joke about how "lucky" they were to find their dream home two blocks away. Dan eventually knew better. Frannie and Van weren't wealthy, but Frannie knew his mom would need the help, so they moved nearby. That way, Dan could go to Frannie and Van's after school, have a home-cooked meal, and do school work while his mom kept up her hours at work.

Frannie and Van didn't have kids. So despite losing his dad, Dan ended up with a family and a half. Van taught him how to throw a football, how to ride a bike, how to deal with bullies, and, a few years later, how to pick the ponies.

Chapter 7

A FEW STEPS past the kiosk where he bought his program, Dan spotted the boy with the limp and tattered ball cap sitting on the top railing of the whitewashed fence surrounding the paddock. From where the boy was sitting, he could see the entire paddock and be near the horses as they departed through the tunnel to the front of the racetrack.

The incident from Crok's kitchen the previous day haunted Dan, and the memory created an instant buzz kill for his opening day euphoria. His failure to assist the boy was one thing, but the behavior by the three men was barbaric. What caused them to pick on someone as small and unimposing as the boy with the limp? Sure, he was different, but his problem was that he was also weak.

Jungle animals don't attack the different; they attack the weak. They also don't attack a gathering; they attack loners.

Being different, weak, and alone, the boy would continue to be an easy target for those punks. The backside was a society within a society. It was unforgiving. It was the Wild West.

Paranoia and greed drove action. Respect was carved from dominance. Jealousy was borne from fear. Oddly, though, the men feared the boy. If he could do this job well, what did it say about them? Better to run him off. So, they lashed out in fear. By minimizing the boy, they elevated themselves. It was natural selection. If left unabated, it would run its logical course.

Dan couldn't erase what had happened the day before, but just maybe he could alter the landscape of the jungle.

He tapped the boy on the leg. "Hey, how you doing?"

The boy didn't look at him, just said, "Fine" in a quiet voice, like he wasn't sure anyone was actually talking to him.

"Who do you like here?" Dan flashed the program to him just to make sure the boy knew he was talking about the race.

Silence.

When the boy realized that the man wasn't going away, he said, "Four is angry. Three feels strong. One looks relaxed."

A glance at the program determined that the morning line on the four was 15-1, the three was 8-1, and the one was 10-1. "Don't like the favorites?" Dan asked.

The boy swung his leg off the fence, like he was uncomfortable with the questions. He looked down the tunnel as the last of the competitors moved through, toward the track. "Seven is hurting, two looks sick, nine don't wanna race today."

Dan again stared down at his program. The boy had just called out the top three favorites in order, despite the fact that he had no program, not even a slip of paper in his hands.

"Seven. Jasper June. He's hurting? What do you know?" Dan was hoping for some inside information.

"Just watchin'." The boy started rocking like he was about to jump down from the fence.

Dan realized he was coming on too strong. He was spooking the boy.

"Hey, I'm sorry. I'm Dan. Dan Morgan."

He extended his hand. The boy looked down at the hand, and after a pause reached down and shook it delicately.

"What's your name?" Dan said. "You see, when you introduce yourself and give your name, the other guy is supposed to tell you his." Dan laughed, trying to break the ice. The boy didn't react and just treated it like another interruption.

Finally. "AJ."

"Okay, AJ. Nice to meet you. I saw you the other morning in the kitchen, when those guys were hassling you. I'm sorry about that."

AJ just nodded, looking off in the distance.

Like it happened all the time, Dan imagined.

"Look," Dan said. "As long as I'm around, those guys aren't going to bother you. Or if they do, they'll catch hell from me. That's our deal. Okay?"

AJ nodded, looking toward the tunnel.

"I've got a couple horses. Jake Gilmore trains for me." Dan was getting no reaction from the kid. "I heard you work for Latimer. He's a good trainer." Dan didn't know if that was true or not; he just said it. Silence.

"AJ? So what does AJ stand for?"

The boy paused a long time, probably hoping Dan would just move on, but he didn't.

"Stands for Ananias Jacob. Ananias Jacob Kaine."

"That's an unusual name. Is it a family name? Ananias, I mean."

"It's from the Bible."

"That's cool." Dan's knowledge of the Bible wouldn't fill a thimble, but he tried to convey that he was impressed. "AJ, I've got to run. I want to get a bet down before they get to the post." He started to walk away, then stopped and turned back. "Uhm, I don't mean to trouble you, AJ. I'm a lawyer, and we ask a lot of questions. I've just seen you around and—" *And what?* Dan thought. "And if you ever need help, you call on me. Okay?" He held out a business card.

The boy took the card and looked at him for the first time. "Okay, mister."

Chapter 8

DAN SCAMPERED up one of the back stairways to the mezzanine level. He didn't have a strong feeling about the race but thought he would take a flier on the horses AJ touted. "Give me a five dollar exact box, one, three, four," he said to the cashier. What did he mean, the four looks angry? Is that good? "Give me twenty across on the four."

Dan scooped up the tickets and headed out toward the track. From where he stood on the mezzanine deck he could see the whole racetrack. The horses were still warming up, and it was four minutes to post.

◆ ◆ ◆

FROM THAT first day with Uncle Van at the racetrack, Dan was hooked. He followed the stake races leading up to the Kentucky Derby each year like a forensic scientist tracking DNA. The events leading to the midsummer derby, the Travers', at Saratoga were indelibly etched in his mind.

The season wasn't complete without total devotion to the Breeders' Cup in the fall, the Super Bowl of horse racing. They constituted championships for virtually every category of racing. Two-year-olds, fillies and mares, sprints, distance, turf and dirt surfaces.

From the time he was legally old enough—okay, and maybe a few times before that—Dan would be at the track or at some nameless off-track betting establishment to get a bet down.

One summer, between his sophomore and junior years in college, he just handicapped for a living. He had rented a house near the Pentagon with four other guys from college, but rather than take a job painting houses or working on a construction crew as he'd done in the past, Dan just went to the track—every day.

That summer taught him more about money management than any college accounting course. He also learned the complete ins and outs of racetrack operations and the dynamics of preparing horses to compete. It was a master's degree in handicapping. Dan didn't win every day. Anyone who told you he did was a liar, but Dan won enough to pay his rent and other minimalist living expenses. It was total freedom, and he relished every minute.

Dan inhaled deeply and absorbed the excitement in the air as he walked the mezzanine level. The reserved box seats were suspended below him. At one time these had been the high ticket seats, but now dark-paneled luxury boxes were housed inside the exclusive clubhouse one level up. Dan preferred the box seats because the people were real. He also told himself the view was better from this position, just over the apron at the track level.

He spotted who he was looking for in one of the front row boxes just beyond the finish line. He walked over two aisles and skipped down the steps to the three men sitting in the box.

"Gimme a winner," Dan said.

Lennie Davis looked up from his form. "Hey, Danny boy." Lennie was a longtime handicapper and close friend. He had a doctorate in mathematics and no visible means of support. He played the ponies, but successfully enough to stay with it.

Eyeglasses hung on the tip of Lennie's nose, allowing him to read his computer printouts and see the racetrack and odds board with total efficiency. His gray hair was receding, but he made up for it by letting it grow in the back. The long strands were pinned together by a rubber band, and the silver locks extended about a foot down his back. The ponytail matched his rail-thin physique. He wore a flowered Hawaiian shirt over camouflage cargo pants. "Sit down, Danny boy."

The box was four beige folding chairs on a concrete slab, confined on three sides by green painted railing. The open side allowed access to the steps leading up to the mezzanine or down, via a separate staircase to the track's apron. It was nothing like the luxury boxes in the clubhouse, devoid of all glamour and prestige.

But for Lennie and his entourage, it was home. It was a haven for serious handicappers amid the chaos of the casual bettors who milled about the grandstand in hopes of finding the lock of the day. Dan sidestepped Lennie and took the chair next to him.

"Who do you like in here?" Dan asked.

Milton Childers piped up from the chair in front of Dan. "Bunch of fuckin' stiffs. They'll probably all lose."

"I take it you got the favorite?" Dan said. Lennie and the fourth man in the box, TP Boudreaux, laughed hard.

"'Course he has the favorite," TP said. "Whenever he has no clue—which is most of the time—he bets the favorite. Just like usual."

Milton grunted and said, "Who's up today, me or you, Boudreaux?"

Dan reached forward and shook TP's hand. TP was a jock agent, which, for the right kind of guy, was a license to steal. TP was that kind of guy.

A jock agent represented jockeys the way talent agents represented actors. He worked with trainers to get his riders on the best horses and working for the best barns.

There were two critical skills for a jock agent. First, find and sign great new talent and, second, do whatever it takes to get your guy on the best horse and riding "first call" for the best barns. Agents made ten percent of the jockey's fee, which was ten percent of the purse won, plus a nominal mount fee on losing rides.

Ten percent of ten percent wasn't much at first glance, but the jock agent could fill a race card with his riders, take home a consistent paycheck, and never risk life or limb hanging onto the back of a wild animal.

TP was as smooth as they came. He wore a crisp, clean polo shirt over khaki slacks. As a former jockey, he was just over five feet tall, with dark hair parted down the middle and a matching black moustache.

"How's your boy going to do in here, Teep?" Dan asked. TP represented Emilio Juarillo, and he had a mount on the one horse, Vindicate.

"I'll be happy if he hits the board. New rider like Emilio has to ride a bunch of dogs and work his butt off in the mornings to get any of these guys to give him rides. Emilio's a natural-born rider, tough as a bucket of nails, but has no personality. Needs to keep up with his English lessons, too."

TP found many young riders in Peru and the Dominican Republic. He'd sponsor their immigration in exchange for a long-term contract as their agent. He'd done well with a few riders and had the perfect pitchman's demeanor with trainers to get his guys rides.

Lennie leaned forward and looked to the left to see the horses nearing the post. "Got anything working here?" Meaning—did Dan have a bet?

"Yeah, I put the one, three, four together and bet the four across."

TP smiled and nodded, acknowledging that Dan had action on his rider.

Milton quickly looked at his program, then the tote board. "The four? Hollering Hal? What do you know, Morgan? Is the fix in?"

"No, the fix isn't in. I'm just taking a flier."

"Interesting," said Lennie, scanning his sheets. "Hollering Hal's got some back speed. Been off for awhile. Second back off a layoff. Stretching out to a mile and a teenie off a six. Looks to be in a little too tough for my money."

"What do you think?" Dan asked Lennie.

"Well, unfortunately, I'm with Magic Milt on the favorite, Jasper June. He ran a solid Z pattern last time out. And against these types, his Beyer's are strong. The pace will be to his advantage. He might draw off and win by daylight. Hoping to keep him above 5-2," Lennie said, looking up quickly to check the tote board in the infield, "but he's starting to get pounded at the windows."

True to his Ph.D., Lennie was a pure numbers guy, relying on Beyer speed ratings, Ragozin numbers, and pace figures.

The "figs," as they were known, were mechanical calculations of prior performance. They were a means to put math to perceived talent. Many of the figs were available in the public racing program and commercial racing forms. Others were purchased by subscription. Lennie absorbed numbers like a Hoover ate dust bunnies. He could calculate percentages and implied odds with blinding speed and ease.

"C'mon, Dan," Milton said as he took a bite of his hotdog. "Hollering Hal is 18-1. What do you know?"

Milton was suspicious of anything and everything. He was convinced that a fixed race would come by and he would be left out. To compensate, he looked for strange angles or reasons to support long shots, in the bizarre hope that his interpretation would somehow match up with the inside job.

Aside from horseracing, Milt's favorite hobby was eating, and, on days like today, he was able to engage in both activities at once.

Milt was the classic "before" picture for famous weight-loss programs. Bones and muscle surrounded by a thick layer of fat and flab. The "after" picture would never be taken. He wore dress pants that hadn't been pressed in the current decade and a crumpled white dress shirt, adorned with a tie that bore the stains of spilled mustard, barbeque sauce, and anything else that didn't quite make it all the way to Milt's mouth.

Magic Milt worked as an insurance agent. Actually, he inherited the family business, but his devotion to food and horses meant it was just a matter of time before he broke the place. He was content living his life, and the future, for Milt, meant the next race on the card.

Maj was a lifetime hunch player, and, if he didn't have an angle to play, he took the favorite. In North American racing the favorite won about 30 percent of the time, some tracks a little higher, some a little lower, but over time the favorite was always 2-1 odds against. The strategy of only taking favorites, betting chalk, was akin to committing economic suicide on the installment plan.

Maj either didn't care about the percentages or wasn't good at math. Unlike disciplined handicappers such as TP and Lennie, Milt couldn't let a race go by without putting down a bet. He had to have action going. It was a lifetime losing strategy but one Magic Milt followed religiously. Maybe he considered the wagering a tax on his enormous food budget.

"I'm just taking a flier, okay? Nothing's going down, Maj."

Just then track announcer Dean Horn came over the intercom:

"They're all in...and they're off.... Jasper June gets away well.... My Guy up on the outside and Hollerin Hal between horses...past the grandstand for the first time it's Jasper June showing the way...Hollerin Hal up to challenge...and Vindicate trails the field...."

Milton was waving his arms and shouting, "Just like that, baby, all the way around. Stay right there, baby."

Lennie glanced at the time just as the first quarter was posted. "Twenty-three and one, a little quick for this bunch." Lennie watched a horserace the same way a seasoned cardiac surgeon performed a bypass, dispassionate and analytically.

Dan could only recall Lennie raising his voice one time, but he could be forgiven for that as Lennie had a 35-1 shot keyed in a superfecta that paid $466,000. Other than that one time, Dan had never seen Lennie shout, root his horse on, or make a scene. He was the consummate thoroughbred gambler.

"They turn up the backside.... Jasper June leads by two, Hollerin Hal, My Guy, and Minion's Gate.... Topic A is fifth... three back to YaYa Dime, Total Energy, Billie's Dream, Anacka...two more back to Bishon and Vindicate trails...half mile in forty-six and two...."

"Stay right there, seven." Milton was shaking the remaining bite of his hotdog toward the track. "No passing zone, baby. Stay right there."

"That Hollerin Hal is hanging right with them," Lennie stated. "Jock's working too hard on the seven. TP, here comes your boy."

"Out of the turn and into the stretch Jasper June has led every step of the way. Hollerin Hal starts to inch closer on the outside.... Minion's Gate starting to make a move...and Vindicate on the extreme outside is closing fast...."

Milton could sense that Jasper June was losing steam. "Damn it, hit that horse, c'mon."

Dan jumped to his feet. Hollerin Hal was going to do it. He was clearly going to hit the board, but the one horse was moving quickly.

"Danny boy may have a winner," Lennie said.

"*Hollerin Hal surges to the lead.... Jasper June trying to hold on... Vindicate in the middle of the track... at the wire it's Hollerin Hal, Vindicate second, Jasper June holds third and Minion's Gate fourth.*"

Lennie slapped TP on the shoulder. "Hey Teep, your boy almost got there."

TP smiled. "Told you that fuckin' kid can ride. Need to get him some live horses."

Milt sat down disgusted. "Eighteen to one. Shit, Danny, get here a little earlier when you have a tout like that."

Over the years Dan had learned that Milton was a bad loser but a good friend. Inside he was happy for Dan. Of course, he'd have been happier if he had money down on Dan's horse.

"Looks like we need some drinks."

"Hell, yeah," TP shouted.

Dan waved at the cocktail waitress working the section. The good ones always watched for anyone who won the previous race. They tended to get bigger tips that way. It didn't take long in this business to figure out that losers don't tip well. Dan pointed at each of them. No refusals.

"We need three tall beers and a black coffee," Dan said.

Lennie was a recovering alcoholic who drank coffee all hours of the day. It made no difference whether it was ten below zero or ninety in the shade—hot black coffee. Being around drinkers didn't bother him. In a weird way he seemed to like it.

"And a pretzel. With some of that nacho cheese stuff," Milton shouted after her.

She turned and Dan nodded. "Bring him two pretzels. It'll save you some steps later."

She laughed and walked off.

"How many times you have the exacta?" Lennie asked.

Dan had forgotten that he had the one and three boxed with Hollerin Hal.

AJ's horses ran first, second, and fourth, all at better than 12-1. He'd nearly cold-cocked a monster trifecta with no program or racing form. "I had it two and a half times."

"Nice hit," said TP. "You're gonna share some with Uncle Sam."

"What the hell, I'm a patriot." Tickets paying more than three hundred times the value of the bet were cashed with taxes withheld on the spot.

The exacta payoff was going to be close to the line. If Dan did his record keeping right, though, he'd get the money back next April 15.

The race was declared official, and the prices flashed up on the tote board. The twenty across brought back $720, and the exacta ticket was forty bucks shy of two grand.

Hello, taxman, Dan thought. And thank you, AJ.

Chapter 9

ANGRY VOICES knifed through the air as Jake Gilmore entered the building housing the Racing Secretary's office. About one hundred people, mostly men, were packed into the open area and hallway running past the secretary's cluster of offices.

Large spaces of white drywall covered the walls, interspersed with an occasional winner's photo tacked to the wall. Yellow and beige checked tiles on the floor confirmed that every expense was spared to decorate this most functional of spaces. Down a narrow hallway to the left a series of offices hid from sight. These housed the racing secretary, track president, horseman's liaison, and track security.

The meeting was called on short notice; only a few hours after the letters had been delivered to the trainers. Word traveled fast on the backside and at the speed of light when it involved the potential to lose money.

Tim Belker, the chief of security for the racetrack, was near the far wall, motioning to several trainers to calm down. He was tall and muscular, one of those guys who looked like he could still play tight end in the NFL. Following an All-American senior year at that position with Penn State, he'd been taken in the fourth round by the New Orleans Saints. He was cut just after the third pre-season game and cut the following year by the Jets.

The game had passed by his physical attributes. He was a tight end from the 1970s, a stonewall blocker with great hands, but today's tight ends could run a 4.5 forty-yard dash. Tim could never crack 4.7. Despite his talent, he was a relic of old-fashioned football.

He took a job as a private security guard and quickly rose through the management structure. After four years he started his own security company but didn't have the sales ability to sustain it. The position at Fairfax Park opened up, and he jumped for the steady paycheck and the opportunity to place bets at work. That was three years ago.

Belker's hair was dark and close-cropped, military-style. His effort to silence the teeming mass of trainers was having little effect. Allan Biggs, president of Fairfax Downs, and Chase Evert, racing secretary, were also on that side of the room, effectively making it the front of the room.

Jake had torn up his version of the note, but the message was etched in his brain. It was addressed "Dear Partners," as if this creep was something other than an extortionist and petty criminal. It went on to describe how Emerald Stone, a gelding trained by Keith Daniels, had been poisoned and Missing Lens, a mare trained by Juan Camillo, had to be destroyed after a cannon bone fracture.

Unless an animal's DNA carried the strains deemed desirable to carrying on a royal equine blood line, the fracture of a cannon bone was a death sentence, and it was for Missing Lens.

The note also told of the kidnapping of Exigent Lady from Hank Skelton's barn. The movement of horses onto and off the property was a daily routine, but actually kidnapping a horse out from under a trainer's nose was a whole new level of criminal enterprise.

Trainers were warned that future injury was inevitable for their barns unless they agreed to pay a "safety fee." The safety fee was twenty dollars per horse per week. Trainers who agreed to pay the fee were assured that their horses would be protected from these "random acts of violence." Those who failed to pay the fee were at risk for "unfortunate circumstances."

Jake had come to the meeting for information only. There was no way in hell he was going to pay some damn "safety fee." Jake didn't want to put his owner's horses at risk, but he needed all the day money he could get.

Jake never disclosed his financial condition to anyone, but he'd taken a beating since the start of the year. Two owners had dropped him at Delaware Park. They went with the latest pharma-trainer, who juiced the horses and got quick wins where Jake couldn't.

Damn stews needed to crack on these guys. Winning long shots created by these pharma-crooks brought in bets, and the pricks in suits just looked the other way.

The day money from a few horses shipping to his barn this week would help, but only a little. He needed some wins—and fast. He'd tightened up on receivables as much as he could without appearing desperate. His reserve fund was gone. Payroll and vet bills spun around each week like a screen door in a tornado. He needed horses on the track and wins. That would solve everything. It had to.

Allan Biggs waved his arms, trying to silence the crowd and get its attention. Tim Belker put two fingers in his mouth and emitted a shrill whistle that brought the unruly group to an activity level nearing calm.

Biggs was tall and slender, with a healthy shock of white hair that was combed straight back. He was sixty-four years old and had been in the industry for nearly fifty years. He wore a black pinstriped suit with a white open-collared dress shirt.

Although he'd never worked a day on the backside, he'd run just about everything possible on the grandstand side. He was liked by some trainers and tolerated by the rest. Perhaps the best one could say about a track president was that he was tolerated on the backside.

There existed a healthy tension between the front office and the backside. The front office had to set a purse structure likely to bring in good stables. They needed to bring in quality horses to have a product on which people would want to wager, both on track and via simulcast. Tracks made money by bringing in more gambling dollars than they paid out in purses. Trainers demanded higher purses. Tracks wanted purses maintained at a level where increased gambling dollars fell to the bottom line. Trainers talked with their feet. If the purse structure was suitable and they could win at a given track, they stayed. If not, they walked.

Biggs held one hand in the air as he spoke. "Thank you all for coming in tonight on such short notice. I want to assure you that Fairfax Park is doing everything we can to ensure the safety of your stock."

"What the hell can you do?" someone yelled from the back of the room. Several other trainers piped up in agreement.

"Please, please," Biggs continued. "I know this is a difficult time, but please be patient. In a minute I'm going to turn this over to Tim Belker, and he'll tell you about increased security protocols and plans for the facility. We'll catch the person responsible for this. We're working with local law enforcement and the FBI."

"What are you gonna do for us?" Daniels shouted. He was standing on the other side of Belker. "I gotta dead horse. I had day money tied up and planned to run out some good money on purses. Now I got nothing but a dead animal and a whole bunch of owners who wonder how the hell something like this can happen."

"Keith, I'm sorry about this situation," Biggs said. "Unfortunately, the loss is something your owner will have to address with his insurance carrier."

"Insurance?" Keith shot back. "Who do you think it was? Secretariat? There's no insurance on that animal. Hell, probably no insurance on 95 percent of the stock back there," he said, motioning toward the backside. "We're just screwed. My owner's screwed; I'm screwed. This whole place is screwed."

Several other trainers grumbled affirmative reactions, and heads nodded around the room. "Keith, like I say, I'm sorry. Nobody saw this coming." As though he was afraid the mob would descend on him, Biggs turned to Belker. "Tim, can you update us on security?"

Belker stepped forward slightly. "Thanks, Allan. First, I'd like to thank the management of the racetrack. In light of these tragic and horrendous attacks, management has increased the security budget by 83 percent through the remainder of the meet. This will allow us to hire two additional security officers and ensure that we have two security officers on site 24/7. The security officer on the backside will be in addition to the security guard in the shack when you drive in."

"Tim, how the hell they steal my mare off the grounds?" Hank Skelton yelled. The volume was well beyond what was necessary as he was standing about six feet from Belker.

Skelton brushed his scruffy and uneven brown hair away from his horn-rimmed glasses. His head hadn't been near a licensed barber in months. He was tall and lean with jeans that were about two inches too short. The cuffs on his work shirt were rolled back, exposing slender, stark white forearms attached to weathered and grime-stained hands.

They were hands that tended to animals sixteen hours a day. Thirty years at the bottom end of the circuit had stunted his patience and erased any semblance of a sense of humor. Thirty years waiting for the big horse to enter his barn and turn his life around. Thirty years of waiting for his payday to arrive.

"I mean, come on, someone can bring in a trailer, load up one of my horses, and just drive right by your fuckin' security guard," Skelton screamed, pointing a finger at Belker. "What the hell is that? Doesn't do any good to have more people on site if they aren't any smarter than the dumbshits you got now."

"Hank, we're investigating that right now."

"That's bullshit, Tim." Shelton lunged toward Belker like he was going to take a swing. Belker stepped back into a defensive stance. Money would have been on Belker. No one knew that better than Belker. He would have dropped Skelton like a sack of horseshoes. Fortunately for Skelton, two other trainers stepped in and restrained him. Skelton didn't offer much resistance in the scuffle.

"Easy, Hank," said Biggs, extending an open hand toward him. "Let's work together to get this resolved."

Skelton jabbed his nubby finger at Belker. "They backed up a fucking trailer and took my mare right under your noses. I don't care if you put 100 new security guards on site. What the hell difference would it make?"

"Hank, take it easy," Biggs said. "Let Tim do his job." Turning toward Belker, Biggs continued, "Tim?"

Belker paused for a moment to keep his composure and stepped back half a step. Then he turned his attention back to the group. "I have added a night security patrol that will run from 10 P.M. to 6 A.M. We think these are the hours of involvement on the prior incidents, and it's also the time when the fewest people are around and visible on the backside. We'll be increasing our scrutiny of badges for people coming onto the property, including the backside. We'll require 100 percent positive ID for people entering."

Several men guffawed and shuffled uncomfortably.

"Please be patient with the process," Belker continued. "Most of my men know all of you and as a result have waved you through without requiring you to furnish ID. In order to try and get better information, our check-in will require positive ID and documentation when individuals enter and leave the property. This will slow things down some but should give us a chance to catch whoever is doing this."

"Great," said Del Dillingham from the back of the room. "Somebody's messing with our horses, and we're also going to have security lines like in airports. Just fuckin' great."

Belker continued unfazed, "In the next few days we'll be adding security cameras in strategic locations on the backside. It's just a way to get more eyeballs on anything that's happening. We're conducting additional background checks on people licensed with Fairfax Park."

"That include all of us?" Dillingham said. "What is this, the Gestapo?"

"Del, come on," said Biggs. "To find the people involved, we need information. This is a way to get that." Biggs gestured back toward Belker, giving him the floor.

"Thanks, Allan. The review will include everyone licensed—so, owners, trainers, jockeys, vets, grooms, you name it. Anyone who could have access to the backside. There's a strong likelihood that the person or persons involved are licensed and raise no suspicion when they're on the property. We need to track who is on the property and when."

"Tim, this is a bunch of crap. You have no idea who's doing this, do you?" said Skelton.

"Hank, we're investiga—"

"You can't guarantee us anything, can you?" Skelton said. "Other than more scrutiny of us."

"Hank, I wish I could provide a guarantee, but you know I can't. We'll do everything we can to apprehend the people involved. The track management is committed to ending this as quickly as possible. The track's reputation is at stake as well."

"What are we supposed to do in the meantime?" Hank said. "In the letter I'm supposed to be the drop man for the pay-off. So I've been co-opted into being a part of the scheme. If I play along 'maybe' I get my horse back." He turned and pointed aggressively at Belker. "It's because you and your people can't do their damn jobs. If anything happens to my mare, I'm coming after you guys." His face was beet red, and a vein pulsed on his forehead. He then turned and pointed the same finger at Biggs. "Allan, this is on your watch. Fairfax should pay the money to ensure the safety of the horses on the backside. It's your facility. It's your obligation."

A chorus of affirmative sounds and head nods ensued.

"Hank, I know you're upset," said Biggs. "But the track can't be responsible, nor will it be responsible for these payments. On behalf of track management, I can't recommend for or against the payment. I consider it extortion of the highest order, but I can't guarantee anyone's safety if they choose not to be a part."

"Well, I've got to pay," said Hank. "They've got one of my best mares, and if I don't pay, I lose her and maybe some others in my barn. So I'm just screwed."

"I'm not paying," Jake said. "Anybody coming around my barn is liable to get his ass kicked, day or night. I'm not giving in."

"Me neither," several others shouted.

"Hell, I'm as pissed as anyone else," said Sid Martin. At nearly six feet tall and tipping the scales at a shade light of three hundred pounds, Martin commanded the space around him. His oversized Stetson and broad stance created the presence of a Macy's Thanksgiving Day float in the flesh. "And if I catch these guys, you won't have anything to arrest. You'll be able to pick them up with a spatula. But twenty bucks a head isn't worth the hassle. It's nothing. And if my horses are safe, I sleep at night. It's a short meet. I need to run out some money, not sit and worry about whether my horses are safe."

"Anybody talk to their owners about this?" asked Dale Jenkins, one of the trainers who had restrained Skelton.

"This stuff is all over town already," Martin said. "Every owner is going to know about it—probably already do. I can't pass the expense on. Hell, I've got enough trouble getting bills paid as it is." Shuffling and voices of agreement filled the air. Martin continued, "I don't need to throw on an additional assessment. Owners are liable to yank the horses and move them someplace else. That's why I'm going to cover it and not make the cost or risk something my owners even have to think about. The less thinking they do, the better for me."

Several trainers nodded along with the logic.

"I'm supposed to make the drop on Monday night," said Skelton. "If you want in, do as the letter said, give me a list of your horses and twenty bucks per head—cash—in an envelope with your name on it. I'm supposed to get a call where I'm to do the drop. I don't give a shit if any of you are in. I don't have a choice."

"I'll need to see your cell phone after the call comes in to see if we can get a trace," said Belker. Hank stared daggers through Belker, then nodded slightly.

"Maybe we should follow Hank and see who picks up the drop," said Jake.

"The note said I'd be watched," Hank said. "I don't need to get my horse killed because we got some James Bond wannabe."

"Jake, I've got a plan to monitor the drop," said Belker. "Leave that to me."

"You get my mare killed, I'm coming after you, Belker," said Hank.

Biggs leaned over to Belker and whispered, "I wouldn't be too specific about the plans right now. There's more than a slight chance that the guy we're looking for is in this room."

Chapter 10

GINNY PERINO eased the Dodge Ramcharger next to Gimore's barn. He slipped on his cowboy hat, effortlessly hoisted the scarred wooden toolbox from the back, and made his way to the stable office.

At first glance, Ginny wasn't an imposing figure, largely forgettable—five foot eight on his best day. Up close, his features were starkly different. He had a powerful upper body with forearms the size of a young child's legs. His hands were large for his frame and muscular. They introduced him as a man who earned a living with his hands.

The box contained the tools of his trade—hammers, nails, hasps, files, and aluminum shoes. The farrier was critical to the success of equine athletes. He was also a first line of defense for ailments of the hoof. He treated the types of injuries and illnesses that kept competitors in the barn, with potentially career-ending consequences.

Ginny was a farrier.

At least that's what he reported to the IRS. The job kept him on the backside, where he was able to run his more lucrative operation, his much more lucrative operation.

Ginny grew up tough. Boys in Brooklyn named Giovanni Perino either grew up tough or became doormats. Grade school playgrounds were unrelenting for boys like Giovanni, but he soon learned how to deal. Strike first, ask questions later.

Quickly, Ginny had learned that there were two kinds of guys, the intimidator and the intimidated. He vowed early on that he would always be the former. He learned so well that he was permanently expelled from school at age fifteen. The nuns at St. Katherine's of the Immaculate Heart were unable to control him.

He smirked as he recalled looking down at the crumpled and unconscious eighteen-year-old who dared to ask Giovanni if he preferred dating boys over girls. The two friends who accompanied the injured senior had scattered, screaming for the police.

Ginny held the softball bat over his head, perfectly framed below the outstretched arms of St. Katherine, high atop the school's entrance. He gave the curled-up body one more whack across the ribs and tossed the bat into the bushes. Then he picked up his backpack, slung it onto his shoulder, and stepped over the body to begin his leisurely walk home.

Ginny beat him good, but if he had wanted to kill the punk, he would have. The boy had it coming. Ginny just delivered it.

His parents were distraught and grief-stricken. Not wanting to turn him out to the streets of the city, Ginny was sent to his Uncle Dale in Arkansas. It was either that or a tough love camp in Arizona, which the family had no means of affording.

Ginny's uncle was a farrier at Oaklawn Park in Hot Springs. They traveled the Midwest circuit—Oklahoma, Nebraska, Louisiana, and Texas. It was where he learned a marketable skill, at least one of them.

The backside made sense to Ginny. Everything was defined by winning or losing. Competition ruled. There was no mercy shown in this business. You won enough to survive or you got run out. He quickly became adept at trimming, shoeing, and racing.

Becoming a competent farrier was easy. Becoming the "go to" guy for top barns required some tricks and twists. At this, Ginny became the best. For the right price he could apply modified turndowns.

A turndown was a shoe that separated slightly at the back of the hoof. It allowed a horse to dig deeper into a track, get better traction, and push off without the ground giving away as much as it would with a normal shoe. Turndowns were fairly common for racing on wet or sloppy tracks as were mud caulks. But in the right circumstances a properly applied turndown could significantly improve performance on a dry track.

Of course, turndowns were illegal unless conditions warranted, but Ginny knew the rules and for the most part stayed within one zip code of the rules. He also used his investigative skills and managed to get dirt on most paddock judges who might otherwise call him on an illegal shoe. Except for egregious cases, he could get them to look the other way. No one wanted to tangle with Ginny.

Yes, Ginny stayed within the rules, the rules as he manipulated them.

Two things drove his life, winning and scheming. He'd become a capable handicapper and occasionally had inside information that was timely. But gambling was merely a hobby. Making money was his business. Betting was sport. Even the best handicappers survived on razor-thin margins.

Ginny learned about making serious money. That included sure things and guaranteed payoffs. He lived by two rules. First, never lose money and, second, hurt anyone who interfered with rule number one.

As with many old-timers on the backside, his Uncle Dale died from a lifetime of smoking and heavy drinking. Ginny took over his book of clients and quickly grew it into a thriving business, at least from what the IRS could tell. Ginny buried his uncle two miles from Remington Park in Oklahoma City. The grave digger, two trainers, and Ginny paid respects. His family was gone, one by death, the others by choice.

He poked his head into the office and rousted Jake, who was writing up training schedules for his barn.

"Hey, Ginny."

"Jake."

"Yo," Jake shouted past Ginny. "Nino, get in here." He then addressed Ginny. "Need you to look at Pristine Fiend. She's getting out on the turns, and her front left don't look right. Also, Aly Dancer will need some racing plates." Ginny nodded and backed out of the office. Nino motioned Ginny toward the correct stall.

"Oh, and Ginny, stop back when you're done. I have something else I need to talk to you about."

Ginny knew what it was. He followed the game closer than anyone. He knew where everyone stood. Ginny smiled to himself as he lumbered behind Nino down the shedrow.

He knew what Jake needed, and he'd be more than happy to oblige. Ginny Perino was always available for a sure thing.

Chapter 11

TIM BELKER entered his office and elbowed the door shut. Once behind his desk, he extended and bent his left leg several times. He was able to avoid significant injuries through four years of Big Ten football, but one wicked hit in his first NFL mini-camp had left a permanent calling card.

He took a sip from his first cup of coffee, leaned back, and cracked open the day's racing form. He studied the entrants in the first race. Fucking goats, he thought. Disgusted, he flipped back to the eighth race, the feature on the card. Although a modest stake for Virginia bred fillies and mares, he could at least handicap a race with some quality in it.

His Zen-like tranquility was shattered by a voice booming through the racing office.

"Belker. Get your ass in here."

Despite being separated by three offices, Biggs' voice reverberated through the office like a tsunami wave crushing a village.

"Belker!"

His assistant, Gail, gave him an eye roll as he exited his office. Tim made his way to Biggs' office. Rosalind, Biggs personal assistant, gave him a sheepish, tight-lipped smile as he passed by. Biggs was seated at his desk, though he had his back to the door, concentrating on two computer screens resting on the credenza behind his desk. His pink shirt was framed by black and red checked suspenders. He spun around as Belker entered.

"Gimme the latest."

"Feds are being kind of sticky," Belker said. "Can't see why they should waste time on a bunch of horses when there are national security concerns elsewhere." He paused to let Biggs frame a question. When none came, Belker continued. "Got the Prince William sheriff's department coming out here in a few hours. Going to take statements from Skelton, Daniels, and Camillo. They think—"

"What a crock of shit," Biggs interrupted.

"Got the cameras going up this afternoon." Belker ignored Biggs' comment and kept going. "Called the temp agency, and we got coverage for twenty-four-hour presence."

"No fucking cops on the backside. Hear me?" said Biggs.

"Wha—"

"No cops. Got it?"

"I'm not sure they'll go for it," Belker said.

"I don't care. Don't give them a choice," Biggs said, pointing a finger at Belker's chest. "If they want to interview folks, it should be in your office, with you present." Biggs stared out the window as horses drifted by in morning exercise. Turning back to Belker, he added, "I don't care how you do it, but I don't want any cops on the backside."

"Why? What diff—?"

"You can bet your ass that there are some illegals on the backside."

"So what?" Belker said. "They don't work for the track. They work for the stables. If anyone is in trouble, it's the trainers, not us."

"Don't matter who employs them," said Biggs, framing "employs" with finger quotation marks. "You ever heard of Carl Lambert?"

"Lambert? What are you, nuts? Everyone's heard of Lambert. His colt won the Preakness and Travers last year."

"Yeah, well about ten years ago, as he was building his stable, I was PR director for San Antonio Downs. Lambert had about forty head on the grounds, about a dozen stakes caliber horses. Anyway, INS agents show up one day and shake down his barn. I'm sure 'cause some other trainer dropped a dime on him."

Biggs rose and walked to the wall of windows overlooking the track. "They cart off two of his workers. Bad deal. But the next week, they come back and shake him down again. Lambert raised holy hell with track management, and he was right." Biggs crossed his arms and gazed out the window to the track. "I tried to help, but Cliff Gantrell said it wasn't his problem. Was between Lambert and the INS guys. Meantime, help from all the barns starts disappearing, acting dodgy, showing up late. You get the picture."

Biggs turned and face Belker. "So, sure as hell, the agents come back the next week and shake Lambert down again. Know what he does?"

"Blast track management?" asked Belker.

"Nope. He backs up his trailers and takes every fucking horse off the track. Said 'screw it' and moved his stable to Louisiana Downs. Put a large hole in our entries. Never came back. Point being we don't want to jack around our trainers by making the help edgy. Sheriff or feds want to interview someone, bring them over here. I don't want cops on the backside."

Belker shrugged. "I'll do what I can."

"You'll do what I say, not what you can." Again with the air quotations on "can."

Geez, thought Belker, that was ten years ago, old timer.

Biggs went back to his seat behind the desk. "And I got that damn Jason Cregg nosing around." Cregg was the race-track beat reporter for *The Washington Post*.

"Yeah, he called me," said Belker. "Left a message last night."

"I don't want you talking to him. Send him my way."

"Gladly," said Belker, leaning back and crossing his arms.

"Idiot wouldn't say a nice word about us if his life depended on it. All the fucking freebies we give him, you'd think he'd show some kind of respect."

"He had a nice piece about Hudgins' mare last weekend," said Belker.

"Oh, he writes good stuff about horses and horsemen, but he goes out of his way to trash the track and management. This extortion thing will make him wet his pants. Can't wait to stick a knife in us. We gotta keep this under wraps. Keep everything as low key as possible."

"We can't keep a lid on this," Belker said. "Cregg will go to the trainers if we stonewall him."

"We can try," Biggs shot back. "Lots of these trainers will want to keep it hush hush. Don't want their owners to know what's going on."

"Going to be hard to—"

"I don't give a damn," Biggs shouted. "Do it. We only have to keep it quiet until you catch the bastard doing this. So don't give me all the lame shit. Go do your job. Now get out of here," Biggs said, spinning around to face his computer monitors.

Rosalind kept her head down as Belker walked past. She'd heard everything. The whole office heard every word.

Belker closed his office door, sat behind his desk, bent his knee several times, took a sip of cold coffee, and turned his attention back to the racing form.

Chapter 12

FRIDAY MORNING brought Dan to the backside early. Plenty of work awaited him at the office, but passion drove him to the place he loved the most, the racetrack backside. For Dan, being an owner was more than paying bills and getting photos taken in the winners' circle.

He loved the process of getting horses ready to compete. He loved the smell of fresh straw being carted to the barns and the pungent liniments slathered beneath bandages on tender bones. He loved the strategy in bringing a horse up to a race, the works, the morning drills, the equipment changes.

He studied the chalkboard outside Jake's office. It displayed a chart for each horse's daily activity—who would walk, who would work, who would jog the track, who would get new shoes, and who would get vet treatment. It provided the map of assignments, and as each day built on the prior, horses would be prepared to compete.

As most owners did, Dan had started off buying a claimer. These horses were the bottom of the racing barrel. Horses that didn't have the ability to run for large open purses such as allowance races and stakes were relegated to the claiming division, which means they ran for a price tag.

Races were scheduled for different claiming values, and the horses could be bought or "claimed" for the stated price. These claiming values ran from $5,000 to—in some areas of the country—as much as $100,000. The ability to compete at given levels was dependent upon the horse. The price established the competitive level. Horses in the $5,000 claiming events were also called nickel claimers. If horses couldn't win as nickel claimers, they became dog food.

In the game, owners claimed a horse and, with the trainer's promise ringing in their ears, tried to move up to higher claiming levels with ascending purse structures.

Dan went "halvsies" on a nickel claimer with Pug Wheatly, a seasoned local trainer. As the old saw went, the best way to make a small fortune in horse racing was to start with a large fortune. The prize was Sasha's Diamond. Pug was able to get her competitive for a dime, and she ran a few seconds and thirds that first year.

The training and vet bills ate all the proceeds, plus some, but Dan was in the game, and Sasha's Diamond ran under his blue and white silks. Dan had his own sports franchise, meager though it was.

He learned quickly that winning wasn't a luxury to be afforded. It was a necessity. Owners don't want to be the last people holding the bridle on a tired claimer. Dan and Pug did what most smart owners did and ran her down their throats. Pug put her back in the $5,000 level and won. They kept running her there with the unstated intention: "Beat me or buy me."

It was dangerous to fall in love with a horse, given the short careers. Make money or go broke. Pug didn't want to drop her down at first. The trainer's job is to keep the horse in the barn making day money, but he also knew he would lose an owner if he didn't cooperate. She was claimed from them after her third win, and Dan was happy.

Dan learned that he didn't want to partner with trainers in the future. The conflict of interest was too strong. They would be his horses and ultimately valued by him.

Jake Gilmore had approached Dan about buying a yearling at auction. Young horses can be bought at auction either as yearlings or two-year-olds in training. The two in training sales mean that the horse could be ready to race in several months following the purchase. A yearling needed to be boarded and trained for a year before an owner would know whether he's got anything.

The selling price for a yearling was generally much lower than a two-year-old, but the carrying costs added up over time. To get a potential bargain, it made more sense for Dan to buy a yearling, if he could be patient. With a purchase at auction, there was always the dream that the horse could turn out to be stakes quality.

When a claimer was purchased, at least the new owner had an idea how the horse could perform. But claimers rarely moved into allowance or stakes company. With a horse purchased at auction, the sky was the limit. It could be a performer or it could be a complete bust.

Over the years Dan had experienced both performers and busts. The idea was to make hay with the performers and get rid of the busts as quickly as possible. If that strategy was followed, there was a chance to make money as an owner, but only a chance. Horses were an asset of uncertain value and would depreciate rapidly at some point.

With that in mind, he was always open to selling a horse if the price was right, even a young horse that was displaying great potential. It was easy to fall in love with a horse. After all, it carried the silks and the pride of the owner's stable. But in the crazy market of thoroughbred race horses, the upside of a promising young animal was steep.

Everyone wanted a winner, and people were more than happy to overpay to get one. Much as it hurt emotionally, Dan occasionally made the decision to sell and never regretted it from a financial standpoint. He had been fortunate to make a little money over the years.

His current stable consisted of four horses, a three-year-old gelding named Hero's Echo, an unraced two-year-old filly named Aly Dancer, and two yearlings. The gelding was a solid allowance horse that couldn't quite crack the stakes competition. He had a breathing problem, which Jake attempted to resolve through surgical intervention. Hero's Echo would be returning to the barn today after laying up from surgery.

The filly was by Closing Argument, a colt that came within a shadow of winning the Kentucky Derby. Her momma was Techie Becky, who placed in a Grade III stake as a three-year-old and knocked out about a quarter million bucks in her career.

Dan was lucky to get her at auction. Buyers of bluebloods thought the filly's legs were a little crooked. They were right about her lack of conformation. Had that not been the case, he never could have gotten her. She would have been bid through the roof.

Like all hopeful owners, Dan thought he got a real steal but then had to put his emotions aside and wait. She was only a yearling and would have to grow up.

After the start of the year, the shared birthday of all horses, she became a two-year-old and was broken and began her training to become a racehorse. Two-year-olds typically don't race until the summer. Some tracks would write races for two-year-olds earlier than that, but it was risky.

The pressure to get in race shape can damage a young horse, and the potential would never be achieved. The knees of two-year-olds continued forming until well into the summer. Most trainers wouldn't think of starting a two-year-old until July.

Reports of Aly Dancer's progress were always upbeat and promising, but then again, the message came from the person who had a vested interest in managing the horse for a long time. If the trainer said the horse was a bum, he'd cut off part of his revenue potential, even though it might be in the owner's best interest.

Dan had come to trust Jake Gilmore as a first-class horseman, but he learned early that, in this game, he had to trust himself first. It was his money, his name, his stable, his sports franchise. If Dan wanted to stick around this game, he'd have to learn everything and question everything. His background as a lawyer served him well in that regard.

Hero's Echo had just been off-loaded from the trailer and settled in his stall. Dan and Jake briefly debated bringing him to the track, given the attacks, but he didn't make any money resting on the farm. He'd been galloped several times at Kenny Laughlin's farm, but he was probably a few weeks away from being able to make a start. The recuperation from throat surgery had gone well, and, according to Jake, he hadn't lost that much conditioning as a result.

Beth DeCarlo, one of Jake's newest grooms, was in the stall with Hero's Echo, scratching the side of his neck and cooing softly to him. She was the size of an Olympic gymnast. Maybe one hundred pounds if she wore work boots and had a few horseshoes in her back pocket.

She had soft features, almost childlike. It was hard to determine her age. She could pass for either eighteen or twenty-eight. Her demeanor and command around horses clearly put her at the top end of the scale. Her grayish blue eyes and youthful looks gave her a pixie-like quality. Despite her size and compassion, she was in complete control of the relationship with her equine subjects. Her blonde hair was trimmed short, pageboy style. It made good sense working on the backside.

Although Dan had seen her around Jake's barn, today was the first time they had met. She would be the groom, the principal caregiver for Hero's Echo, as she was for Aly Dancer.

A noise from behind Dan caused him to turn around. A stocky man in jeans, white pearl buttoned shirt, and blue sport coat approached. Pretty dressy for the backside, Dan thought.

"Hey, Jake. How you doing?" said the man.

"Good, John, and you?"

"Rumor is you got a nice filly on the grounds," John said, peering into the stall nearest him.

"Got a lot of nice horses," Jake said, starting to move past the man.

"Yeah, well, I know what I know." The man eyed Beth, then shifted to catch Jake before he went by. "If she's going to be the best, you need to match her with the best. You know, guarantee that you get the maximum from her."

"I got a rider," Jake said.

"Jake, we'll give you first call on any three horses in the barn—give us a shot with the filly. You won't be disappointed. There's a reason Dagens has been the leading rider here for the past two years."

"Thanks, John. I'll give you a call if I need a rider," Jake said as he continued walking away.

"You name it, Jake—first call on any three horses." John skipped forward to catch Jake. "Hey, while I'm here, I wanted to invite you to a steak fry tomorrow night. My place. Tidewater Court, you know it?"

"Yeah, I know it."

"Stop by if you can." John turned to Beth. "You're invited too. You're *always* invited, honey."

Beth shot him a deadly stare.

Jake stopped and turned back. "All right, you said your piece. Now move along."

"Call me Jake. Seriously," John said as he walked out of the shedrow toward the road.

Dan jogged the few steps to catch Jake and fell in alongside. "That was awkward," Dan said.

"Some guys have no class," Jake said.

"Jock agents by nature generally have no class," Dan said. Jake harrumphed.

"But Jake," said Dan. "Why wouldn't we put Dagens up on Aly Dancer? Guy's right; there's a reason why Dagens wins."

"Hands are too hard," Jake said.

Dan stopped; a puzzled look ran across his face. Jake continued around the corner of the shedrow.

Chapter 13

AFTER ENSURING that all was in order, Dan left the barn and sauntered down the road to Crok's for a cup of coffee. Beth came scampering up behind him.

"Mind if I walk along? I'm just going to Crok's," she said.

"Not a problem."

"Thanks," she said, jogging up alongside. Her blonde hair bobbed in time with her steps.

"Want a cup of coffee? I'm buying." He turned, looking over and smiling.

"Nah, just gonna grab a soda. I need to get back to do some wraps. Another time maybe."

Another time? he thought. That's interesting.

"That filly's a good one," she said.

"Aly Dancer?"

"Yep. She's got black type all over her."

Black type referred to the pedigree book, where past accomplishments of mares and stallions were listed to show the progeny's family. Black type meant winning graded or restricted races. Beth meant that the filly had the ability to win those kinds of races. It was a high compliment. Owners of untested two-year-olds were told that, mostly by the stable hands and trainers who were paid to maintain the animals. Beth's remark seemed more sincere than most.

Dan knew better than to put faith in the opinion of backside help. But he couldn't help himself. He liked this girl. He didn't know why.

"Hope you're right about her. Hey, I asked Jake about putting Dagens up on Aly Dancer," he said.

"You don't want him," she said, her disgust apparent.

"Why not? His record speaks for itself."

"He's a good enough rider. I just think he's a weirdo."

"What makes you say that?"

"Oh, he hangs around the backside when he don't need to. Nights sometimes. Guy's a little freaky."

"Jake said something about Dagens' hands being too hard. Thought I'd heard it all. What's that?" Dan said.

"He's very rough with horses, not abusive, but aggressive right to the line," Beth said. "With a filly like Aly Dancer, you want a rider who can get the best from her but also be conscious of her experiences and development. Soft hands if you will." They walked a few steps in silence, then Beth turned to him. "These are highly strung, temperamental animals. Good riders will keep the horse happy and give them confidence. That's how you build a champion."

"So who's he going to ride?" Dan asked.

"Don't know. He's had a few guys over to exercise her. I don't think he's decided," she said. "As you've seen, word's getting out on her. But you know Jake—never one to rush a decision."

Dan turned to her and in a hushed tone asked, "Jake okay?"

"Yeah, I s'pose. Why?"

"He just seems off somehow." They moved slowly on the side of the asphalt roadway. "Never in my life would I question how he manages and develops horses, but I can't understand why he won't pay the fee to protect the stable."

"He's got one of us on the grounds around the clock, since this all happened," she said. "We'll be okay."

"I don't want to be okay. I want to be safe. I want to be sure. He's taking a risk he doesn't need to take," Dan said. "Won't even talk about it with me."

"He can be hard-headed. I guess, all good trainers are a little hard-headed." She chuckled; Dan didn't.

"I can't be the only owner who's upset about this," he said.

She shuffled along a few steps. "Nope. He's gotten a few calls. But he says we can handle it. If you feed the bears, they keep coming back. He's not going to get started. I admire him for that."

"I think it's unnecessary," he said. "Why take a risk you can easily avoid? Better hope they catch this guy before something happens."

They walked along in silence several strides.

"So how long were you married?" Beth asked.

Dan looked at her with stunned surprise.

"Jake told me."

Of course he did. Probably shouldn't bother me that much, he thought. It just seemed odd to be hearing it out loud for the first time.

"Eight years."

"What was her name?" she asked.

"What difference does it make?"

"Just curious, you know," she said.

"Vickie."

"You don't look like someone married to a Vickie."

"Where the hell were you eight years ago? Could have saved me a lot of trouble. What are you, a fortune teller or something?"

She chuckled and looked down.

"Actually, I really loved Vickie," Dan said. "At least at the start. Not so much that we fell out of love as I guess we just moved apart." He couldn't bring himself to say that maybe he resented her success. He certainly couldn't admit it to himself.

"Kids?"

"Well, aren't you the forward one."

"Just wondering. Don't mean no harm."

They stopped as a rider on a lead pony tugged on the bridle of a racehorse pounding reluctantly toward the track. The jockey in tow gave Beth a long look-see as he passed by. Beth's attention was drawn to the back legs of the animal as it crossed in front of them.

"Nope. No kids," Dan said. "That was part of the problem. She was so committed to advancing through her law firm that—"

"She's a lawyer, too?"

"Yep. Met in law school. She went for the big firm life. Now she's managing partner of their M&A practice."

"What's that?"

"M&A? Mergers and acquisitions. They help companies buy up other companies," he said.

They stepped off the gravel road to allow a pickup to roll slowly by.

"Sounds like she makes a lot of money," she said.

Great, thought Dan. You, like everybody else, think we got divorced because I couldn't handle the fact that she made more money. Why does everyone go there?

"You do that too?" She noted Dan's stunned look. "M&A, I mean," she said.

"No, I was in the litigation group of a large firm. Couldn't stand it. I'd just sit in a room for fourteen hours a day looking at paper. After a year of that, I said 'bullshit.' Quit the firm and became a prosecutor. Tried a bunch of cases, which is what I wanted in the first place. Then three years ago I started my own practice."

"How many lawyers in your firm?"

"You're looking at the whole firm." He expanded his arms and chuckled. "So what's the deal? You torture everyone with questions like this or just me?"

"Oh, probably everyone," she said. "I just kinda like to know about people. You know, where they're from, what they've done."

"Names of their ex-wives," he said deadpanning.

She cocked her head upward and smiled, sparkling eyes peaking past her blonde hair.

"So, what's your story?" Dan asked.

"Not much to tell." She gave him a sheepish smile, tucked her hair behind her right ear, then began laughing.

Dan was game for the challenge. "Gonna make me drag it out of you, huh? You know that's what I do for a living. Okay. Where's home?"

She raised her palms, shrugged, and looked around. "Here."

"Fairfax Park?"

"No. The backside. All up and down the East Coast. Monmouth, Delaware Park, Pimlico. This is the only place I know. Daddy's a trainer, so we moved around a bunch."

"And mommy?"

"Mommy ran out on us. Not even sure I could recognize her if she walked by me. She left when I was ten. That was that."

"Sorry to hear it."

"No worries. Used to bother me. Kinda tough being a girl growing up on the backside, changing schools every four months, living in hotel rooms. In hindsight, would've been nice to have a woman's perspective growing up. Might've made fewer mistakes, but what are you gonna do?"

At a loss for words, Dan gazed at her. She smiled in return.

"Tough place to grow up," he said finally.

"Especially tough for girls."

"Where's dad now?" Dan said, altering the conversation.

"Fingerlakes."

"And?" Dan said.

"And what?"

"Why are you here with Jake's barn?"

"Little disagreement about business practices."

Dan stared, demanding more.

"Oh, nothing big," she said, flashing a smile that lit Dan's insides. "Kinda hard to be a daughter and a business partner. I want to train someday, and I knew I needed to see some other operations. To learn more. I learned everything my dad could teach me."

"So you're going to be a trainer. Got any owners?"

She smiled, cocked her head slightly, and batted her eyes. "Not yet. I'm a ways off. I've got a lot to learn. I just love this business, and the way I can control things is to run my own business. I don't want to be dependent upon anyone else. Jake's a good horseman. Fair. Really cares about the horses. Some, they don't. Anyway, I need to keep learning, then get my license. Probably take a few years. But I'm gonna do it."

Dan stepped up onto the landing to enter Crok's. Beth turned left toward the vending machines, fishing change out of her jeans pocket.

"Okay, last chance." He motioned toward Crok's front door.

"See ya," she said, smiling.

Got that right, he thought.

Chapter 14

DAN EASED open the screen door and noticed AJ sitting at his usual table. Across the room Dan eyed two of the three men who had badgered AJ just days before. They were headed toward AJ's table. Dan quickly moved in that direction, pulled out one of the chairs, and plopped down in it. He crossed his arms and glared at the men as they moved toward the table.

"Retard," the shorter of the two mumbled as he moved past.

"What's your problem?" Dan asked.

"What's it to ya?"

"This guy is my friend." Dan gestured toward AJ and stood. "I want you to knock it off. Leave the boy alone."

"What are you gonna do? Beat us up?" The men looked at one another and laughed.

"Well, Romeo," Dan said, staring at the taller of the two. "Here's what I'm going to do. You see, anything happens to this boy, and I'm coming after you." Dan pointed at him. "Not your pal or the other guy. I'm coming after *you*. Don't matter who does it—where or when. That's how it's going down. Something happens to him, you get a visitor. So you might want to watch your back from now on. Either that or change your tune and get your Neanderthal pals to follow suit."

Dan took a half-step toward him, and the two backed away. "Your call," Dan said. "But you sure as hell better hope nothing happens to this boy. That's our deal. Got it? Just makes life easier for all of us. Don't you agree?"

"You're nuts, man," said the one Dan called Romeo.

"Try me," said Dan.

The shorter one turned away from the table and said, "Come on, Paul. Let's get outta here."

"I'll be seeing you," Dan called out after them.

Crok came scurrying over with a steaming cup of coffee. "On the house, mister," she said. "Been waiting for someone to set them boys straight." She gave AJ a little pat on the head and walked away.

They sat in silence for several moments. "You didn't need to do that," AJ said while looking down at his plate of food.

Dan leaned in toward him and said quietly, "You're my friend, AJ. Friends take care of each other. Understand?"

Dan was hoping that he wouldn't have to make good on the promise. He regretted having to resort to their level of discourse, but sometimes the only message that worked was the one the audience feared.

Dan sipped coffee, and AJ chomped away at his breakfast. Dan sat, wondering whether he was still able to fight a twenty-year-old. He put his coffee cup down and watched AJ.

The boy's eyes were always down and away, either focused on his plate of food or looking to the left at the floor. Somehow it just made Dan feel better, sitting there with him, even though they weren't talking.

"Hey, AJ, thanks for the tip the other day. Hollerin' Hal really came through." AJ just nodded as if he'd just told him the current weather report in Alaska. No excitement, no emotion. He had to loosen this kid up. "So, AJ, you like anyone today?" The boy shifted in his seat, still looking at his plate, and began swinging one leg back and forth under his chair.

"Won't know 'til I see 'em."

"Got it. You're one of those visual handicappers. Got to see how they react in the paddock, how they warm up, how they move. Guys like you make all those numbers guys go kookoo." AJ didn't react. Dan had gotten more feedback from a store mannequin. What was it about this kid? "What do you look for?"

"Don't look for nothing. You can just see it." His leg swung back and forth under his chair.

Did that mean he was nervous or getting more comfortable?

"Well, maybe you can, AJ. I sure as heck can't. Let me know if you have a pick you like."

AJ sat and continued to eat. Finally, AJ stole a glance at Dan, cleared his throat as though annoyed, and said, "Hudgins has a horse in the fourth."

Then nothing, Dan leaned forward. Just let him talk, he thought, don't rush him. Dan waited.

"Used to be in our barn," AJ started up again. "Got claimed off us at Delaware Park last spring." Leg continued swinging. AJ looked down at his food.

Dan waited and waited.

Finally, AJ looked at Dan, then back down at his food. "Horse can run some."

Chapter 15

EVERY DAY at a racetrack was a good day, as far as Dan was concerned. But Fridays were the best. Maybe it was the fact that the weekend had arrived. The Friday cards weren't as strong as weekend cards, but somehow the attitude and emotion around the racetrack was different. People had fun, they drank more, they made strange pooled bets with coworkers and friends. It was casual. There was hope. For those who made it to the racetrack on a Friday, there really was a tomorrow. It was called Saturday's race card.

While walking across the mezzanine, Dan spotted Milt coming from a concessions counter. In one hand he had a soda about the size of a Buick with a tall straw in it. In the other he was balancing three cardboard wedges that each contained at least one slice of pizza. He was sliding sideways, trying to balance the three wedges. Dan rushed forward and grabbed the pizzas just before they toppled to the ground.

"Gotcha, Milt."

"Thanks, Dan. Fuckin' place. You'd think they'd have people here who can serve." He hitched his pants with his free hand and took a slurp from the straw.

"Goin' down?" He nodded, and they made their way to the box seats.

TP was studying the latest condition book, a publication the racing secretary released to horsemen about what types of races the track planned to schedule in coming weeks. Trainers used the condition book to find the races where their horses were eligible and had a shot at getting a purse. Agents used it to argue that their boy could ride a certain style or distance, for which a race had been written.

Good jock agents knew every horse on the grounds and were aware who had first call and what kinds of races each horse was eligible for. A savvy jock agent could look at a condition book and know which barns and which horses were likely to enter.

From that information, the jock agent could, with re-markable accuracy, predict which jockeys had conflicts. That was where the jockey had previously ridden two horses that would be entered in the same race. The jock could only ride one at a time, so the agent had a pitch to make to one or both trainers. Knowing the horse and the race, the agent would tailor the pitch for why his boy would be perfect for that ride.

The agent would also get the kid over to the barn early in the mornings to shake hands, smile, laugh, and say, "Oh, your rider isn't here yet? Let my guy work your horse this morning."

If the kid was presentable, respectful, and could ride worth a damn, they had a shot at getting a mount. It might also take some cold beers after the work day, but day after day, you chipped away and built relationships to get rides eventually. If the agent got his kid on a horse, he better ride hard to keep the mount, or the guy behind him got the next shot. So, despite the beautiful weather and picturesque race-track setting, TP was working.

So was Lennie. Milt squeezed his way into the box and over to his seat.

"Hey, Dan-o," said Lennie. TP scribbled some notes and threw his hand back toward Dan to shake. "Good to see Milt finally found someone to carry his food for him."

"Right," Dan said. "Damn near killed an old lady with a pizza avalanche up there. Lucky I came along when I did, Milt, or I'd have to represent you for assault with a deadly pepperoni."

"Screw you guys." Milt laughed. "You're just jealous that I can eat like this and keep my girlish figure."

"Got that right, Maj," said TP.

Dan glanced at the tote; it was eleven minutes to post for the fourth race. "Lennie, you see anything in Hudgins' horse?"

"Funny you ask. I've been looking at him."

"Who you talking about?" Milt jumped in.

"Film Star," Lennie said. "He's been off for six weeks. Likes a layoff, though. He's got the back speed to run with these guys. Kind of interesting that Hudgins moved him from fifteen thousand to twenty. The purse differential between Delaware Park and here makes that almost a double move. One might think he's over his head, but he's shown he can compete."

Dan knew that Lennie was too much of a pro to ask whether Dan had been touted on the horse. Lennie could handicap a race without the noise of other opinions. His career had proven him right. Milt, of course, couldn't hold back.

"Morgan, what do you know? He's 7-1. What's the deal? Is the fix in?" he said, leaning forward as if Dan was about to share some unknown clue to a treasure quest.

"Nothing big, Maj. I've got a friend who used to work in the barn where Film Star was claimed up at Delaware. Thinks he's got some talent. I'm going to play him, but, Maj, take it easy. This is no mortal lock, just a friend who thinks the horse will run well today."

Lennie studied his sheets. "I do like him coming off a layoff. Only one work and that was okay, nothing special. At those odds, it's worth a little action. I'm going to tie him up with the nine and twelve. The way the track's been playing the last few days, I can't leave those live frontrunners out."

They all got up and headed to the windows. At the top of the mezzanine stairs they split off and got in separate betting lines. Dan put twenty across and boxed Film Star with the nine and twelve as well. Word from Lennie was good enough for him.

Milt made it back to the box just as the horses were loading in the gate. He had a bag of cotton candy under his arm as he balanced his racing form and program. A ballpoint pen was sticking out of his mouth.

"Good lord, Milt," said TP. "Pepperoni pizza and cotton candy. You going for the heart attack this afternoon?"

"Breakfast of champions, boys. Breakfast of champions," Milt said as he collapsed with a grunt into his box seat.

The bell rang, and they were off. Film Star trailed the field by three lengths as they went past the grandstand the first time. Milt shot Dan a glance as if to say, What gives? Dan shrugged back in reply.

"He's okay," said Lennie. "They're going too fast up front for this bunch. Long way to go."

At the three-sixteenths pole Film Star still trailed, but he was in high gear, and the front runners were getting ragged. Milt jumped up. "Come on, baby. Bring it home." Two strides later Lennie casually called out "Winner" as though he was watching a memorized segment on *Jeopardy!*

Film Star got outside in the stretch and was mowing down horses with each jump. He collared the leaders with about fifty yards to go and went on to win by three parts of a length.

Milt was up, dancing and shouting, "Yeah, baby. Yeah." It would be the most physical exercise he would have for the week.

Dan sat stunned and silent. He'd been touted on horses plenty of times, and he'd been around great handicappers like Lennie. But AJ's ability to spot long shots was unbelievable.

Film Star paid $16.40 for every $2 win bet, and the exacta with House of Joy, the twelve, paid $116. They all got healthy that race, and the cocktail waitress was most appreciative.

Dan happily cashed the tickets, but he felt a certain emptiness inside. It felt like he was taking advantage of a friend. Despite Milt's exuberance and his dramatic display of bowing with arms extended toward him, Dan felt bad.

He tried to talk himself out of it. Just be happy with the big win and get more picks from AJ—but it didn't help. By all appearances AJ lived a life of near isolation, and here

Dan was celebrating with his friends, and AJ wasn't a part of it. Dan needed to get to know that kid better.

And not just for his ability to pick live horses.

Chapter 16

THE MONDAY night crowd at Clancy's was concentrating on ingesting as much alcohol as possible, all without the necessity of verbal interaction. A raised finger or nod to the bartender produced another bottle or glass. Words weren't needed here.

The man in the baseball cap walked in and ordered a beer. The non-verbal types at the bar looked his way, then back to their drinks. The one who had disturbed them moved to the booth at the far wall. Even the men shooting pool had little use for words. Their actions carried the game. An aimed cue stick called the next shot. Multiple jabs of the cue designed intricate combination shots. A pointed finger asked whether another beer was needed. The questioner picked up the bottles in one hand, placed them on the bar, and without a single word, the bartender replaced the empties with full bottles.

Raven entered and ordered a beer. The patrons at the bar again looked to see who had disturbed their unspoken existence. He quickly joined the man in the baseball cap. Classic rock music pounded through the bar and made it possible for them to have a private conversation without disrupting the non-verbal ecosystem of the bar.

"How'd we do?"

"Just over eight grand." Falcon pulled an envelope from his back pocket and slid it across the table. Raven quickly slipped it into his pocket without examining the contents.

So far, so good, Raven thought. Getting Falcon to do the dirty work was the trick to the whole scam. Blood on the other party's hands was what cemented a partnership like this. Before that it was just blind trust. Now that Falcon had done his part, some of the pressure was off. It wasn't a complete trust, but Raven knew he owned the guy.

"Thought we'd do better?" said Raven.

"Hard to predict. Just the first week."

"We don't have that many weeks. Need to ratchet up the fear. When do we increase?"

"Don't think we want to go up any 'til we got about eighty percent of them. Maybe two weeks."

"Who's on the list?"

"Which list—the paying list or the not-paying list?"

"Only one list. The guys putting their horses at risk. Stupid bastards."

Falcon produced a slip of paper. On it was a list of trainers at Fairfax Park in alphabetical order. There were two rows of names that nearly covered the entire page. About a third of the names were crossed out. He examined it on the table in front of him, then spun it around so Raven could read it.

"A kidnapping and two dead horses, and this is all we've got?" Raven stared at the page for a long time, memorizing the names on the list. "We need to double the take. Fast."

"They start seeing how this works, and a bunch will join up next week." Falcon took a long pull off his beer, then continued. "Plus, nobody gets a pass. To get off the list, they gotta pay from the start. Ain't no free weeks. How's it going on your end?"

"Lot of tough-guy talk," said Raven. "But nothin' I can't cover. I know what's happening before it happens. We just keep 'em in the dark and grind on 'em. They'll pay. They'll all pay."

Raven pushed the page back, got up, and went to the bar. He held up his empty bottle, raised two fingers, and two beers promptly showed up. He sat back down, sliding one of the beers toward Falcon. "Who's next?"

Falcon pointed at the list of names. "One of these three guys." Raven smiled. Ferrare, Simpkins, or Oliver.

"Big barns."

"Yep."

"I like it. How you gonna do 'em? Everybody's guard will be up," said Raven.

"Sometimes it's easier to have someone else do the dirty work," said Falcon. "They'll never see it coming."

Chapter 17

"WHERE'S MILT today?" Dan asked as he moved into the box. Lennie had the place to himself today.

"He's got some kind of insurance seminar today. You know, figure out more compelling ways to sell folks something they'll never use."

"Probably driving him nuts to miss an afternoon at the track."

"Depends." Lennie paused and slid his reading glasses onto the top of his head. "I heard a lot of those insurance company seminars have killer buffets. Milt's probably packing his arteries as we speak."

"I love the guy, but he's a walking heart attack," said Dan.

"Hey, speaking of insurance, what's the latest on the protection racket running on the backside?"

"It's serious. People are getting edgy over there," Dan said. "They need to catch the guy."

"I don't get it. Twenty bucks a horse? That's hardly worth the effort, isn't it?"

"Well, 1,500 horses on the backside," said Dan. "Thirty Gs per week ain't so bad. Enough to get someone interested. The guy will probably raise the stakes once people start paying in. That's how these things usually go. At least that's what happens on *The Sopranos*."

"Still, not much money," said Lennie, crossing his legs and tucking his sheets under an arm. "I mean, the guy's killing horses. Who does that?"

"Puts these trainers in a tough spot," said Dan. "They charge over a hundred bucks a day per horse for training, so the twenty bucks a week seems fairly cheap, but with payroll, feed, rent, and upkeep, there isn't much margin there. Some of the guys are turning to the owners to pay the fee. Others are afraid to mention it to their owners."

Lennie pulled his glasses down off his head and onto his nose. He picked up his stack of sheets and began studying. "It's a universal truth, you know. There are two things that account for ninety-nine percent of all corruption and criminal activity."

"Two things, huh? What are they?"

"The first is money." Lennie glanced up at the tote board. "The second is people."

They sat in silence, each studying their racing forms and materials. Five minutes to post, Dan spoke up. "Who you like in here?"

Lennie let out a long breath and gazed at the tote board. "Think I'm going to try Oliver's mare here."

"The seven? Chesterton?"

"Yeah, she's dropping down in class. Had a good tightener last time out. Put Dagens up on her. This is also a horse for a course."

"Saw that," Dan said.

"Hit the board in all four outs last year, winning two," said Lennie.

"What's not to like?"

They climbed the stairs to the mezzanine to bet and had just returned to the seats when Dean Horn called them all in line.

Chesterton broke well along with Party Tyme, the two, and Ricky Rover, the three. That trio led the field by two lengths as they entered the far turn.

"Just what I was afraid of," said Lennie.

Dan turned to look at Lennie, then back to the race.

"...*coming out of the turn its Ricky Rover by a head... Party Thyme and Chesterton challenging on the outside...two back to Angler's Angle, followed by Tipper Terry, Envelope, and Penny Vane...Bisconti Road trails...down the stretch they come, and it's Party Thyme by half a length, Chesterton on the outside, and Ricky Rover on the rail...*"

"She's in the death," said Lennie.

"In the what?"

"In the death, the death seat."

The crowd stood and cheered as the two horses approached the wire. Party Thyme held sway and won by half a length. Chesterton ran second.

"What did you say about? What was it? Death?" Dan asked.

"It's called being in the death or in the death seat."

"Never heard of it."

"When you've got a known frontrunner but another speed horse is inside, you're in the death seat." Dan just stared. "The outside horse has to travel farther than the inside horse—just math," said Lennie. "But when the pace is hot and your need-to-lead horse is outside a legitimate frontrunner, you're in the death seat."

"I thought it was supposed to be a stalking position, just outside the leader."

"Depends on the pace. If you win, you were stalking. If you lose, you were in the death seat."

Chapter 18

THE FILLY stood nearly still. She looked out into the darkness beyond the stable lights and shifted her weight slightly. Her coat twitched nervously, as if shoeing off flies. Beth kept her calm, and she busily worked through her tasks.

"That's right, girl: You are the real deal." Beth tenderly combed and cut the filly's mane.

"I trimmed your tail off in a block. That always looks best, and after I finish your mane, honey, I'm going to brush you down again."

Aly Dancer's head nodded up and down, and she snorted in approval.

"You moved so well on the track today. You handled your lessons at the starting gate just great. First time can be kinda scary, huh. Sometimes those guys can be hard-headed, but you were just great."

She hummed a tune while she swept the trimmed hair from Aly Dancer's mane. "You and me girl, we're gonna stick together. Yes, indeed." She began brushing her hind quarters with the wooden hand brush. Beth stopped and gestured with the brush. "You know what, girl? Not only are you the fastest filly on the grounds, but damn, you're good looking too." She laughed and went back to brushing down the filly. Crouched on her haunches, she methodically stroked the lower part of Aly Dancer's leg.

"I'll tell you what—"

Before she could finish, Aly Dancer shifted backward, startled by movement ahead of her. Beth fell onto her backside. From the corner of her eye she spotted a head in the stall doorway.

"Hey, how's my girl?" Jim Dagens said.

"What the—"

Dagens gave her a toothy grin. His face was framed by brown hair cut into a mullet, as if he hadn't heard the 80s were over. "I'm talking to the filly," he said, patting the filly on the nose and glancing toward Beth. "But if you want to be my girl, I'll see if I can squeeze you in."

"Get the hell out of here," Beth said. She scrambled to her knees and barrel rolled at his legs. She tumbled under the webbing into the path in front of the stall.

The jockey nimbly sidestepped her and leaned back against the stall with his arms crossed. As an athlete and tireless workout freak, Dagens had the body of a power lifter, though as a jockey, his physique was contained in a travel-sized package. His cockiness wasn't similarly confined. A receptacle hadn't been designed that was big enough for his ego.

Beth shot to her feet, crouched forward. "Get outta here. You got no business being here."

Dagens cocked his head and made a pouty face. "We going to wrestle?" He chuckled. "I bet you're pretty good on top."

She threw the brush at him, but he ducked, and it caromed off the stall wall.

"Beat it, loser," she said. "You got no reason to be here, 'specially this time of night."

"What are you going to do? Kick my ass?" He said, sneering at her.

"She don't need to." The words came from a voice behind Beth. She spun around, and Jorge crept forward. He held a steel-tonged rake like a baseball batter. Admittedly, a 110-pound cleanup hitter, but one with the business end of the rake facing Dagens. Jorge stepped closer and raised the rake, preparing to strike.

The palms of Dagens hands slowly pushed forward, and he backed away. "Hey, easy, Pancho Villa. Don't need to get your panties all in a bunch. We were just having a conversation."

"Get off the property," Beth said, pointing emphatically. "Get."

"Hey, dial it down, guys," Dagens said, laughing and continuing to back away. "I'm just checking out the filly. I hear she's a good one."

"Move along," said Jorge.

Dagens stopped and smiled. "You tell big boss man that if he wants the best out of that filly, he'll put Dagens up on her.

"Fat chance, pinhead," Beth said. "Move it."

Dagens turned and walked out of the stable, disappearing into the darkness. Beth turned back. "Thanks, Jorge."

"What the hell he doing?"

"I don't know," she said. "But I don't like it. Don't like it one bit. I'm going to have Mr. Gilmore take it up with the stews." She stared in the direction Dagens left. "Jocks shouldn't be out roaming the backside this time of night. And with the guys attacking horses, what's he thinking?"

Jorge rested the rake on his shoulder and shook his head. "I'll be in the office," he said. Beth nodded slowly.

She slipped back under the webbing and put her arms around Aly Dancer's neck. "Nothing bad's going to happen to you, girl. Okay? I promise you. Nothing."

Chapter 19

ASIDE FROM the competition between barns on a backside, there was also a supply-and-demand relationship for other services. Veterinarian services were no exception. A backside typically was home to four or five different vet companies. Many were one-man shops, and they hustled for business like a jock agent. Some had developed longstanding relationships with established barns. Others positioned themselves in second place, ready to jump at a new account if a relationship changed.

Vets had a few rules to live by. First, they did nothing that could put their license at risk. Their ability to earn a living was dependent upon a license in good standing with the State. So they kept good records and were subject to oversight by the track, the medical board, and the state thoroughbred licensing commission.

The other rule was keeping client receipts current. Trainers on a bad streak got slow in payment. Nobody wanted to be the vet of record when a stable went bust, so vets had to be glib and persistent about being paid. If they weren't, the system would take advantage of them. Folks who were taken advantage of in this world went broke.

Dr. Vic Dancett moved slowly but efficiently. His actions bore the precision formed by a lifetime of exercising an abundance of caution. He was tall and straight, like a walking pool cue, with shocks of white hair and a puffy white moustache. He did nothing quickly, but he did everything correctly. Vic was sixty-five and had worked the backside for nearly forty years, the last thirty as a licensed vet.

Dancett had seen it all. Every kind of ailment a horse could suffer, every kind of racing injury, stress fracture, and infection, every kind of bad luck, hard knock, and tough break. Roaming the backside of a racetrack was all he ever wanted. He lost his wife to breast cancer two decades before. Dancett's life was animals and the backside community. It was his family. Yes, Dancett had seen it all—or at least he thought he had.

The hours were brutal, but most vets worked in the game because they loved it. They lived to see young horses develop, and they challenged themselves to solve problems that helped horses get better. More than occasionally, they cashed a ticket or two based upon things they could see that the public couldn't. The betting public rarely looked at the animals in a race before they broke out of the starting gate. Their analysis solely focused on the history of their performance, like they were machines and the race was simply comparing different machines.

Horses were far from machines. They performed based upon physical conditions. Little in a racing form told one about current physical condition, but vets knew physical condition firsthand. Sometimes it helped cash a bet.

The day typically started at 5 A.M. with rounds, consults, and preparations for morning works. On race days the afternoons were filled with examinations of returning warriors and administration of medication before and after racing. As with medical doctors of the human world, the stress of competition created nicks, injuries, and assorted stress in equine athletes. Vets who wanted to keep their book full were available until the evening for advice and therapy. Then they would get up the next day and do it all over again.

Over the years bans had been implemented over the use of race-day medication. Most were pain relievers or blockers to dull the sensation of pain in the course of a race. Horses who couldn't feel the pain would over-perform, leading to breakdowns and career-ending injuries.

Even small injuries that kept an animal from racing cost everyone money, and no one wanted to pay for an athlete who couldn't perform, so there was always tension to push the envelope to get animals to the track.

The best trainers were patient with small injuries because they maintained high winning percentages. Trainers lower down on the list needed numbers. They needed runners, so any advantage was sought, sometimes to the detriment of the competitors.

One race-day medication available and legal in nearly every state was Lasix. During heavy physical exertion, the capillaries in a horse's lungs could explode. This resulted in blood seeping into the lungs. A horse with blood in its lungs couldn't run fast. At times the bloody discharge would fly out of the nostrils, covering the jockey and the horse itself. Obviously that wasn't the image the thoroughbred set liked to foster. As with the human world, the industry's answer was chemical.

Lasix was a powerful diuretic, which if given to a "known bleeder" would reduce the body fluids in the animal and prevent bursting capillaries in the lungs. Unlike most medications, the name Lasix had no connection to the chemical makeup of the substance. Lasix was a term coined because the effect of the diuretic lasted six hours, hence Lasix. It was common knowledge that Lasix could improve a horse's performance, and sometimes the improvement could be dramatic. Many handicappers looked for first-time Lasix runners because history has shown a horse could improve five to six lengths over its pre-Lasix performance.

By regulation, the tracks and information services had access to race-day medication information, and that was shared with the betting public. Lasix made horses lighter because of the water weight loss, and since there shouldn't be excess fluid in their lungs, they ran faster.

To be prescribed Lasix, the horse had to be examined by a vet who scoped the lungs following a race or workout. If evidence of bleeding was present, the horse could go on the Lasix list and be treated on race day. The actual degree of bleeding, or presence at all, was a subjective determination made by the vet. If the vet said there was blood, the horse could get Lasix. End of discussion. Once on Lasix, the saying went, always on Lasix. As long as the horse ran in jurisdictions that allowed Lasix, it would race with the substance.

To hit the optimal time zone for administration of Lasix, a vet would travel from barn to barn on a schedule to allow several hours for the Lasix to kick in. If the vet's clients had horses running throughout a race card, he would time his visits to the barns to administer the medication. Then he would check off the horses as the day progressed. Giving the medication too late or too early could have adverse effects, so vets operated on a strict schedule.

A vet van was a virtual cornucopia of pharmaceuticals, all identified and stocked in plastic trays similar to a carpenter's workbench. In this case there were several workbenches fastened to the interior of the van, along with rubs, wraps, and other therapeutic devices.

Although vet vans were required to be locked when not occupied, most vets would park near a barn and leave the side or back doors open. They administered the required therapy, returned to the van, and moved to the next barn.

A vet on his rounds was like a milkman. He made deliveries, provided services, and moved onto the next location. If someone knew the relationships of a specific veterinarian and could match up horses scheduled to receive Lasix injections, the person could fairly accurately predict the path of the vet as he distributed services. Most people didn't care and never knew the difference.

◆ ◆ ◆

FALCON KNEW the difference.

The card had set up perfectly for Falcon. Two unprotected trainers, Dave Simpkins and Kenneth Oliver, had race-day Lasix performers in the same race, the eighth. So while Dancett was giving an injection to a horse scheduled to race in the seventh, Falcon was able to get to the open vet van door. He pulled open the drawer holding the Lasix, withdrew all four boxes, and replaced them with two identical boxes.

Then he disappeared.

◆ ◆ ◆

DANCETT DROVE to Simpkins' barn and pulled a Lasix box containing the med and pre-packaged hypodermic needle from the drawer. He frowned because he thought he had more than just the two boxes left. At least he had enough to finish today's entrants. He made a mental note to stock up in the morning as he never wanted to be short of such a valuable product. Lasix was a medication that moved through the vet vans quickly, so he shrugged and injected Simpkins' gelding with the substance. Then he drove to Oliver's barn and repeated the process.

◆ ◆ ◆

NEITHER SIMPKINS' nor Oliver's horse won that day. In fact, neither got a check.

Both dropped dead before being led over for the eighth race.

On another part of the track, Raven smiled as Dean Horn struggled to explain to the racing audience why two entrants in the eighth had to be late scratches.

Fear on the backside was palpable. Raven witnessed it firsthand every day. Confusion and uncertainty filled the air. It was a stench that intensified with time.

The backside smelled of fear. Raven only smelled the money.

They had no idea what was coming.

PART TWO

ONTO THE BACKSTRETCH

◆ ◆ ◆

PEOPLE ATTACKED WHAT THEY FEARED.

It was simple. It was predictable.

They feared what they chose not to understand. The possibility that an event was beyond the realm of the cogent or the logical was not to be tolerated. Reality existed only in what man chose to believe. If it did not match beliefs, it could not be true. It had to be evil. It had to be destroyed.

That's why some were labeled witches and burned at the stake.

That's why gifts from the obscure were callously rejected and distrusted.

*That's why bloodletting was deemed
the highest evolution of the medical arts
for two thousand years.*

*That's why eugenics was roundly
accepted as morally beneficent science.
Mankind had faith only in what it chose to
believe, in what it chose to see.*

*It was logical. It matched belief systems.
It didn't challenge their fears. It was
understandable. It didn't cause them to question.*

*Yet the human spirit wearily
cried out for a miracle.*

*The miraculous was scoffed at, ridiculed,
and rationalized as a quirk, a coincidence, a
random act. The miraculous was written off as
a parlor game, hucksterism, or infested vermin
that had to be eliminated so that the ledger of
logic was again balanced and true.*

*When the alchemist practiced on metals,
people waited breathlessly. They wanted to
believe. The alchemist who toiled with the
human soul was shunned, marginalized,
and justified out of existence.*

*This was the lesson taught generation
after generation. Who would dare to change it?
Through this worldly existence each would
bear a gift, even the boy.*

Chapter 20

THERE WAS a rhythm to mornings on the backside.
Before heading to the office, Dan grabbed a cup of coffee at Crok's and walked the four barns to Gilmore's stable. He didn't have any particular business most days—just liked the sounds, smells, activity, rumors, and, above all, the horses.

They were beautiful and the center of this universe. They were treated like princes and princesses and cared for like a mother cares for her infant. It was a hard life for the grooms, hotwalkers, and stable hands. Most made little to no money, but the horses needed them, and, in the same way, they needed the horses.

He walked down the gravel road, stepping quickly to the side to get out of the way of a veterinarian's van heading toward him. As Dan moved toward Gilmore's barn, he stepped into the grassy area just off the shedrow path. He pulled up a crate and sat down, watching the grooms and hands care for their charges.

Beth was washing down a young horse. It looked like Welling Green, a promising three-year-old in Gilmore's barn. Nino was walking a hot along the shedrow. Jorge was mucking out a stall, which involved scooping out all the straw, including parts left behind by the inhabitant.

The straw was raked into a pile, hoisted onto a hand cart, transferred to a larger cart, and eventually taken to a larger pile, hopefully downwind from the backside. Once that was completed, new, clean straw was laid down in the stall. Then the process was repeated twenty or so times until every stall was mucked.

Everyone on the backside had mucked a stall. Everyone on the backside hated mucking out stalls. If it was a better job, it would have a better name. But mucking out stalls happened every day, and the "new guy" at a stable, routinely became the "chief mucker outer."

Jake occupied the trainer's office, but Dan was content to sit and take in the morning. He took the lid off his cup, blew some steam off the coffee, and sipped. All around was activity, all centered on a horse and making that horse confident and strong.

It was a place for dreamers. Could this young horse be a champion? Will he fight down the stretch? Does she have the will to win in a nose-to-nose duel? And there were smaller dreams. Could this older claimer keep winning? Will this gelding stay with us another year? The hands poured their hearts into these horses, and the vast majority of the time their hearts were broken. But they came back the next day, and the day after that, and the day after that. They still believed. They were dreamers. They were God's gift to the racehorse.

Jake stepped out of his office, stretched, and yawned. Then he glanced Dan's way and quickly snapped into character. "Dan, how are you? Didn't know you were coming by."

"Just killing time before I head to the office. Only have the carnival in town for three months. I need to make sure I get value for the e-ticket I bought."

Jake walked over and started talking quietly. There was enough background noise at the time. He didn't need to be secretive. "I been meaning to call you. That filly is turning into something. We're gonna work her from the gate tomorrow morning right after the break. You're gonna wanna be here."

"That's great. I need a runner with Hero's Echo on the shelf for a few more weeks."

Jake shrugged like he'd been insulted. Dan was just being honest.

"We'll have Hero running before the month's out," Jake said. "But this little filly's got fight and a good turn of foot. She's passing all her lessons."

"Who you going to ride?"

"Got Kyle Jonas up on her tomorrow. Kid's a little green, but he sits well on a horse, and she really moves for him. If she does what I think she can do," Jake said, under his breath.

Dan nodded and sat silently. This is what owners hoped for. The reason they got in the game, to get a good one. He did his best to keep emotions in check. As was often quoted at the racetrack, being too close to the game would break your heart. Dan had experienced the broken heart part and planned to be close to the sport as long as he could, but he'd learned to temper his feelings. It was okay to dream; it was deadly to expect.

"Kid's got soft hands?" Dan asked.

Jake looked puzzled, then smiled. "Yep, soft hands."

Dan decided it was time to turn serious. "Jake, I think you've got to pay the money. There's too much to lose and not enough to gain."

Jake spit on the ground in front of him. "I don't give in to punks. Never started, never will."

"Jake, it's about keeping the horses safe. It's about keeping your business. They'll catch whoever is doing this, and it'll probably be real soon. It just doesn't make sense to take the risk."

Jake glanced off into the distance, like he'd ended the conversation, then continued. "When I was a kid in middle school, we had some bullies from the nearby high school who would shake down my friends on the way home. They demanded money, tennis shoes, anything of value. Had some kids so scared they were stealing money and stuff from their parents to pay them off." He spit again. "Anyway, they came after me one time, and I said I wasn't going to pay."

"What happened?"

"They beat the crap out of me."

"Inspirational story, Jake."

"Well, the next day, I came by. I looked like I'd been in a cage match with a grizzly. They ask me if I'm gonna pay up. I said 'nope.'"

"Don't tell me."

"Yep, they beat the living crap out of me again. But you know what? They never bothered me after that, 'cause I beat them at their own game."

"How do you figure?" Dan asked.

"It was a shakedown, and I wouldn't give in. So their only recourse was to beat the shit out of me. When they saw that it didn't work, it just wasn't worth it to them. They went after the easy targets and just left me alone."

"This is different," said Dan.

"No, it's not. If I give in, it's like giving in to those bastards from the high school. Not then. Not now."

"But this time it involves other people's property. Mine, for example. Don't let your pride cost you your business. It's only twenty bucks a head. That's nothing compared to what you've got invested in your business—and to make yourself a target as everyone else opts out?"

"Everyone else hasn't opted out."

"Enough of them have and more will. If you don't, the odds go up dramatically. I've finally got a few good runners; I don't mind the payment as long as I know my horses are safe. They're tracking this guy down and will probably catch him. Can't believe they aren't onto him already. Jake, it's not forever, and right now I need the security. Horses like Aly Dancer don't come along every day. I need to know what's going on, and I need to know my property's safe. I could step in and pay on your behalf, but I'd rather we agreed on it rather than just jumping in. It's not about the money."

"You're right; it's not about the money. Nothing's ever about the money." Jake watched Nino go by, looking at the hind legs of the colt. "Well, there's a trainers' meeting tonight over in the secretary's office. I wasn't planning to go, but if you want, I'll take you."

"Why wouldn't you go?" Dan asked.

"'Cause I'm not paying, and I don't give a da—"

The calm of the backside was shattered. A horse cried out, and hooves cracking the wood of a stall brought everyone to attention. Dan spotted AJ charging toward the neighboring barn. He ran on one leg and hopped on the other, but he was motoring as fast as he could toward the sound. Dan threw out his coffee and jogged with Jake over to the edge of the adjoining barn.

Three men were gathered outside a stall halfway down the shedrow. "He loco, boss. Loco." One of the grooms was trying to reach into the stall but jumped back as the horse neighed loudly and snapped at the man. The trainer, Champ Hudgins, reached in to get a hand on the halter.

"Shit," he screamed out and jerked his arm back. There was blood coming off his arm, and half his shirt sleeve was missing. The horse cried out and kicked the stall.

AJ moved toward the group of people assembled in front of the stall. He dropped to the ground and skittered between the legs of the groom and trainer, crawling beneath the webbing into the stall.

"What the hell are you doing?" Champ yelled, clutching his forearm to staunch the bleeding. "Stupid kid, that horse is gonna kill you. Jesus H. Christ. Who is that kid?"

The groom was yelling, but all that could be heard was "*Mal, muy mal.*"

Suddenly the horse went quiet. Champ and the groom leaned in closer to the stall door. Jake and Dan moved a few stalls closer.

"Move the colt next door." The voice was AJ's, stern and confident.

Champ shouted, "What the hell do you think you're doing?"

AJ yelled with urgency and command, "Move the colt next door!"

"We just offloaded that colt from the trailer," said Champ. "Hasn't been there ten minutes."

"Now!" AJ shouted.

Champ looked at the groom, and the groom shot over to the stall on the far side of the one that AJ had entered. The colt was whinnying and snorting from all the disruption. The groom put a cinch on the horse's bridle, unhooked the webbing, and walked the colt out into the shedrow path.

"Put him in number nine, Philippe."

AJ shouted again, "Get the goat out of there, too."

Champ walked into the stall and brought out a small white goat. Some animals were so high strung that they needed company in their stalls. Occasionally, trainers would put a goat or dog in a stall to calm a horse. Champ walked toward Phillipe, who had set the webbing for number nine, and passed him the bridle on the goat.

A few minutes later all was quiet. AJ slipped under the webbing back out into the shedrow.

Champ grabbed AJ's arm and pushed him into the wall of the shedrow.

"Hey, just a damned minute," Dan said. He stepped toward Champ. Jake grabbed Dan's shoulder.

"Kid's got no damn business messing around my barn. Don't work for me."

"Seems like you need someone like him," Dan said. "He did you a favor. You should just say 'thank you' and let him go." The *thank you* came out a little more sarcastically than he'd planned.

"Got no business bein' here." Then he turned to AJ. "Go on, get the hell out of here."

They stepped back and moved away. Jake leaned toward Dan. "Champ's right. Kid has no business being over here. And with all that's going on, everybody's on edge about strangers near their barn. Kid should've known better."

"He helped him." Dan gestured back toward Champ. "He fixed his problem. Would it kill him to say thank you?"

AJ came by, heading out of the shedrow.

Dan reached down and touched him on the shoulder. "You okay?"

He kept walking, looking down. "M'all right."

"What was going on? That horse gone crazy?"

"Horse is fine." AJ looked over his shoulder back down the shedrow toward the stall. "Just was mad about that colt and the goat being next to him. Really upset him."

"How'd you know that?"

AJ stopped and looked at Dan. Then looked back down and kept walking. "He told me."

Chapter 21

JAKE AND Dan drove in silence from the backside around the track to the parking lot next to the racing secretary's office.

How can someone get access to these horses and not be noticed? Who would do this to an innocent animal?

Dan needed more clues. "What's the name of Skelton's mare that was kidnapped?"

"Exigent Lady. Five-year-old."

"Never heard of her."

"She's a quarter claimer on her best days. She probably don't have much run left in her anyway. Had seven outs between Keeneland and Churchill this spring."

"How do you think he pulled it off?"

Jake put his pickup in park and turned off the ignition. "Don't know." That seemed to be the common answer to any question about the extortion scam.

"Which trainer's lost horses yesterday?"

"Simpkins and Oliver."

"Were they poisoned?"

"Beats me. The track management and medical board rode ol' Doc Dancett like a rented mule over the incident.

Looks like someone put some other substance in a counterfeit Lasix box. Poor bastard just did what he does a thousand times a year. Only thing is, this time two horses dropped dead."

"Dancett wouldn't behind this, would he?"

"Hell, no. Man's been around racing since he was a kid. Can't imagine him hurting a horse on purpose. He was set up, sure as hell."

"How do we know it won't happen again?" Dan said as they got out of the pickup and walked toward the building.

"Dancett had to tap dance like a motherfucker just to keep his license. He won't be leaving his van unlocked anytime soon. All the other vets are just damn happy it wasn't them. They won't be leaving any doors unlocked either."

Just inside the doorway, Dan noticed a brick outhouse of a man with arms folded.

"Jake," the man said as they entered.

"Ginny."

The three stood there for an awkward second. When Dan realized that Jake wasn't going to introduce them, he stuck out his hand.

"Dan Morgan." He would have exchanged some pleasantries but locked his mouth to avoid squealing like a schoolgirl from Ginny's crushing handshake.

"Ginny Perino."

A few more seconds and Jake spoke. "Ginny's a farrier."

"Oh, okay," said Dan. "I've seen you around."

Ginny nodded.

"Dan owns Aly Dancer and Hero's Echo."

"Nice filly," said Ginny.

"Thanks, hope so."

Ginny stared directly at Jake. "Everything okay, Jake?"

"Fine. Fine, Ginny—and you?" Jake said, returning the stare.

"All good."

Jake turned sideways, gesturing for Dan to continue farther into the room. Dan took his cue.

"Nice meeting you," said Dan.

"You, too," said Ginny, with his eyes never leaving Jake. "Take care, Jake."

Jake half waved without turning back and kept moving.

"Jesus, Jake," Dan whispered. "Think the guy broke three bones in my hand," he said, shaking and flexing his fingers.

Jake didn't say anything.

"Man of few words. Been around long?" Dan said.

"Few years," Jake said, looking around the room.

There were about two dozen folks in the room outside the racing secretary's office, mostly grouped in threes and fours. Hank Skelton was on the opposite side of the room, talking with Champ Hudgins and Del Dellingham.

"Thought there'd be more trainers here," Dan said to Jake.

"Those who are paying probably don't give a damn about any update and those who won't, well, if it weren't for you, I wouldn't be here either."

Allan Biggs and Chase Evert walked out of Evert's office, and the attention of the group was focused on them. Chase raised his hand and waved people over. "Tim will be joining us in a few minutes. But let's get started." He gave the group a few moments to step closer. "I wish we had more information for you, but here's what we know so far. Whoever is doing this has kidnapped a mare and killed four other race horses. At some time the last two Tuesdays he left a list in the overnights box near Crok's." Biggs held up a piece of paper. "The list identifies each of the trainers with horses on the backside and those who are paying the fee."

Hudgins shouted from the back, "Call it what it is, Chase. Extortion."

"Champ, it is what it is," said Evert. "But those who are paying have their names crossed off. What we figure is the uncrossed names are those he's targeting. At least that's what we believe."

"What the hell is the track doing about it?" Dellingham yelled. "Seems like not a damn thing, far as I can tell."

"Del, we're on it. Tim will be here in a minute to update everyone." Biggs gestured with his arms to quiet the mob. "One other thing I want to talk about before Tim takes over." He swiveled his head around like he was going to have a private conversation with the group. "There are probably some reporters going to be asking around. I can't tell you who to talk to, but I can tell you that it's in all of our interests to keep this contained as much as possible."

"Just trying to cover your own ass," Hudgins shouted. "Might help to have a little public exposure to crack this."

"You're wrong, Champ," Biggs said. "The industry's in a tough enough spot as it is. You know that. Bad publicity is good for no one. Not your owners, not the betting public, and certainly not us," he said, extending his arms to the group. "Be careful who you talk to and what you say. I don't want a bunch of rumors and theories floating around in the press, and I sure as hell don't want PETA reps protesting out front. I'm having conversations with media folks right now. Feel free to send them my way if you want. Let's make sure we don't make this worse than it is."

"It's damn bad right now, Allan. Jesus, how could it get any worse?" Dellingham asked.

Tim Belker walked into the area from his office down the hallway. Biggs and Evert turned as if to say *you take it.*

Jake stepped forward and grabbed Belker's forearm as he walked toward the front of the room. "Tim, you talk to Dagens yet?"

"He don't mean nothing," Belker replied. "He's just trying to round up some rides."

"He don't ride for me," said Jake. "Got no business being at my barn. If he comes around again, he's going to get hurt, and I won't be responsible. Got me?"

Belker eyed Jake, nodded, and continued toward where Biggs and Evert were standing.

He turned to address the group. "Del," Belker said, "I was just on the phone with the FBI. They're helping run a trace on all the licenses for everyone on the backside. Should have some feedback from them soon."

"Shouldn't that be done by now?" said Skelton. "What takes so damn long?"

Belker motioned for calm, then continued, "Please be patient. With law enforcement assistance, we're getting the best of the best. They've dealt with this kind of thing before and know what they're doing. We've got the extra cameras up, and the additional staff has been put on. We're gonna catch this guy."

Angry grumbling rang out from the back of the room. "And we're just supposed to pay or what?" someone shouted. "What's the track gonna do?" another yelled.

Biggs stepped forward. "We're doing all we can to track this guy down. Tim and his staff have been working round the clock on clues and working with other agencies on information. We learned there was a similar threat at Louisiana Downs a few years back, but it never got off the ground. This might be the same guy."

"We've also tried to track the drops, but it's been kind of difficult," said Belker.

"What's so damn hard about it?" Jake said.

"Well, Hank, why don't you tell them about the drops?" said Belker.

"Yeah, what the hell—I'm the guy getting screwed the most here. Guy kidnaps my horse right under your nose and makes me his friggin' chamber maid. I'm going to sue you bastards for everything you got."

Belker interrupted, "Hank, that's not helpful. Just tell them about the drops."

Hank settled himself. "As you know, the letter says to put the cash and names in a newspaper with a rubber band around it. Then I'm to leave the park after eight P.M. on Mondays."

"Why Mondays?" Dan asked. Some of the trainers looked at him as if to say *why the heck are you here?*

"Guess because it's a dark day at the track," said Evert.

"Anyway, I drive away and get a call on my cell phone," Skelton continued. "Some guy directs me to the drop point. Both drops have been different. I get two or three separate phone calls on each trip. The same guy each time. Says he'll kill Exigent Lady if I don't follow the instructions exactly. He tells me that they're watching to see if I'm being followed."

"Where have the drops been?" Del asked.

"Both have been in D.C. I was told to drive toward Alexandria, then as I approached I was told to get on 395 into D.C. Then, after a few minutes, a call came in and told me to take Connecticut Avenue through downtown D.C. As I approach the bridge where Connecticut crosses Rock Creek Park, I get another call, and I'm told to throw the newspaper off the bridge down into the park."

"That would sure make it hard to track," Dan whispered to Jake. "Can't get down there on foot, and by the time you drove your car around to anywhere near that spot, whoever it is would be long gone."

"The second drop was similar. I was directed toward the city and instructed to cross Key Bridge into Georgetown. I get another call. This guy is watching because he knows exactly where I am all the time. Anyway, I get another call and was told to veer right onto Whitehurst Freeway and throw the newspaper off the right side into the park below. Says if I don't make a good throw, he'll put my mare's head on my desk."

"Yeah, same thing," Dan said. "Again, the person will be long gone before you could get your car back down K Street, which runs below Whitehurst. Also, anyone following Hank is in the same position. Can't jump off the bridge."

"As long as Hank gets these messages while driving, there isn't much anyone can do in terms of tracking," said Belker. "Even if you are tracking, it wouldn't do any good. It's all under the cover of darkness, and the drop points are places where you can't pull over and stop your car. You have to keep moving."

"Guy's pretty smart," Jake whispered to Dan.

"That's what bothers me."

Chapter 22

KYLE JONAS drove west on Interstate 66. At 4:30 in the morning the traffic was light. He would be at the track in twenty minutes. Three years on the circuit and he was still hustling rides in the morning. This meant riding training mounts for free in the hope that he could get on some horses in the afternoon. Jocks were supposed to be paid for working horses in the morning. Sometimes they got paid; sometimes the trainer "forgot," and it was considered bad form to remind a person that he owed money, when you were looking for a favor.

TP Boudreaux had handled his book for the past year. Being a former jockey, TP knew the life, and he knew how income drops to zero without the right mounts and a deep relationship with a big barn. TP worked Kyle's butt off.

Kyle's former agent, Skip Dawson, was a full-time gambler with a part-time interest in being a jock agent. The jock agent status allowed him access to the backside to find information that he could convert into some kind of wager. He found Kyle at Meadowfields racetrack and brought him to the big time—or at least at the time it seemed like it. Skip helped Kyle's career, but he was more interested in cashing a big bet than in helping Kyle move to the next level. Kyle moved to TP's book at the close of the Fairmont season last year.

Although Kyle had shed his apprentice bug two years before, he was still considered inexperienced by many. Some barns would only ride guys with ten or more years' experience. There was one thing that changed the hierarchy—winning.

Kyle had to start winning races that he shouldn't win or else run big long shots well above the level of their prior experience. He could get attention by either ramping up his win and in the money percentages or by hitting the board with long shots.

It made him angry to get up at the crack of dawn to ride works on horses, only to see jocks ahead of him in the standings get the mount in the afternoons. Jocks, who because of their win percentage, could afford to sleep comfortably while Kyle busted his ass. But being second on a trainer's list was one of the only ways to get those mounts, so he was up at four to be available for training mounts and workouts.

Jockeys got hurt, spun to other horses, or were called out of town for rides at other meets. In those cases the guy second on the list got his shot. If he could win, he had a chance to keep the mount. If he couldn't win, he would have a difficult time holding that ride.

Since top jockeys get the best mounts, they many times will have first call to ride two horses in the same race. Logic would dictate that the jock will "spin" or get off the horse with the lesser chance to win that day. Handicappers had poured plenty of cash down that rat hole of a theory.

The factors that went into who "spun" involved myriad calculations. The equation included which other horses were in each stable, which barn the jock agent had been working, and, most critically, how the trainer would react to being "spun." Would he put the guy back up next race, or would he "spin" him from all mounts? It was a touchy and political exercise but one that occurred every racing day.

Jocks needed their agents to deliver the news to a trainer and work to stay in a relationship with the barn. This was where the jock agent really earned his money. "Spinning" in this world wasn't unlike agents for movie actors making decisions about what scripts to read, what movies to perform in, and which production houses to support.

Jockeys advanced their careers by making the best decisions, just as actors and actresses who won the Academy Award were guided by an agent who consistently made the right choices.

Kyle's stomach rumbled. It was a feeling to which he had become all too accustomed. He needed to keep his weight below 114 pounds; 112 was even better. If he went off his daily regimen, he would balloon up to 125 in a matter of days. It would take him a week in the hot box and near starvation to get back down to racing weight.

In all thoroughbred races, horses were assigned a given weight to carry. In most situations all horses carried the same amount, known as level weights. In situations where fillies ran against colts and geldings, the filly would get a reduced weight assignment, usually two or three pounds.

Apprentice jockeys received allowances between five and ten pounds off the assigned weight. It was known as the bug because of the mark printed in the racing program to designate the apprentice allowance. In reality, a trainer was balancing the effect on his horse's performance under reduced weight against inexperience in riding. A capable apprentice jockey was favored by nearly all trainers, and the "bug boy" had a full racing card until the apprentice status expired either by time or wins.

In handicap events, the racing secretary assigned weights to each entrant, with the favorite carrying the high weight. The concept operated on the belief that adjusted weights would even the difference in perceived ability and "handicap" the chances for each horse to win. It was a system developed over decades and consistently applied by most racetracks.

For Kyle—and other riders—it meant he had to keep his weight under 114 pounds to ride most races. Being "overweight" was a disadvantage to the mount since the horse had to carry the extra weight. So if Kyle's horse was assigned to carry 118 pounds, with tack, Kyle had to be below 115. If Kyle weighed in that day at 117, then with tack the horse would be two pounds over.

This change would be broadcast to all at the track, essentially saying Kyle couldn't make weight for 118. That was damaging to his chances of getting other mounts, as trainers wouldn't risk riding a guy who couldn't consistently make weight. He could be the next Willie Shoemaker, but if consistently overweight, he risked interfering with a horse's performance.

If an overweight rider lost a close photo, the trainer, along with the betting public, would blame the jockey. Carrying the extra two pounds cost the horse the difference between winning bets and losing bets, between a first place purse and a second place purse, between having the mount next time and being spun for another hustling jockey who could assure the trainer he'd make weight.

It damaged a trainer's winning percentage, his income, and his ability to lure new owners. Being overweight was simply a risk Kyle couldn't take.

His ration of calories each day was strictly monitored, and he took a battery of vitamins and supplements as the exertion of riding headstrong animals demanded physical strength and endurance, despite the restriction on carbs, proteins, and fats.

Unlike other riders, Kyle avoided pharmaceutical aids to keep weight off. Some jocks did Lasix. It essentially drained all excess fluids from the body quickly. Kyle also avoided what was known in the trade as "The CB" or Clenbuterol.

Though a proven treatment for asthma in humans, the equine version was a synthetic metabolism accelerator, and, of course, designed for a 1,200-pound animal. In a 120-pound human, the results were staggering. As a result of its miraculous weight-loss properties, it had quickly become the illegal substance of choice among the Hollywood set.

The saying was it burned fat from the inside out, but it burned up everything else in the human body. The CB allowed some to make weight, and that was all that mattered in the end. A few vets on the backside had been known to "lose" a vial or two of CB in exchange for a "found" C-note.

Kyle also wasn't like many riders who "flipped their meals." He avoided that activity except when necessary, like after a big dinner thrown by an exuberant owner at a local steakhouse. With those rare exceptions, Kyle stuck to his diet. It was a requirement for continued income. He took a big swig of his iced tea. That 32-ounce jumbo cup should help fill his empty stomach for a few hours. He tugged his ball cap down on his forehead and kept driving west.

◆ ◆ ◆

KYLE GALLOPED Aly Dancer on the outside of the track clockwise. Horses near the rail raced by, going the "right way." It was customary in morning exercise to warm up against the grain and far away from the inside rail. Aly Dancer had her head forward and tugged on the bit. Kyle kept a tight grip on the short reins and steadied her pace to a light canter. They approached the starting gate.

Jake and Dan climbed the steps to the clocker's perch on the backside of the track. Mickey Gains, the clocker, held court with several trainers as they entered the small room overlooking the track. Some nods were exchanged before Mickey picked up his binoculars and focused on the starting gate.

"Evaline working," squawked over the walkie talkie on the counter. The gate crew called out the horse for Mickey to record the official work from the gate. Aly Dancer was behind the gate and moving away to avoid being too close to the gate when the other horse worked.

Evaline stood in the gate for nearly a minute when she was finally sent off. Ben Webber, her trainer, moved closer to Gains and clicked his stop watch. The horse spun through the turn and raced down the homestretch toward the finish line. The jockey urged the horse on, and the horse responded. She hit the finish line, and the jockey eased her up.

Mickey's binoculars had a built-in stopwatch, which he controlled with buttons on the top of the device. "Forty-eight and four," he called out.

Webber looked at his watch. "Yup." He didn't seem too happy about the result. He stepped away and moved toward the door. Jake slid closer to Mickey.

"Hey, Jake," Mickey remarked. "One of your babies this morning?"

"Yeah. Filly. Aly Dancer. She's a little green in the gate. We been working with her on her manners lately. Want to qualify her today."

Young horses had to learn to be comfortable in a starting gate. Trainers would start by walking them through an open gate and eventually stop them and close the gate in front of them. As they became more comfortable with the process, they would willingly enter the gate and break when the gate flew open.

If the training was successful, the horse would be "gate qualified," which meant it could be eligible to start a race. No matter how fast or well-bred a horse was, if it wasn't gate qualified, it couldn't race.

"Aly Dancer, next," the starter sent over the walkie talkie.

Kyle eased Aly Dancer toward the gate. One of the gate hands came forward and grabbed the bridle. Aly Dancer bristled. Kyle patted the filly on the neck, and she calmed somewhat. The hand led her toward the gate. Aly Dancer moved slowly toward the gate and reluctantly entered. She stood calmly as the hand jumped onto the ledge inside the stall. Kyle got ready for the break.

The starter made her stand, and after a prolonged delay, hit the button.

Aly Dancer bolted away from the gate. Dan was unable to draw a breath until she was out of the turn and moving down the homestretch. Dan had so much money and time in this young filly. He should have been nervous seeing her break from the gate for the first time. But in this moment, Dan was totally in awe of her strength and power. "God."

Jake looked at Dan and nodded confidently.

KYLE HELD Aly Dancer with a firm grip. The reins slapped the filly's neck as she tugged forward against him. Kyle didn't release her head. She skimmed like a feather over glass, not like those old claimers he rode that rocked and shimmied like ancient washing machines. All her effort went in one direction, all generating speed.

She chugged in forceful breaths, all in sync with her motion. Damn, thought Kyle, she's moving.

The wind whipped her mane, and they entered the turn. Kyle shifted his weight, and Aly Dancer perfectly changed leads, to power through the turn. Her ears were perked and flashed forward and back. She was enjoying this; she hadn't pinned her ears in stress or anger as many horses did. She was having fun as they ate up ground.

The pair hit the finish line, and Kyle stood in the stirrups to slow her. She wanted to keep going. Kyle knew they went fast. He didn't know her time, but he knew one thing. Nothing was going to get him off this ride. She was the one he'd dreamed of. This was the one that could vault his career. Whatever it took, no way was he giving up the chance to ride this filly.

♦ ♦ ♦

DAN'S HEART was pounding like a jackhammer as she hit the finish line, and Kyle eased her. She went fast—Dan knew that much. Jake clicked his stopwatch and looked at it.

Mickey glanced over at Jake in astonishment. "Forty-six and one?" The question said it all. A two-year-old being gate checked wasn't supposed to go that fast. "Solid work, Jake," Mickey said.

Another trainer who had entered the clocker's shack asked who the horse was. "Just a baby," Jake said. Then he motioned for Dan to leave.

At the bottom of the stairs Dan turned to him. "Forty-six and one? Good lord, that's fast. For a two-year-old? Are you kiddin' me?"

Jake motioned him closer. "More like forty-five and four," he whispered. "That's what I got her in."

"But, Mickey said—"

"Forget Mickey."

"What? Did he miss it?"

"Nope," Jake said, walking away. "Mickey got it. Saw it same as you. That filly can flat fly."

Chapter 23

"LOOK AT that tote," Milton said. "Likatious is 8 to 5. Damn thing would run second in a one-horse race."

Lennie studied his pace and speed printouts like a scientist pouring ingredients into a test tube. "Don't be so sure. He's been off for three months and worked well coming back. Throw him out at your peril."

"Dan, you got any winners like Hollerin Hal? Y'know, just a flier that you can't tell us about? You know, 'til it's too late to get a bet down?" Milton dipped his finger in the cup of nacho cheese sauce, then stuck it in his mouth.

"Hey, I remember you cashing a bet on that last horse I gave you. Don't be greedy. If I've got something, I always share. Just don't blame me if the horse runs up the track."

Lennie made some pencil marks around the numbers on his sheets. "Hey, you work your two-year-old?"

Dan beamed. "She was beautiful this morning. Just a thing of beauty."

Lennie turned from his sheets and gave him a big smile. "I hope you got a real runner in that one. How'd she do?"

"Mickey got her in forty-six and one."

"What? That's quick," said Lennie. "And for a two-year-old? Wow."

"And she did it so easy," Dan said. "Kyle Jonas didn't move a muscle the whole way 'round. Strange thing, though. Jake said Gains clocked her in forty-five and four." Lennie's eyes nearly popped out of his head.

"Geez, Dan," Milton piped up. "You going to let us get in the winner's circle picture?"

"For you, Maj. Anything."

Lennie had a big smile he was trying to keep to himself.

"What?" Dan asked finally.

"Danny, she went forty-five and four, maybe faster. Mickey is going to write her up at forty-six and one. May not be a big deal to many people, but I think Mickey's going to try to cash a ticket when your filly runs." Dan gave him a puzzled look. "Clockers have been known to miss a killer workout because, if they put it down as it happened, it would knock down the odds. It wasn't a totally dark work, but I guarantee you, he's got his eye on your filly."

Milton edged his way around Lennie to get out of the box seats. "I'm going with the three and gonna play him with the four and seven in exactas," Milton said. "Likatious is gonna be a bust today. I can't play him as the chalk. You guys want anything?"

They weren't sure whether he meant a bet or libation. Dan shook his head no. As Milt neared the top of the steps, Dan said, "Heck, if I ordered a sandwich, he'd eat it before he got back to the box anyway."

"Tough card today, Danny boy," Lennie muttered. "They're going to make it hard on us."

"Where's TP?" he asked, looking down on the crowd milling around on the apron below them.

"Emilio's got a ride here. He may be buttering up the trainer in the paddock."

"Or practicing his excuses," Dan said, which raised a chuckle. "Lennie, were you in the seminary once? Am I remembering that right?"

"Yeah, I was. Mom was so proud," he said. "For the whole three months. Then I came to my senses and went back to Princeton to get my math degree. That was an odd time." Lennie stared at the tote board and put his pages on his lap. He lifted his glasses and rubbed his nose. "I'm going to pass this one. Likatious may run out, but he might as easily draw off and win by five. Can't play this race."

"Does the name Ananias mean anything to you?"

"From the Bible?" Lennie asked. Dan shrugged and nodded. "Well, you're talking about Ananias and Sapphira. It's a biblical story that theologians have debated through the ages. Some think it has to do with tithing, and others think it's about deception."

Dan looked at him, waiting.

Lennie continued, "As the story goes, Ananias was married to a gal named Sapphira. Ananias sold some land and was preparing to short his contribution to the apostles. You see, early Christians gave everything they had to the apostles. Didn't believe that they owned anything—just held it for the work of the church. Anyway, Ananias kept some of the money and only gave part to the apostles." Lennie eased back in his chair and looked out over the track.

"And?" Dan asked.

"And God struck them both down. Killed both Ananias and his wife."

"Killed them?"

"Well, in the scriptures it was known as 'giving up the ghost.' You just dropped dead. So 'kill' might be a harsh word, but they died spontaneously. So you tell me the cause of death. They were just taken out. Boom."

"Why? I don't get it," said Dan.

"That's why scholars have debated the story for centuries. One theory is that he didn't give the right amount to the apostles. Ergo, they were killed. Another theory is that it wasn't about the money. It was about deception. If Ananias had been honest about how much money he got from the deal and only wanted to give the apostles so much, he wouldn't have been struck down. I'm not sure either one is completely right. You know, there are some strange stories in the Bible, and I've always wondered what was lost in translation or about errors in transcription. To me, the story seems like it's missing some pretty important pieces."

Dan looked down and tried to imagine why someone would name a child Ananias.

"So, what sent you on this biblical trip down memory lane?" Lennie asked.

"Oh, I met a guy with the name Ananias, and he said it was from the Bible, and I wondered what the story was."

"Quite a tag to hang on someone," said Lennie. "What did they do, name his brother Pontius Pilate?"

Milton came back, carrying a tub of popcorn, and he had two hotdogs wrapped in foil in his jacket pocket.

Lennie scooted back as Milton slid past him. "Bet the favorite, didn't you?"

Milton looked at him like he just ruined a birthday surprise. "Damn straight. Dellingham wouldn't bring him back and put him in this spot if he didn't think he'd fire. Plus, lot of barn money coming in on him late."

The tote showed Likatious at six to five. Track announcer Dean Horn called them all in line.

Likatious ran middle of the pack and never fired. He finished last. A total non-factor.

Milton threw a half-dozen tickets in the air as the leaders were halfway down the stretch. "Damn it. I told you he couldn't win a one-horse race. Didn't I tell you that?" Milton said in total frustration.

"That you did, Milton," Lennie said, licking a finger and turning to his pages for the next race. "That you did."

Chapter 24

THE MORNING sun hung low in the sky but presaged a blistering, humid day. The movable outside rail on the backside of the racetrack was shifted over, leaving a thirty-foot gap, which allowed horses and riders to get onto the track from the backside.

Morning works were in progress. Some would be official works, some in company, and others galloped and cantered around the track as the daily exercise. Jake wasn't at the barn, so Dan wandered over to the break.

Those who loved this game could stand for hours and watch horses go by. With experience, the exceptional athletes could be spotted much the same way one could watch a group of boys playing basketball and rank-order their ability. It was called "watching their action"—how they moved over the ground, how eager they were to be on the track. Some would show reluctance; some would be so full of themselves they would drag the rider around the track, throwing their heads in a plea for a loosened grip.

Exercise riders had been given instructions for each mount, whether that was a canter just to stretch the legs, a two-minute mile clip, or a bullet work. Horse and rider had to cooperate, or it was a constant tug of war between man and animal. Man had the leverage; the animal had its will. On good days, they fought to a draw.

He spotted Beth standing on the left side of the break, leaning against the rail. Her tiny frame mirrored the posts holding up the rail, with her blonde hair swaying slightly in the breeze. She was looking up the track, past the clocker's tower, probably watching one of her charges go through its exercise regime.

Riders going past made sure to catch a good glimpse, and those going to and from the track gave her an in-depth once over. Some shouted to her or at least in her direction. She ignored them, keeping her eyes on the long backstretch.

"Who you got out today?" Dan asked.

She shifted her weight and looked over, brightening. "Tom Crater's mare, Breaking Dawn. Just giving her a little air." This meant a moderate workout, just to aid in conditioning. "She's a tough customer. Doesn't like working in the mornings. Would rather sleep in."

"Mare's done all right. She runs well in the afternoons." Dan had cashed a bet on her a few times. He knew the ins and outs of Jake's barn, and even though he didn't have an ownership interest in the horse, she was on the same team.

"Yeah, some of these characters only want to race. Problem is, unless we get them sharpened in the mornings, they won't have any legs for the afternoons."

"Makes you wish you could talk to them, explain the purpose."

She smiled and looked him in the eye. "Oh, we communicate. Believe me. May not be with words, but after a while they know the drill. They may not like it, and they can be stubborn as hell, but they know. Never want to take the chip off their shoulder. Want them to have that edge, but like dancing, somebody's got to lead and somebody's got to follow."

"Who's who?"

This raised a chuckle. "We lead." Beth gazed out over the track, watching for Breaking Dawn. "Well, most of the time anyway."

Dan gave her a quick glance, then looked up the track. "Which one?"

"Emilio's got a green shirt under the vest."

He found them in the middle of the track, just out of the turn, pounding toward them. "What's he doing? A two-minute clip?"

"S'posed to. Hell, he may have to go to the whip to get that out of her."

They watched in silence as the mare came toward them. From straight on, it was difficult to determine how fast she was moving, but Emilio bounced up and down, indicating that he was working somewhat to raise her interest level.

Dan spotted the man coming down the stairs of the clocker's tower that adjoined the track twenty yards from the break. He was the man he met at the trainer's meeting, the one who nearly broke his hand. The farrier. *What's a farrier doing in the clocker's tower?*

The man approached, and Dan caught his eye, or at least part of his eye. Most of his attention was on Beth's backside. "Ginny. Right?" He didn't bother to offer a hand to shake.

Ginny nodded. "Dan." He kept moving past, giving one last glance at Beth's backside.

Breaking Dawn moved past them, and Beth's head followed the arch into the turn. She turned and saw

Ginny moving away, then focused her eyes back on the horse.

"Guy's bad news," she said.

"Ginny?"

"Yep."

"What's his deal?"

"Stay away from him," she said, still focusing on her horse, halfway through the turn.

"No, seriously. Guy's a farrier isn't he?"

"All I know is what I hear. He's trouble."

"Make sure you never shake hands with him. He nearly crushed all the bones in my hand," Dan said, trying to get a laugh out of her.

She wasn't going for any of it. "Heard he beat a guy to death down at Louisiana Downs."

"If that's true, why isn't he in jail?"

"Who knows? Maybe he had a crafty lawyer like you get him off." She looked over, not smiling. Two horses working in company blistered past them near the rail. Both were drawn to the action and competition. One jockey pumped his arms furiously, trying to get his horse to take the lead over his counterpart. They watched them spin into the turn, then Beth turned back.

"He's been ruled off two or three other tracks, I've been told. Threw a jockey through a plate glass window once. Man's crazy. I mean it—if there's a problem, that guy is always in the neighborhood. Been hanging around the barn a little too much for my comfort."

"Jake knows what he's doing," he said.

"Yeah, maybe. I'm telling you, stay away from that guy. He's not your friend. The guy creeps me out."

Chapter 25

KYLE LEANED forward and hooked his toes into that familiar position around the stirrup. He wrapped horse hair from the mane around his index finger and prepared for the break. He would time it perfectly to be on his toes, leaning over the horse's neck. The acceleration would balance him, and his forward position would keep him from falling back and yanking the reins. Men who worked as gate hands were scrambling in and around the starting gate.

"Two out."

More shifting and movement could be heard behind him. One gate hand was standing on the foot ledge inside the stall with Kyle and Aly Dancer. He held the horse's bridle and unwrapped the leather strap that had run through the bridle to lead the horse into the starting gate stall. On the break he would release the horse, hopefully in a straight course.

"One out."

The clanging of the stalls slamming shut told him they were all in. Jack Meeks shouted "No, no, no." He was trying to steady his mount, Arestie, in the six hole. Meek's plea was directed toward the starter, who stood on a high platform just inside the rail.

"Whoa, whoa," said jockey Jim Dagens, in chorus with the gate hand next to him. Mystic Prose in the number one shoot had reared back. Dagens' foot had come out, and he was desperately trying to hook it back in the stirrup.

The starter would try to accommodate the jockey's requests, but when he sensed them all standing well, he would hit the button. The magnetic field holding the front of the gates closed would be cut, and the two piece gate would spring open. Kyle sensed the break and leaned forward up on his toes.

"They're all standing well...and they're off.... Mystic Prose broke well on the inside.... Undaunted Cem moves up from the far outside to contest the early pace. Magnet Time is third.... Aly Dancer is placed well inside in fourth...with Arestie just outside her in fifth.... Big Bad Bess is half a length back, holding sixth. Prized Piece is next...two back to Gypsum Doll, and Yellow Bellow trails the field."

Kyle steadied Aly Dancer. On the break Prized Piece bolted left out of the four hole and slammed into Aly Dancer, nearly knocking her sideways and into the two horse, Gypsum Doll.

Dagens got Mystic Prose away well from the rail. Aly Dancer didn't break stride but absorbed a good blow. Prized Piece got the worst of it. Aly Dancer straightened well and took up chase.

Kyle looked over his left shoulder and guided Aly Dancer to the rail. He gathered the reins and held position. Magnet Time was alongside, and another horse was outside him. Kyle couldn't see who it was, and it didn't matter for the time being.

He had two horses in front of him and a good spot on the rail. He could wait it out from here. Kyle decided to let the front runners extend themselves a bit and gave Aly Dancer a light tug on the reins. She pulled hard on the reins and pinned her ears back. She wanted to run.

As the leaders moved from a one-length lead to two, Kyle drifted Aly Dancer half a lane right to avoid the dirt spray coming from the front runners. If he stayed directly behind the leader, the spray would hit his mount in the face. This could annoy and frustrate any horse, but with a young horse like Aly Dancer, it could be a negative experience that might affect her racing career.

Kyle had to restrain her but also keep the horse's courage and confidence up. They were going pretty good up front for the first quarter. Kyle calculated it was just a few ticks too fast for these types. Unless one of the horses in this field was a superstar, the race would come back to him. He pulled down one of his pair of goggles under his chin, leaving three clean pair stacked over on another.

He felt Aly Dancer relax and get a good rhythm.

He waited.

"Mystic Prose and Undaunted Cem are heads apart... the first quarter in 22 and 4.... Aly Dancer tracks them in third.... Arestie is fourth on the outside...Magnet Time between horses...break of three back to Yellow Bellow, Big Bad Bess, and Prized Piece in eighth.... Gypsum Doll follows."

Kyle watched the horses in front of him. He was looking for any evidence that one was tiring. As the race stood now, he was in a strong stalking position as they neared the far turn. If the horse on the rail tired, she would start to drift away from the rail. This would be Kyle's preference as he could sneak past the leader on the rail, and everyone else would have to go wide to catch him.

If Undaunted Cem started to drift out, he could split the frontrunners, but he'd have to get there first as the horse outside him would be going for the same spot. The worst case would be if both horses ahead of him maintained pace. In that case he'd be blocked like a pick in basketball; the horses outside him would get by the leaders, and he'd be trapped inside.

Kyle looked over at Arestie for any clue. Was the horse laboring? Was the jockey urging? To his disappointment, the horse was moving well, and the jockey was sitting chilly. They started creeping ever closer to the frontrunners.

"The leaders move into the turn...45 and 3 for the half.... Undaunted Cem and Mystic Prose continue to lead.... Aly Dancer moving well...Arestie outside her says, "I'm going to get a piece of this".... Magnet Time is losing ground. Big Bad Bess moves along the rail.... Yellow Bellow keeping pace... Prized Piece is fading.... Gypsum Doll is starting to make a move from the back of the field."

Damn it. The frontrunners weren't giving it up. He could move to the rail, but if he was shut off, so were his chances. Splitting the frontrunners would be dangerous, and, given their position, they could all end up in a heap on the track. Kyle and Aly Dancer edged closer to the leaders.

He saw Meeks look over from Arestie. *Arrogant prick.* He knew Kyle had a lot of horse and was in a bind. Kyle looked back to his left and saw a horse beginning to move into striking distance on the rail. He still had enough room to take the rail, but he would have to decide fast. If he let the other horse advance along the rail and get position, he couldn't move left down on top of him.

◆ ◆ ◆

JAKE SLAPPED his racing form on the rail in front of him. "Shit. He's got a ton of horse and no place to go. Find someplace to run." He and Dan stood on the upper level of the mezzanine, giving them a view of the entire track. Jake held a small set of binoculars up to his face with one hand. "C'mon, Kyle, get her outside, God damn it!" Jake yelled.

"Out of the turn, Arestie is moving well on the outside.... Undaunted Cem puts his head in front.... Aly Dancer is fourth.... Big Bad Bess moves along the rail...and Gypsum Doll is moving powerfully on the outside."

◆ ◆ ◆

KYLE SAW Arestie start to make her move around Undaunted Cem. He looked back to his left, barely enough room.

Fuck it, that's not Seattle Slew up ahead. Now or never.

Kyle threw a cross with the reins and yanked Aly Dancer's head to the left. He shouted, "Haaah," loosened the reins, and ground on the horse's neck with his knuckles. Aly Dancer responded to the lane shift, then seemed to balk as if to say, *Are you serious?* Kyle scrubbed her neck with knuckles, and she knew he meant business.

Kyle saw Dagens on Mystic Prose peek over his left shoulder at Aly Dancer. He turned back and kept riding.

He's not going to budge off the rail, Kyle thought. There wasn't enough room to get through.

There was no place to go.

◆ ◆ ◆

"COME ON, kid," Jake muttered. He'd laid all but $200 of the remaining loan from Ginny on Aly Dancer—all on the nose. She had all the ability in the world, especially against a bunch of maidens. Running well wouldn't cut it. Jake needed a win.

"Come on, Kyle. Find a lane," Dan yelled as if he was hoping his positive vibe would counteract Jake's defeatist tone. "Come on, baby, get room."

"Arestie surges to the lead.... Undaunted Cem tries to keep pace.... .Mystic Prose on the inside...and Gypsum Doll moves four wide into the stretch...."

◆ ◆ ◆

KYLE HUGGED the rail and waited. Even if he got through, the horses on the outside were moving well and unimpeded to the finish line.

Just then it happened.

It was the slightest move, almost imperceptible, but Mystic Prose drifted slightly to the right. Could have been a result of tiring through the fast early fractions or the distraction of seeing horses outside her moving well, but she drifted.

Kyle pulled his whip and gave Aly Dancer a full crack. She responded and quickly filled the gap when Mystic Prose drifted off the rail. She wasn't through the hole yet. Kyle scrubbed with his knuckles "C'mon, c'mon, haaaah!"

◆ ◆ ◆

JAKE HAD a poor angle to see the shift, but years of experience told him there was a hole on the rail. "Get her through there." He slammed the racing form against the rail. "Get through there." Suddenly, she had a chance. A ton of ground to make up, but she had a chance.

"Gypsum Doll moves outside Arestie, and the two of them are kicking on.... Undaunted Cem is third.... Mystic Prose is losing touch with the top ones...Aly Dancer trying to get through on the rail."

◆ ◆ ◆

MYSTIC PROSE kept drifting slightly to the right. Kyle flashed the whip on the right side of Aly Dancer's head. Keep her focused, get through the hole. Dagens tried to move Mystic Prose left to hold the rail, but he was fighting a tiring horse.

Kyle could feel Aly Dancer dig down and accelerate. "That's it, girl. C'mon." Aly Dancer moved past Mystic Prose, but she was still a length and a half behind Arestie and Gypsum Doll, who were moving well on the outside.

Kyle re-gripped the reins and started driving forward on Aly Dancer's neck. He turned the whip in his hand and cracked the horse on the right flank.

They still had work to do.

"Aly Dancer moves up to third along the rail.... Gypsum Doll has a head in front on the far outside.... Arestie battles on."

Kyle kept pumping with his arms and driving. The horse was giving him everything she had. They were catching the frontrunners, but there was less than a sixteenth of a mile to go. Kyle put his head down and pushed. He flashed the whip past Aly Dancer's head. No need to abuse the animal; she was already running her guts out.

"Arestie leads on the outside...Aly Dancer driving strongly on the inside...Gypsum Doll third...Arestie...Aly Dancer... these two to the wire...Arestie...Aly Dancer...at the finish, it's...."

◆ ◆ ◆

"GET UP, get up, get up." Dan pounded on the rail as the horses hit the wire.

"She got 'em," Jake said, throwing his fists in the air. "Yes!"

Voices from the crowd around him questioned the finish.

"Too close."

"Outside horse held on," one said confidently.

"I don't know," one muttered.

Jake had seen enough races; he knew. He started moving through the crowd toward the track. Jake was sure she got up to win. Cashing the ticket would give him breathing room for a few days, until he could get more runners to the track. Yes, she won.

She had to have won.

Chapter 26

KYLE DROVE Aly Dancer through the finish line. He thought he got it. He extended his legs and stopped pushing. A few strides past the finish line, he looked to his right at Jack Meeks on Arestie. He could see it in Jack's eyes. Aly Dancer won. It might be some freaky head bob, but they both knew Aly Dancer was moving best at the wire. Kyle let out a whoop, slapped Aly Dancer on neck, and rode her out. They got home first.

◆ ◆ ◆

DAN WATCHED Aly Dancer ease up after the finish line. She was flying at the end. He was breathless and spent. Aly Dancer looked like she could go around the track again. She was full of herself, prancing and nodding. All the time, money, energy, and interest in these animals—and this moment was what it was all about.

"Hell, yes," he shouted, throwing his racing form in the air.

That was a killer move she made down the stretch. Not only was she talented, but she showed the will to win. This was the one he'd dreamed of.

In his revelry he didn't notice that Jake had left him to go to the winner's circle. It didn't matter. When your first time starter won like she did, you were entitled to jump and shout and generally make a fool of yourself. She had won, right? At least he thought she had. Jake was sure. Damn right, she won, he thought as he made his way to the winner's circle.

Dan hustled down the steps to the apron. He couldn't contain his smile, and pride nearly burst from his chest as he zigzagged through the crowd to the winner's circle. Win or lose, she had performed. She fought through the stretch. Despite a troubled trip, she showed ability and fire.

Outside the enclosure Dan noted the groom he'd called Romeo among the group waiting for the entrants to return to the unsaddling area. The horses, winded and caked in dirt, trotted clockwise past the clubhouse turn, back toward the finish line. Jockeys stood in their stirrups, bent over at the waist; some sat and bounced as they returned from the rigors of the competition.

Which horse was Romeo connected with? He's just a punk, why should I care?, Dan thought. Then Romeo reached forward for the bridle and sponged a handful of water on the muzzle of his horse. Of course, it was Arestie. How fitting, Dan thought. He wanted to win that photo even more.

Arestie and Aly Dancer circled in front of the winner's enclosure, awaiting the photo. Beth circled Aly Dancer in a large arching turn, the smile on her face matching Dan's as she chatted up Kyle. By appearances, there was no question who won. Kyle was more reserved, but the animation in his conversation with Beth revealed his excitement. This filly was the real deal.

Minutes later the photo sign came down, and for half a second time stood still. A large three flashed up on the top of the tote. Dan was airborne, thrusting his fist in the air. "Yes, yes," he screamed. Cheers and moans rose up from the grandstand. Gypsum Doll held third.

Dan slapped hands with Kyle as Aly Dancer was led into the winner's enclosure. He patted the filly on the neck.

Perspiration from her coat soaked his hand, but Dan could care less. Standing in front of his now undefeated two-year-old filly, Dan held the reins and bridle as they posed for the winning picture.

◆ ◆ ◆

AFTER THE photo, Kyle jumped down and patted Aly Dancer on the neck. He un-cinched the saddle and slid it over his arm to carry to the scale. Jake put an arm around Kyle's neck and bent low to whisper in his ear.

"You got lucky," Jake said.

Kyle looked back in amazement. Jake wasn't smiling.

"I put you on the best horse in the race," Jake whispered. "And you nearly got her beat. I'll tell you what I'm gonna tell TP. If you can't keep 'em out of trouble, I'll take you off fucking everything. You hear me?"

Jake didn't wait for an answer; he walked off. Kyle weighed in and passed the saddle to a valet. He walked just outside the rail bird's fence as he headed back to the jockey room.

"Great ride, KJ," one shouted.

"I knew you had that six horse measured at the head of the stretch," another said.

Several stuck out hands for high fives. Kyle smiled and walked past. He loved the attention, but after Jake's parting shot, he wasn't in the mood for glad handing.

He was lightly tapping his whip against his boot as he entered the jockey's room. The next thing he knew, he was falling backward into the lockers, just inside the door. Dagens was standing over him.

"You're dangerous out there." Kyle tried to get up, but Dagens kneed him and knocked him off balance and onto his back. "You try that again, and I'll put your ass through the rail."

Phil Gillette and Meeks pulled Dagens back, allowing Kyle to scramble to his feet. A security guard also stepped toward the door.

Dagens gestured at Kyle. "That's the last time. You ride like that, you're gonna put guys on the track. I'm puttin' you through the rail, you crazy bastard. Where the fuck you learn to ride?"

Gillette was able to push Dagens backward and away from Kyle.

Dagens wasn't done yet and motioned with a crooked finger extended from his fist. "Through the rail. That's all I got to say."

Chapter 27

THE ROUTINE in the bar had become near clockwork. Raven walked into Clancy's, nodded at Falcon, and moved toward the bar. He knocked on the bar, got the bartender's attention, pointed at a half-empty beer bottle in front of a 300-pound biker sitting precariously on a bar stool, and raised two fingers. Two beers were produced, tops popped off, money exchanged, tip left behind, and Raven walked to the booth.

"Anybody follow you?" said Raven.

"Nope."

"How can you be so sure?"

"I drove all over around hell and back. No way anyone followed me through all that."

A Van Halen tune pounded out of the jukebox in the corner. Guitar riffs and heavy bass lines filled the air. Two guys at the pool table were laughing and setting up trick shots, apparently for tequila shooters.

Raven leaned in. "How'd we do?"

"Sixteen."

"We're getting there."

"Six guys came current," said Falcon. "That gave us a boost."

"How many are out?"

Falcon produced the sheet of paper containing the trainer names. "Eleven." He turned the page around and slid it toward Raven.

"We'll have to try and help motivate these leftovers."

"We're doing okay now," said Falcon. "Got the pump primed. We can cool it for a while."

Raven just stared at him.

Falcon continued, "Seriously. We've got the money coming in. No need to take on more risk. Not that much to be gained. Everybody is ramping up their security. Hell, you can hardly walk around outside the barn without being interrogated. Let's just play it cool for a while and let the cash roll in."

Raven just nodded like he was agreeing, then stopped suddenly. "No way in hell I'm letting those fuckers off." He pointed at the list. "They owe us too much money."

"You're taking this too far."

"I tell you what. Once we have all the names crossed off, we stop. 'Til then, these bastards are fair game."

Falcon shook his head. Raven reviewed the paper in front of him. He tapped on Gilmore's name. "Fella's got a nice filly. Lotta talk about her on the backside. Be a shame if anything happened to her." Raven could see the stunned look on Falcon's face.

"I thought we were only gonna hit old claimers. Horses nobody'd really miss," said Falcon.

"Never said that."

"That was the deal," Falcon said. "This is bad enough. I don't wanna be killing two-year-olds. 'Specially good ones. No point in it." Falcon looked down at the table and shook his head. "Just wrong."

Raven pressed on, "I don't need you wimping out on me. Too much money to make. You stay cool. I'll take over the wet work for a while. You just worry about holding up your end."

"What are you going to do?"

"You ever study biology?"

"Never studied nothing but a racing form."

"Nature has a way of evening out life's odds. When you know what you're doing, you can put the odds in your favor." Raven tipped his head back and killed off the last half of his beer. "After that I've got an even better plan. I don't even have to be near the damn horse to kill it. It'll be a thing of beauty." Raven slid out of the booth, swooping up the envelope of cash. "All in due time, my friend."

Then he walked out of the bar.

Chapter 28

THE WASHINGTON *Post* broke the story Wednesday morning, under Jason Cregg's byline. An unnamed source, had confirmed the death of four horses at Fairfax Park, including two scheduled to run in the same race the previous Thursday.

Details remained sketchy. It wasn't clear whether an outside force was responsible for the deaths or some kind of battle among rival stables on the backside. The report was less than three column inches at the end of an article that recapped the upcoming stakes schedule. But now the story was out. A storm was coming.

Track President Allan Biggs had no comment as an internal investigation was currently underway. He did express deep regret for the loss of some of the track's most courageous athletes. He vowed to use all available resources to uncover who was behind these heinous acts.

Biggs threw the paper onto his desk. *Who the hell was his source?* There was no mention of the extortion demands, but that was just a matter of time. The internal investigation line would work for now, but Cregg was persistent. He was dangerous. The knuckleheads on the backside were primed to blow it at any moment. *Can't believe Cregg didn't get more dirt from them. Maybe they're holding together, as he'd asked them. No, he could never get that lucky.* He was running out of time.

He leaned back in his chair, then shot upright. "Belker! Get your ass in here!"

◆ ◆ ◆

MOST OF the jocks had cleared out. Those who didn't ride the last race had long since evacuated the jockey room. When the final horses hit the wire, the crowd emptied out of the grandstand. The few remaining winners had cashed their tickets, laughed, bought the last round of beers, and marveled in their mastery.

Tomorrow would be a new day for the early departers. Those who closed down the concessions bragged about their day, mostly to concession workers who wanted to clear out and head home themselves. Cars snaked their way off of the property and dumped onto the freeway. Soon the parking lot turned to its normal shade of black.

Kyle leaned back against his locker, exhausted but happy. He didn't dare smile. Today he'd broken through. Two wins, a third, and one race up the track. The wins moved him into the top ten at the track. He still trailed Dagens and Masterson, who led the colony this meet, but he was gaining.

Neither winner was a favorite. He rode so few favorites, but if he could keep up the pace, he would start attracting attention from the better barns. Gilmore's filly gave him a legit shot at stakes money—if he could keep the mount. Even though several days had passed since that maiden win, Kyle was still exhilarated by the ride. She was the real deal.

But he had to keep improving. Today's third place was a legit long shot at 15-1. He leaned forward and pulled his boots on, then slid back and rested his head against the locker.

After several minutes of enjoying the solitude, Kyle walked out of the jocks' room and moved toward his car. His path took him down a narrow corridor and past the employee entrance.

Cyndi would know the results before he got home, but he would give her the blow by blow of each race as he did on days he won. She would have calculated his take for the day. When he didn't win, they seldom talked. She'd learned. Growing up on the backside, she knew the code.

There were no paychecks in his world; there was only performance. When he won, they dreamed. When he lost, they worried. Tonight they would dream.

"Hey, punk." It was Dagens. He was standing at the end of the corridor with two other jocks, Skip Delacroix and Jose Moreno. Dagens stepped forward. "I've about had it with your shit, Jonas."

Dagens ran second on a heavy favorite when Kyle won the tenth race. Kyle had gotten through on the rail again and beat Dagens' horse in the last two jumps. Beaten favorites were the death of jocks. Fans jeered, owners complained, and trainers got antsy. The jock was where the rubber met the road.

Kyle stopped about five feet short of Dagens. "That's the way it goes." Delacroix and Moreno stood back, smiling with their arms folded.

"That's not the way it goes, dipshit. Not around here." Dagens stepped forward and pushed Kyle in the chest. "I told you once, not gonna tell you again."

Kyle couldn't remember the last time he was in a street fight. Come to think of it, he hadn't been in one since grade school skirmishes. The last thing he wanted to do was tangle with Dagens. "That's horseracing," Kyle said, hoping to diffuse the situation.

"Bullshit."

Dagens was moving forward with fists clenched.

Just stay calm, Kyle thought. He's bluffing. He just wants to appear tough; then, he'll throw some more verbal abuse, and it will be over.

"I told you I'd put you through the rail, fucker. But I think I'd rather just kick your ass right here."

He's bluffing. One more tirade and it'll be over. Stay cool.

"You'll get ruled off," Kyle said. The stewards would give him days for fighting. Everyone knew that. Dagens wouldn't risk days over a fight. It's almost over. Stay calm.

"It'll be worth the days to teach you a lesson, shithead."

Kyle put his open hands forward. Dagens kept advancing.

He won't do it, Kyle thought. He wouldn't risk it.

Dagens was catlike quick, and an overhand cross ripped across Kyle's face. The punch caught him flush on the side of his face, smashing his nose against his right cheek. Kyle spun and fell forward onto his hands. His eyes watered from the searing pain in the place where his nose used to be. He looked up. Delacroix laughed. Moreno kept a lookout for anyone coming into the corridor.

"Get up—I'm not done with you."

Through most things Kyle was able to keep his anger in check, but the reaction by the two other jocks bothered him more than the punch. He sprang at Dagens and tackled him, throwing both of them onto the ground. Dagens rabbit-punched him as they went down. Kyle brought his fist down, hoping for Dagens' face, but only glanced off his shoulder. He lifted himself, pulling away from Dagens' grip and swung again. This time he connected, but the close quarters meant there was little energy behind the blow.

Dagens swung him off and scrambled to his feet. Kyle was up breathing hard. Blood was running from his nose, and he wiped it off with the back of his hand. His eyes were still stinging. They circled to the left. Kyle clenched his jaw and snuffled blood into his throat. He looked for an opening. Dagens smirked. That was it.

Kyle lunged and delivered a right cross. Dagens deflected it with his hand, but it still connected. Keeping his momentum, Kyle pushed Dagens. The move surprised Dagens, and he slammed against the wall. Kyle hit him again, this time catching Dagens flush on the cheek. Kyle's knuckles screamed out in pain. Dagens threw an upper cut that buried his fist into Kyle's stomach. Kyle doubled over and drove his head into Dagens, jamming him into the concrete block wall.

Kyle wasn't done yet. He threw a left, a right, another left. They weren't crushing blows but had cumulative impact. He saw fear in Dagens' eyes for the first time. Blood from Kyle's hand had been transferred to Dagens' cheek. Kyle kept throwing punches.

"Hey, someone's coming," Delacroix yelled.

Kyle turned to look. He instantly knew it was a mistake. Dagens made him pay with another right. Kyle stumbled back but kept his feet. A man in a suit came around the corner. "Hey, what the hell's going on here?" Men in suits at a racetrack this time of day meant management.

Dagens wiped his nose and turned toward the man. "Guy dropped something. Was just helping him find it."

"You okay?" the man in the suit said to Kyle.

"Yeah," Kyle said, snuffling in blood and pulling his hand over his lip to mop off the blood. "Yeah, no problem. Like he said, just dropped something."

"Right," said suit. "Well, take it somewhere else. I don't have time for this."

Dagens moved past Kyle and whispered, "We're not done." He walked past the suit. "We're just going out to get a few beers." The three jocks turned and walked out toward the parking lot.

Suit watched Kyle. "You sure?"

"Fine," Kyle said, wiping more blood from his face.

"Your nose is pointing over your shoulder. Might want to have that checked." With that, the suit followed the jocks toward the exit.

Chapter 29

THE HORSES had just come onto the track for the third race. It was a good card for a Sunday. A light rain from the night before had broken the heat wave. The track dried quickly, before the morning works were finished. The track was again labeled fast.

Lennie hit the first two races and was building a ticket for the pick six. A wager depended upon selecting the winners of the third through eighth races. It was a daunting task but one that had the possibility of paying off handsomely. The carryover for the bet was $230,000. It was worth the long odds if Lennie had some races he could narrow to one or two horses.

"I think I've got solid singles in the fourth and sixth. The seventh is a crapshoot. We may want to go deep there. I have a ticket that'll be $420," Lennie said.

"Put me in for ten percent of whatever you do," Dan said.

"I'll go in for twenty," added Milt.

"TP? You want in?"

"You got Emilio's ride in the seventh?"

Lennie checked his sheets, "Yep, sure do. Would love to have him bring that one home."

"All right, give me ten percent. Emilio thinks that horse is live. I don't know if he knows something or is just hopeful. He'll give him an aggressive ride; I can guarantee you that."

Lennie got up, carefully laid his printed pages with myriad calculations on his chair, and moved out of the box to place the wager. They would settle up after the bet was placed. Sometimes Lennie would make last-minute changes, but they were all in, regardless of what he wanted to do.

Lennie had cashed three pick sixes in the past two years, one for $130,000 and one for $85,000; he also hit one for $235,000, but a series of favorites meant the pool was divided among five winning tickets. He had cashed so many five of six tickets that no one could keep track. If Lennie went to the window for a pick six ticket, smart money was along for the ride.

"Lennie, would you grab a hotdog on the way back?" Milt called after him.

Lennie half turned, then resumed his walk up the steps. It was even money whether Lennie would return with sustenance for Milt.

"Hey, I saw Kyle this morning," Dan said to TP. "What the hell happened to him? He wouldn't talk about it."

"Walked into a door," he said, gazing at the toteboard.

"Sure he did. What's the door's name?"

"Jim Dagens. But you've got to keep that on the QT. If the stew's find out, they'll give both guys days." The code of silence allowed each of them to keep riding.

"What happened?"

"Little disagreement about etiquette on the racetrack. Been brewing for a few weeks. Dagens is a hothead. Figures if he gets beat, it's 'cause the other guy cheated."

"Kyle okay? He seemed fine, but I don't need him getting his brains rattled a few weeks before that filly stake."

"Yeah, he's fine. Sometimes you just gotta fight a guy to end the tension," said TP. "It's amazing. I remember punching guys and rolling around on the floor in the jock's room when I was still riding. Then two weeks later, we're out having cocktails. It's a respect thing. Not that much removed from the school yard in junior high. If you don't fight, those guys will just punk you on the racetrack every chance they get."

"Sounds like the mafia."

"Yep, it's the code they live by. Kyle can handle himself."

Lennie slid back into his seat. "Four forty, went five deep in the seventh."

They pulled out cash and handed it to Lennie. "Hey, how 'bout that hotdog?" Milt said.

"Oh, did you say something to me when I was going to bet? I must not have heard you," Lennie said, smiling.

"Great," Milt said. "I'm gonna go play the seven here anyway. And I'll get that hotdog I ordered." He had his bankroll in one hand and motioned visibly to TP and Dan. "You guys need anything?"

They waved him off. "Hey, Maj, you're not going to make a bet with that?" Dan pointed toward the $50 bill on the outside of his bankroll.

"Why not?"

Lennie looked up and noticed the same thing. "Bad luck. Nobody ever cashed a ticket on a bet made with a fifty dollar bill. Where you been?"

"That's BS. Watch and learn, gentlemen. Watch and learn."

Several minutes later Magic Milt made it back to his seat, accompanied by two hotdogs, a large lemonade, and a bag of peanuts. He was just in time to see the break. His seven horse ran fifth, but Lennie's pick won. They were alive in the pick six.

After dramatically tossing his tickets in the air, Milt began unwrapping one of his hotdogs. "And I still say that fifty dollar bill thing is a bunch of crap."

"Keep trying it, Milt," Lennie said. "Can't beat fate. Kind of like doubling up to get even. That's a game you can't play unless you wear long pants. Even then, you better have some serious cash behind you."

"Yeah, yeah," Milt mumbled with half the hotdog in his mouth. He swallowed hard and said, "Any break on the extortion scheme on the backside?"

"Not as far as I can tell," Dan said. "They've increased security, and folks are guarding their barns like Fort Knox, but two more horses were hit this week."

Lennie pulled down his glasses and shook his head. "I had money on one of those. Damnedest thing I ever saw. Two horses in the same race."

"They autopsy either horse to see why it died?" asked Milt.

"They don't autopsy dime claimers," Lennie said, then turned toward Dan. "Are there guys still holding out? I heard almost everyone was paying, at least to buy time 'til they catch this guy."

"Heard Dillingham was still out," said TP. "And Jake's out, isn't he, Dan?"

"Yeah, for now. I told him I'd pay for my stock, but he's pretty pissed off about it. More trainers agreeing to pay puts a bigger bull's eye on those who don't. Need to catch this guy."

"Ya know," said Milt. "They catch this guy, I know what to do. It's what they talked about if they ever caught bin Laden. Don't need a trial or any legal proceedings. Just announce the time they were going to release him at Times Square in New York. They catch this guy, they oughta just release him on the backside. The problem will take care of itself." With that, he jammed the remainder of the hotdog into his mouth.

"It has to be someone with a license," said Lennie. "I mean a trainer, groom, owner, vet, someone with a license to access the backside. Can't believe anyone in this game could harm one of these horses. Just makes me sick. This keeps up, owners and trainers are gonna pack up and go somewhere else to race."

"A few have," Dan said. "But it's tough to get stalls anywhere now that other meets are in full swing. Whoever is doing this knew the timing would be good. You either take your horse home, in which case you have no chance to make money, or you risk being here. That's why a bunch are just paying. It gives them a chance to make some money."

"That's why we're all here," said Lennie. "Chance to make money."

Emilio's horse won in the seventh and paid $28. They all got well there, but the single in the sixth lost a photo, and they ran out in the eighth. Four winners of six didn't pay, but it was always a good idea to be with Lennie on exotics. There was always tomorrow. Over time, he was going to win more than his share. Like he said, they were all there for the chance to make money.

Chapter 30

COWBOY HAT wasn't wearing it tonight. Darkness had fallen on the backside, and he smiled to himself. He was like the invisible man. He could walk anywhere on the backside and not draw attention. Many barns had sentries posted as fear gripped the backside. Raven had created the fear, and there was nothing any of the sentries could do to stop him.

Two nights before, a raucous fight had erupted on the backside. A groom from Hudgins' barn was caught prowling around a neighboring barn. Three stable hands jumped the guy, then beat and kicked him until he was unconscious.

An ambulance took the victim. Prince William's sheriff's department took two of the assailants. The third disappeared, yet to be seen again.

Protecting the horses was the justification. In the backside's court of public opinion, the beat down, though brutal, was deemed righteous. Raven smiled at the thought.

Prior to tonight's mission, Raven had checked the list of unprotected trainers and zeroed in on Gilmore and Tom Posten. Gilmore had that kick-ass filly that wowed everyone a few days ago. Damn, if someone got to that horse, then everyone would know that there was no protection. If Gilmore had only come clean and paid up, that filly would turn into a hell of a horse, but pride was one of the seven deadly sins. Pride would kill Gilmore's precious filly.

Raven wore a light jacket. The weather was sweltering, but he needed the pockets to carry his little packages. He approached Posten's barn. A short Mexican stepped out of the shedrow. "*Que pasa?*"

"*Nada,*" Raven said. Then he walked around the side of the shedrow out of the man's sight. At the sixth stall he turned and leaned on the webbing slightly, just enough to retrieve the plastic baggie and empty the contents into the feed tub. He stroked the horse's neck as he crumpled the emptied bag in the other hand.

Raven leaned back and quickly deposited the bag into his jacket pocket. He walked back to the side of the shedrow where the Mexican was standing. "Take care, *amigo.*" The Mexican waved back. Raven walked to the end of the shedrow and ducked around the corner.

Gilmore's barn would be a little more difficult as that hot chick and some Mexican were keeping a constant vigil. Raven waited in the shadows. After several minutes he heard the babe tell Ricki Ricardo that she was going to Crok's for a soda and did he want anything. Raven needed to get to the fifth stall on the far side of the barn. Ricki moved to a chair and leaned back on the rear legs, tipping against the outside wall of the Gilmore's office.

This was his opening. Raven didn't hesitate. He zipped around the far side of the shedrow, then after scoping out the scene, he raced to the fifth stall, and as he had done at Posten's barn, emptied the contents in the feed tub.

"That a girl, eat it up," he whispered, as the horse dipped its head into the blue tub. He chuckled to himself, scratched behind the horse's ears briefly, then zipped off into the darkness.

The substance was largely harmless and, in proper use, made a beautiful garden. Not many people knew about the more unusual properties of *Taxus cuspidata*. Raven was able to pick up a large plant at the nursery in Merrifield, Virginia.

It was a gorgeous plant, but he cut it up and trimmed the piney needles from the branches. He mixed the trimmings with a little molasses to make sure the horses would lick out the tubs, hopefully cleaning up all traces of the substance. And the horses would eat it, Raven knew. *Hell, they'll eat anything you put into their feed tub. Stupid animals.*

Yes, *Taxus cuspidata* was largely harmless. Funny thing, though: If ingested by a horse, it proved fatal. At the nursery the non-scientific name was Japanese yew.

For centuries, this plant formed the centerpiece of intricate and stunning Asian gardens. The health of the plant bore directly on the beauty and stature of the garden, and as a result the face and prominence of the garden's owner.

Each plant told a story. Only a skilled gardener knew how to bring out the best in the plant and the unique way to trim it. Only through years of study and reflection could a master alter the growth of a *Taxus cuspidata*. The gardener and the plant were forever connected. An error in trimming the plant forever changed its character and, as a result, the character of the gardener.

The amount Raven had dropped in the feed tubs would slow the horses' heart rates, and within twelve hours, both horses would be dead. Nothing could stop it. Nature was a beautiful thing, Raven thought. The strong survived; the weak got their just desserts. Stupid bastards should have paid up.

◆ ◆ ◆

BETH WALKED back to the barn, carrying her plastic bottle of soda. She'd been in the business her whole life, yet she was amazed by how Jake individualized the regimen for each horse. Each horse had a personality. Each was unique, and rather than treat them like widgets on an assembly line, Jake got into the heads of each of his horses. He made them happy and confident. Happy horses trained better; confident horses won purses.

She loved how he managed Aly Dancer's daily experiences, from workouts with older horses to allowing dirt to be kicked in her face to changing the physical environment constantly.

If this filly was what they thought, she would be on the move frequently. If she could compete at the top of the game, she would ship from track to track, attempting to take down big purses.

That filly was special.

There was nothing going to separate her from this one, nothing.

Chapter 31

BIGGS PACED in his office. Jason Cregg was stopping by soon, and he pondered how to play his hand. He couldn't keep stonewalling the guy. Biggs had ridden that strategy as long as he could.

Normally, he would do a walking interview with a reporter and show off the customer improvements and upgrades like a used car salesman. Today the meeting would be in his office and only in his office. He didn't know who to trust and sure as hell didn't want to bump into a horseman or official that Cregg could latch his teeth into.

Biggs had done his research. Cregg had been with *The Washington Post* for the past two years; prior to that he had been a beat writer for the *Daily Racing Form*, based in Southern California. He'd put out feelers on the guy with his network in the racing community. The feedback was that Cregg was fair-minded as a reporter but typically bore a bias against management. He was always angling for the little guy, and management was just a means to keep the little guy down.

Cregg did an exposé on impoverished backside workers at San Gabriel Race Track in 2006. With that effort he'd won a nomination for an Eclipse Award. And that was the problem. The track took the hit. The legislature wanted to pull funding and made a huge human rights stink over it. In the end the backside help worked for the stables, not the track. But why address the problem when there's a big bad corporation that can be strafed for publicity's sake?

How can anyone be in this business and not see management's side? We take all the risk. We provide the purse structures. We do the advertising and promotion. We invest in structures, barns, and amenities for horsemen. In the end, we get treated like we're the problem.

His phone buzzed, and Rosalind came over the speaker. "Mr. Biggs? Mr. Cregg to see you."

"Send him in."

Biggs positioned himself behind his desk, the power spot, as the door opened. "Jason, how are you?"

A slender thirty-something with long, uncombed blonde hair walked forward and shook Biggs' hand. He wore a wrinkled blue polo shirt over faded jeans and muddy tennis shoes. The shoes indicated he'd been on the backside already this morning. A black satchel was slung over his shoulder, and a pad and ballpoint were gripped in the other.

"Good, Allan, I'm good." Cregg sunk into a side chair and crossed an ankle over the other knee.

"Rosalind!" Biggs shouted. "We need some coffee in here." Pointing at Cregg, he asked, "Black?"

"Fine."

"Two, Rosalind, both black."

"Thanks for meeting with me, this morning," said Cregg. "How's the investigation going?"

"Always takes longer than you think. We're making good progress, but—"

"Allan, cut the crap. What's going on? I was just on the backside. I watched them drag a dead horse out of Gilmore's barn this morning. Posten woke up to a dead animal in his barns as well. Hudgins had a groom nearly beat to death a few nights ago. Guy's still in the hospital. What the hell's going on?"

"Hold on," Biggs said, extending the palm of his hand. "We think the deal with Hudgins' groom is separate. You've been around. Fights break out all the time. We don't like it, but what are you going to do? Couple of hotheads get together, and the next thing you know you gotta brawl."

Hudgins' groom was a victim of the ramped-up tension on the backside. With his jaw wired shut, it would be a while before he'd be telling folks why he was in the other barn late at night.

"That's bull. People get in fights; they don't send each other to the freakin' hospital. Something's up, and you don't want to be covering it up, 'cause it's coming out," Cregg said. "May not be me, but it's coming out somehow."

"What, are you trying to win that Eclipse this time?" he asked sarcastically.

"No, Allan. I'm just trying to tell the truth. You ought to try it." He flipped his notebook shut and glared at Biggs.

Rosalind knocked on the door, then walked in bearing porcelain coffee cups with saucers and set them delicately on the desk.

The pause allowed Biggs to calculate a response but also released some tension from the room. Biggs leaned forward and sipped his coffee.

"Okay, I'm going to give it to you all. But I want a promise," Biggs said.

"I'm not into promises. That's not how I work."

"Make an exception here," said Biggs. Cregg nodded. It wasn't an "I agree" nod. It was a "Let's see what we have" nod. Biggs wasn't going to do any better by begging, so he continued. "I don't need to remind you that both of our jobs depend upon a strong thoroughbred industry, especially in these times."

Cregg nodded, the "I agree" variety this time. He reopened his notepad.

"Okay," Biggs said, exhaling loudly. "The night before opening day, two horses were killed and another was kidnapped. The next day someone put a note in each of the trainer's message boxes demanding twenty bucks a horse per week protection money."

The pen in Cregg's hand scribbled frantically as Biggs recounted all of the events, including the trainer list, the drops, and the barns involved.

After several minutes Cregg collapsed back in the chair and whispered, "Jesus." Biggs nodded.

"I need your help. Just for a little while," Biggs said.

Cregg cocked his neck, as though considering the request. "This is too big," he said finally. "This story's getting out one way or another. Trainers and owners, you can't count on them to keep quiet. Can't believe they've held it this long. What's the track doing? Who's involved on the law enforcement side?"

"Tim Belker's our lead security guy. He's working with local authorities, but we want to keep it low-key on the backside. Don't want a show of police force over there."

"Maybe you could use it," Cregg said.

"We've increased security and carpeted the backside with cameras. For now, we need to focus on catching this guy, not putting the backside in turmoil," Biggs said. "Hard enough for the barns to keep their help as it is." After a pause, he continued. "Just give us some time, Jason. You're the only reporter I've given this to. And you'll be the only one. Give us a few weeks."

"Few weeks? You can't keep the top on this for that long."

"Okay, one week. You know what a story like this could do to our handle and attendance. I'm being straight with you. I won't give this to anyone else—just give us some time to resolve it. If we get a break, I'll give it to you. Just play ball on this one. Having an exclusive after we catch the guy will be better than a piece that just rips us and damages everyone."

Cregg nodded slowly but didn't speak.

"I respect you," Biggs said. "If you feel like you've got to run with this, just let me know first. At least give me a shot to get our side out."

The reporter leaned forward and took a long sip on his coffee, then stood and walked toward the door. "Thanks for the coffee."

Chapter 32

DAN DIALED Jake from his office. He'd timed the call to be around the mid-morning break. It was when the track was reconditioned between early and late works. If he called any other time, Jake wouldn't pick up. He was pretty good about returning calls, but Dan knew the best times to get a hold of him, and they needed to talk.

Now.

Dan made a decision, either Jake was going to pay the fee, or Dan was going to yank his horses from him. He hated the decision, but he might never get a filly like Aly Dancer again and couldn't take the risk. He'd move her to another barn or just get her off the grounds.

It wasn't worth it. It killed him to think that he might have to take a pass at the filly stake, but it was just one race. Just one race he desperately wanted to win.

Jake's only option was to accept. It was the only answer that would allow Jake to keep the horse in the barn. Dan had fired trainers before, and it was never easy. Everything was personal, but this was his money—his horse, his shot. He either agreed or that was that. The phone rang, and Dan took a deep breath. He didn't even give him time to exchange pleasantries.

"Jake, I've been thinking, and I don't think we can wait any longer."

"They tried to kill the filly last night."

"What?" Dan shouted, jumping out of his chair. "I thought we had her under watch. Jake, this is bullshit. It has to stop. I'm going to—"

"Already done. I'm going to pay. Son of a bitch, if I ever get my hands on him."

"Jake, I think it's the right thing. I'll cover the cost of my horses."

"Nope. I've got it."

"What happened?"

"Guy threw a bunch of Japanese yew in the feed tub."

"What the hell is that?"

"Beats the shit out of me. Dancett says it's some kind of plant, but if eaten by a horse, it kills them. Killed Bob Crater's mare, Breaking Dawn, and Tom Posten lost a horse last night, too. Same thing. Dirty motherfucker."

Bob Crater was one of Jake's biggest owners. Jake had half a dozen of Crater's horses at any one time. The call Jake had to make to Crater this morning made Dan shutter. He probably lost an owner because of his pride, certainly lost day money because he had an extra empty stall and probably more to follow when Crater yanked the rest.

Jake continued, "Doc Dancett was here this morning. Said he'd read about this kind of thing in vet school but had never seen it in action. Apparently, it slows down the heart rate of the horse to the point that it just drops dead. Found traces of it in Posten's feed tub and figured Crater's mare was the same."

"Why do you think they were after the filly? I thought Beth and Jorge had twenty-four-hour watch on her."

"They do. Aly Dancer was in that stall yesterday. I had Beth move her. Trying to get her used to new surroundings and changes. Bastard had his sights on her, sure as hell."

"Jesus, Jake. What if you hadn't moved her? Good lord."

Jake was silent. Dan knew it killed him to give in to the extortion. If it was just him, he wouldn't give in. The idea that property in his possession was harmed made all the difference. Dan had visions of Jake standing bloody in front of those high school bullies, saying, "I'm not paying"—but pride can take you down alleys you can't escape.

"Jake, I know you hate it, but it's the right thing."

"Whatever. Gotta go."

JAKE HUNG up the phone and leaned back, his hands covering his face. The catch up for the safety fee to the start of the meet, plus the juice he owed Ginny ate up all his cash. Despite the purse from the maiden win and his cash on the bet, Jake was nearly underwater again. The funds for the purse money were released the day before. He had withdrawn his ten percent share and deposited the balance in his owner's trust account. By agreement with his owners, he could tap that account to offset trainer, vet, transportation, and farrier bills.

Farrier bills. He shook his head.

Fifteen years in the business and he'd never tapped that account to meet his own needs. Keeping them separate was the price of integrity. With the load he'd owe for extortion come Monday, plus Ginny's juice, he'd be stone-ass broke. He had three horses entered the next two days. He had to get purse money out of them, but even if they did get checks, the funds wouldn't be released by the track until the following week. He hated making receivable calls on his owners. He was just plain bad at it. He could pull some funds from the trust account and replace them. No one would know. Then again, he would know.

Crooks took money from trust accounts. Jake wasn't a crook.

He had Gentleman Tim, a six-year-old gelding that he owned outright. Jake had claimed him a year back, and he consistently hit the board between a dime and twelve-five claiming. He could drop him in for a nickel. He'd lose him sure as hell but get the five grand out, plus the purse. Thing was, even if he found a race for him in the next week, the funds wouldn't clear in time to help. A private sale would be at bargain basement prices and a flashing sign of desperation to the world.

Jake picked up the condition book and looked for an open $5,000 claiming race. Maybe Ginny would let him slide a week on the juice. He didn't want to get crosswise with Ginny, but he needed time.

Time and some wins.

Chapter 33

THERE WAS one sound that struck fear into the hearts of horsemen everywhere.

It wasn't a sound made by their animals, though they were always on the alert for signals from their stock that something was amiss. It wasn't a sound emitted by stable hands, veterinarians, or backside help. It wasn't a sound that someone unfamiliar with a racetrack would deem significant—noticeable but not terror-filled.

That sound was the loud tone broadcast through the track speaker system that signified "loose horse." Just after the break on Thursday, Jake and Dan were sitting in the makeshift office off the shedrow, reviewing vet bills, when the alarm sounded. The response was instantaneous.

Jake shot out of his chair and shouted down the shedrow for Jorge and Beth. "Count 'em." He ran down the line of stalls, checking inside each one. "Secure them."

The horses sensed the panic as they reacted to the alarm over the speaker system. They whinnied nervously, rocked, and stomped in their stalls.

Jorge pushed a wheelbarrow out of the way and raced to the far side of the stable to check the horses. Beth moved toward Jake, stopping every five feet to poke her head into a stall to make sure the stock was where it belonged. They met halfway down the shedrow. Jorge came spinning around from the far side. "It's okay, boss. It's not us."

This dance took about ten seconds and had been replayed in every stable on the backside. Once it was determined that their stock was safe, it was time to look outward to find the loose horse.

Jake turned and rumbled back toward the office. Over his shoulder he yelled, "Beth, stay here and keep them calm. Jorge, let's go." When he reached the end of the shedrow, he turned out toward the main road, looking left and right for the loose horse.

What little motor traffic there was had stopped. A loose horse was a frightened horse and could do anything and come out of anywhere into the path of any moving vehicle. Several other trainers and stable hands were out looking for the horse as well. Lynn Johnston pointed toward the break in the track, and all eyes moved that direction.

A jet black, rider-less horse sprinted past the break, just inside the track surface. Two men on horseback were trying to corral and contain the animal, but the jet black would have none of it. It dodged left, then right, haltingly in one direction, then sprinting for a hundred yards up the track.

The two men were trying to steer the horse away from the break in the track. Keeping the horse on the racetrack was safer than allowing the horse onto the stable grounds.

Two more riders on horseback were moving from the far end of the track to lend support. The jockey's racing saddle was on the black horse, and the reins dangled loosely around its neck. It reared on its hind legs and kicked out toward its pursuers. The loose horse let out a whinny that shrieked through the air and caused many other horses on the backside to join the equine conversation. The men on horseback moved toward the black horse slowly, trying to limit its ability to escape.

The two horses from the far side of the track were approaching rapidly, and, between the four of them, they were quickly containing the loose horse. Jim Dagens raced down from the clocker's station and jumped the railing onto the track. He ran stiffly through the loam and sand in his cowboy boots—hardly the equipment for running on a racetrack. When he was about fifty feet from the horse, he slowed considerably to avoid spooking the colt.

The alarm continued sounding, causing the men to shout and gesture in exaggerated motions to communicate with one another. The horse was jumping with his front legs back and forth. It spun around and would run twenty feet, then turn and run twenty feet the other direction, then bounce side to side.

Dagens stepped closer and closer. He extended his hand to the side and slowly moved toward the horse. The riders were closing ranks, reducing the area by penning the horse against the inside rail and limiting any avenues of escape.

Dagens reached out to grab the loose rein. The jet black horse bolted, rearing on its hind legs like a desperate boxer striking at an opponent. Dagens fell backward, and the horse shot past him, between the men on horseback, and sprinted toward the break.

Several people moved toward the break, but they were too late. The horse shot up the track and through the break and was now loose on the backside.

"Whose is it?" someone shouted.

"Jenkins' colt" was the breathless reply, and the group ran to get position to corner the horse. "Threw Biggers."

The backside was a more dangerous place for a loose horse. More places and obstacles it could hit or be hit by. A scared horse could do just about anything from running through a shedrow fence to ramming into a pickup truck or getting out the main entrance into the traffic outside the racetrack.

The gated entrance had been secured by several vehicles. Men were waving hats and making noise to keep the colt away. The black horse raced between two shedrows and turned right, moving away from the entrance. It slid on the gravel as it slowed to change directions.

"Keep him moving that way," Jake shouted, waving toward the right. There was no way for the horse to get out if they moved him to the right. This had become a community event. All stable hands were out, and they formed a makeshift line to keep the animal moving toward the back corner of the backside. "Get over that way." Jake gestured toward the right. "Don't let him get by you."

The line moved forward, closing in on the horse. Several stables separated the horse and the corner of the backside. The black horse ran up into the yard of one stable, crying out. The horses in the stable answered back. The loop of the loose reins dangled precariously. If the reins got caught on something, a fence post or railing, the horse could snap its neck.

The black spun around and sprinted through the shedrow, exiting on the other side. The line of stable hands on that side continued the horse toward the corner. The horse turned quickly and nearly fell when the gravel slid out from under him. He regained his balance and ran to the right, jumping a wheelbarrow.

The men on that side of the line moved forward and re-directed the horse back toward the corner. They waved their arms with cowboy hat in hand, their broad, quick motions causing the horse to shy away.

The jet black moved to the corner. It made a quick move like it was going to jump through the wooden fencing, then changed its mind at the last second. It turned and snorted, digging the ground with its front feet. The line of stable hands slowly closed ranks. "Don't spook him," someone shouted.

The horse was cornered, and it jumped back and forth on his front legs, throwing its head side to side.

Dan caught a glimpse of AJ moving between two men off to his left. He was so much smaller than the men around him. His arms were extended to the side, and he was walk-ing slowly toward the horse. His head was tipped slightly backward, and it looked like his eyes were closed.

"Get that damn kid out of there," someone shouted from behind Dan. "He's gonna get killed."

AJ was about ten feet from the animal and walking clos-er. The horse snorted and reared on his back legs. His front hooves slashed through the air. The kid was unfazed. He didn't even flinch, like he couldn't see the danger.

"Look out," Jake shouted. The men instinctively backed away.

"AJ, move away," Dan yelled.

The boy kept moving forward, his arms still extended straight out to the side. He was mumbling something that couldn't be heard over the shouting of the men and the shrieking from the horse.

The horse jumped left, looking down toward the boy, then jumped back to the right, turning nearly sideways. AJ leaned forward and stretched his arms toward the horse. The colt shimmied and shied away.

"Stupid shit, get out of there," someone shouted from Dan's right.

AJ stepped closer, reaching for the horse. The horse reared up and slashed at AJ with its hooves. One hoof caught the bill of AJ's cap, knocking it askew. AJ didn't back away. He couldn't sense the danger around him. AJ continued reaching out and found the withers of the jet black with his right hand, then quickly put his left hand on its neck.

The jet black instantly became silent and stood stock still on all four legs, perfectly calm. AJ's shoulders started to shiver and quake, then his torso shook, and his legs began to buckle. AJ was able to keep his balance leaning against the horse. He was making guttural sound, like someone in a deep sleep, struggling to escape a nightmare.

"Get a shank on him," someone yelled.

Dan couldn't pull his eyes off the boy. He was quivering and muttering like someone possessed. A stable hand stepped forward and clipped a shank on the horse's bridle. He yanked down hard on the shank and began walking the horse through the crowd. AJ followed with his hands on the horse and eyes closed. Matt Jenkins stepped forward and shoved AJ to the ground.

Dan shouted, "Hey, leave the kid alone." Jenkins looked over and scowled.

The jet black jumped sideways and reared. The groom holding the shank grabbed on with the other hand and yanked downward. The horse reared and pulled the opposite way. The cowboy was nearly lifted off the ground, and he slid forward on his boot heels.

Another hand raced forward and slapped a shank on the other side of the bridle. Between the two of them they were able to get the horse under control and led him away. The crowd began to disperse, most shaking their heads, feeling glad it wasn't their horse that got loose.

Dan stepped over to AJ and helped him up. He dusted off his jeans, picked up his ball cap, and began walking away.

"Hey, wait a minute." The boy kept walking. Dan took two quick steps and grabbed his shoulder. "AJ, what was that?" He pointed back over his shoulder to where he had calmed the horse. The kid shrugged and looked back toward his barn. "How did you do that?" Dan asked.

The boy looked at the ground. Apparently believing that Dan wasn't going to let him walk off without an answer, AJ inhaled deeply and said, "Dunno, just helping."

"No, AJ, that was…that was…. What was that?" He stammered. "This, and the deal at Hudgins' barn last week."

The boy rolled his head side to side like he was annoyed. "I just touch 'em. They talk to me, tell me what they feel." He was still looking down at his feet.

"What do you mean? They talk to you?"

He looked over at his barn like he needed to get over there. "They tell me. I touch them and feel what they feel. I help calm 'em down."

"You were shaking and talking, making noises, whatever. What was that?"

"I dunno. Just helping." He turned and walked away.

Dan watched the boy limp along the gravel road back toward his barn.

Alone.

Chapter 34

THE MAN standing in the shadow of the shedrow waved at AJ. The gesture wasn't acknowledged; AJ just continued walking. He was making his way back with a cold soda he had gotten from the vending machine outside Crok's. It was after four in the morning, but the heat sent AJ in search of a cool drink.

Since the attacks had started, most stables had posted a groom or hotwalker to stand guard over the barns all night. AJ knew them all by sight, even if he'd never spoken to them. His limp created a distinctive rhythm to his gait, and most on the backside recognized the sound of his approach on a quiet night such as this. With tensions running at code red on the backside, the limp's distinctive sound was an advantage.

AJ walked through Latimer's shedrow and poked his head in on the inhabitants in each stall. All was well. Most were sleeping. He would get an occasional weary glance from a sleepy horse, but everything was in order.

Having circled the entire shedrow, AJ found a spot on the side of the barn where the slightest breeze was detectible. Any advantage to break the heat was taken. He sat on the ground and leaned against the wooden structure. From here he could see through the rows of identical barns. On the far end to his left was the racetrack; to his right stood the overgrowth of trees and brush of Manassas State Park.

There wasn't enough breeze to disturb the haze of humidity hanging in the air. AJ twisted open his soda bottle, wiped his forehead, and took a long drink. As he was bringing the bottle down from his mouth, the gunshot rang out, breaking the quiet of the hour.

AJ had been looking in the direction of the park and saw the blast of light coming from the weapon. Despite the visual clue, the sound startled AJ, and he spilled part of his soda down the front of his shirt.

He locked in on the location of the flash of light. It seemed to be well beyond the fence dividing the racetrack from the park. In the daylight, AJ knew there was a steep hill beyond the fence. Whoever had fired the gun was shooting down from that hill toward the backside. A flash and another gunshot rang out.

Several horses cried out in terror, and the backside was abuzz with horses stirring in their stalls, contributing to the sounds of fear around them. AJ scrambled to his feet and ran in his skip-hop fashion toward the park.

He had to veer left and run the length of two barns to get to the spot where the separation in the fence would allow him to squeeze through. He slid through the opening and was on the park property.

He moved back to his right to get near the spot where he'd seen the flash. His pace was slowed by the uneven terrain, the brush, and the low hanging limbs of the trees. In perfect daylight this would be a treacherous walk; in total darkness, it was virtually impossible. He tripped over a root growing above ground and fell, banging his knee against the base of another tree.

He looked to the right and tried to gauge his distance by the familiar sight of the shedrows. He was still about one and a half barns from where the shot was fired. He got back on his feet and trudged forward. His arms were braced in front of his face to block the tree limbs. AJ entered what seemed to be a clearing and covered ground quickly, entering more heavy brush after about fifty feet.

After scraping himself through more of the forest, he broke out into another clearing. Looking to the left, he could tell he was near the point where the gun was fired. There was a burst of activity to his right where several people congregated around the stall, the targets of the shooting. AJ crouched down and looked for any sign of movement up the hill.

He scurried up the hill, sometimes on his hands and knees, but he continued to climb. After about thirty feet he reached a plateau. He turned and looked down on the backside. This had to be where the shot came from. AJ looked down on the barn below him.

Below him, lights were on, and a pickup had been pulled near to illuminate the barn area with its headlights. AJ stood silently and listened. No sound around him. He started to move to the right when he kicked something solid.

He bent down, and his hand found a rifle. The barrel was warm. He picked it up. He'd never held a gun before, much less a high-powered rifle. As he was examining the gun a flashlight came on and blinded AJ. He put his hand up to shade his eyes and peered into the light.

"Hold it right there," a voice shouted.

PART THREE

INTO THE TURN

◆　◆　◆

HUMANS WERE WIRED FOR JUSTICE.

At least it was comforting to think that.

*The misconception persisted that
right and wrong were easily discerned.
Justice was not static. Justice was simply a
perspective, a matter of degrees, a sliding scale.
Too often justice, like beauty, resided solely in
the eye of the beholder.*

*All lawyers knew that.
Facts were a tapestry woven to meet the
buyer's eye. Good lawyers exploited that.*

*In the abstract, doing the right thing
was simple, an objectively determined fait*

accompli. Justice, as theory, was casually applied in the absence of issues that confront real life.

Who was entitled? Who decided?

One man's justice was another's tyranny. Authority cloaked the few as defenders of justice. But authority was manmade; hence, justice was shaped in authority's image.

The distance between self-defense and murder was one second—a wink, an untimely tic, a frightened gesture. And, of course, it involved delving into the murky minds of the killer and the killed.

Justice became the bedrock of survivors and victors. Their personal histories were translated as justice. Just as dead men told no tales, the vanquished were defined by justice— never ones to define it.

The only test of justice was whether it protected those who refused to fight back.

Justice was never the battle of one man.

It remained the struggle of all men.

Chapter 35

DAN'S CELL phone chirped as he was driving to work. It was just before seven, and he wanted to get a head start on an appellate brief he was under deadline to file. Dan pressed the button on his wireless earpiece. "Hello?"

"It's Jake."

He never called this early. "Jake, what's up? Oh no, don't tell me. We get hit last night?"

"No, we're fine. But two horses from Creighton's barn got shot last night."

"Got shot? Jesus."

"Yeah, well, the reason I called is they arrested someone."

"About time. Who'd they arrest?" Dan asked as he glanced in his rearview mirror and changed lanes.

"The kid," Jake said.

"The kid? What kid?"

"Kid from Latimer's barn."

"What?"

"Thought you'd want to know."

"Come on, Jake, that's insane. That kid wouldn't hurt a horse in a million years."

"Yeah, well, they found him with a rifle. They went through his stuff in the barn and found a syringe, a three-foot length of pipe, and a shit load of cash."

"That's crazy, Jake."

"Just telling you what's going on."

"Where'd they take him?"

"Don't know. They took him away in a Prince William County sheriff's car about half an hour ago."

"Thanks, Jake."

Dan swerved into the center lane, made an illegal U-turn, and punched it. His best guess was they'd take him to the station on Route 28. It was the one nearest the track. *AJ won't last five minutes in lock up.*

Dan torpedoed into the parking lot, jumped from the car, and raced toward the front door. Once inside, he went to the intake desk. The desk officer was a young kid, yakking on the phone. No one else was present.

"I'm Dan Morgan." The officer looked at him like Dan was out of his mind. "I represent AJ Kaine. I demand to see him immediately. If he's being interrogated, I order you to stop."

The officer put his hand over the speaker of the phone and said, "Just a minute."

Dan reached over the counter and disconnected the call. "Don't got a minute."

"What the—"

"AJ Kaine. Is he being held here? If so, I want to see him. Right fucking now."

The officer put the phone down and stared at him. Dan stared back and gestured with his hands like *do something.*

He began lazily punching buttons on his keyboard. "Might take a while."

Dan reached into his pocket and pulled out his pocket dictaphone recorder. "This is Dan Morgan," He looked at his watch. "It's 7:28 A.M. on August 9. I'm at the intake desk of the Prince William County sheriff's department on Route 28. I informed officer—" Dan picked up the nameplate on the counter. "Officer J. Sterling that I represent AJ Kaine. Is all of that correct, Officer?" He held the dictaphone toward Sterling.

The officer pulled back like Dan was holding a snake. "What the hell are you doing?"

He put the dictaphone behind his back, leaned toward him, and whispered, "In case you haven't noticed, I'm making a record of my lawful demand seeking to protect my client's constitutional rights. This recording will come in damn handy in the civil rights case I'm going to file if you don't get me in there right now."

Dan pulled the dictaphone back toward himself and continued. "At 7:27 I informed Officer Sterling that I wanted to see my client immediately and that any interrogation of my client must cease. Isn't that correct, Officer Sterling?"

Sterling reached under the desk, then there was a metallic buzz coming from the door to Dan's left. The officer cocked his head as if to say *go on in.*

The door opened to a hallway with a series of doors on either side. About three-quarters of the way down the hall Dan spotted Tim Belker, talking with two sheriff department officers.

"Who's the officer in charge?"

The taller of the two officers turned. "I am. Who are you?"

"I'm Dan Morgan, AJ Kaine's attorney. I want to see him immediately."

"He's being printed now. You can talk to him when they're done."

"I want to see him now." He glared at Belker as he approached.

The officer turned and continued down the hall. "Follow me."

"I want to know if you've interrogated him, and, if so, I want a record of everything he said."

"We haven't interrogated him yet. Security guy from the track did. Kid said the gun was his."

"Bullshit." He'd have to move to quash that statement in court. No way AJ owns a gun. He better not.

They walked to a booking area. An overweight woman in a blue, tight-fitting sheriff's uniform was talking quietly with AJ as she was rolling his fingertips on the paper form pinned to the counter.

"That's an unusual name. That a family name?"

"No, ma'am. It's from the Bible."

"Well, isn't that interesting."

"AJ," Dan interrupted. AJ looked up and appeared relieved that a friendly face had shown up.

The woman handed AJ a paper towel and squirted some liquid into the palms of his hands.

"That'll clean you up."

"AJ, come with me." He glanced at the officer's nametag. "I need a room where I can meet with my client, Detective Manning."

They moved back into the hallway, and the detective opened a door. AJ and Dan walked in. The boy went over to one of the gray metal chairs behind the scarred metal desk in the center of the room. AJ slumped into the chair and said, "I didn't do it—I didn't do nothing."

"I know, AJ. I know. I'm going to try and get you out of here, but it might be a few days. Here's what I need you to do." Dan pointed a finger at him for emphasis. "Don't you talk to anyone in here—I don't care who it is. I don't care how nice they are to you or what they promise you. Unless I'm here, you don't talk, okay?"

The boy nodded.

"If they put you in lock up, you just keep to yourself."

"You mean I can't leave? Who's gonna take care of my horses? I can't stay here." AJ stood and waved his arms, a reflex to the sudden terror that he couldn't be around horses today.

"They aren't going to let you leave right now."

"Why not? I didn't do nothing."

"I know. Look, I need to ask you some questions, and I need you to tell me the truth."

"I always tell the truth."

"How old are you?"

"Nineteen."

Damn it. Dan was hoping he was still a minor. He could get him assigned to better, safer youth lock down. That idea was blown.

"Okay. Did you tell Officer Belker—you know, the security guy from the track—did you tell him the gun was yours?"

"No. I said I found it."

"Well, he's saying you told him it's your gun."

Dan could see AJ getting fidgety. The idea that he couldn't leave had never occurred to him; now it was beginning to sink in. He wouldn't see his horses today.

"No, sir," AJ said. "He asked me where I got the gun. I said I found it. He never asked me if it was mine."

"What else did he ask you?"

"Nothing. He went through my stuff, then had me sit in his car until the sheriff showed up."

"I need to know what happened last night. Everything." AJ recounted the story about trying to get to the flash of light and finding the rifle.

"Okay sit right here," Dan said. "I'll be right back."

He stormed out of the room and up the hallway to where Belker and Manning were standing. Dick Latimer was with them.

"He never said the gun was his. I don't know what the hell you're trying to pull, Belker, but you got an innocent kid in there."

"I asked him where he got the gun. He said he found it."

"Yeah, like ten fucking seconds before you arrested him. That doesn't make it his gun; just means he found it. What the hell's the matter with you?"

"Hey." Belker put his hands on his hips and leaned toward him. "I hear a gunshot, I go to the spot, I find the kid holding the rifle, two horses been shot. You do the math."

"Where's a kid like that going to keep a high-powered rifle? He saw the muzzle flash and ran up there. That's all he did, and you're trying to pin the whole fucking deal on him." Dan turned to Manning. "You cannot put that boy in lock up. You can't. I want him released. Now. You know you don't have enough to hold him." Dan knew he had a weak argument. With a firearms incident, they could hold him for forty-eight hours on suspicion without even charging him, but he had to try and get AJ out.

Belker didn't back down a bit. "Then I go through his stuff—he's got a lead pipe, a big fat roll of cash, and a syringe that their lab is going to test." He pointed a thumb at Manning. Manning nodded.

"Big fucking deal. The lead pipe doesn't mean anything. We going to start arresting people for having cash? Jesus, man, think. And a syringe? Are you kidding me? Syringes practically litter the backside. Probably not the greatest thing, but that doesn't give you shit to hold this kid." He turned toward Latimer. "Dick, you know it's not his gun. Heck, you'd know if he was carrying around a damn hunting rifle."

"Absolutely." Latimer turned toward Belker. "Tim, there's no way the kid did this. No way. Kid couldn't hurt a horse. Not a chance."

"Can't release him. Kid's a transient," Manning said.

"He's not a transient. He works for this guy." Dan pointed at Latimer. "He has a job. His job just moves from town to town a few times a year."

The other officer came down the hallway and handed Manning a note. He opened it, read it, and looked at Dan.

"Listen, Officer Manning," Dan continued. "Let the kid go; let him work his job. After the work day I'll pick him up. He can stay with me. I'll be personally responsible for him. All these horse attacks have been at night. If you honestly believe that this kid hurt those horses, then I'll take him off the grounds and watch him every night."

Belker piped up: "He'll just start attacking the horses during the day."

"You ever see this kid around horses? It's fucking magical, okay? The idea that he would harm those horses is ludicrous." Dan pointed at Latimer. "Dick, you have the slightest concern about having this boy around your stock?"

"Nope. Not a bit."

"All I know is I got someone attacking horses on the backside," Belker said. "It needs to stop. Some forest fairy might have left the gun, and the kid found it. Who knows? But this is the best angle I got to go on, so pardon me for trying to do my job by keeping a suspect off the premises."

Manning refolded the paper message and slid it into his shirt pocket. "We're not going to charge him. For now." He pointed at Dan. "We'll consider it an open investigation. If we want to question him, you better have him here pronto, you understand? We need to find him, we're coming to see you," he said, gesturing toward Dan. "I don't know what's going on over at the racetrack. That's not my problem. Officer Sterling will have some paperwork for you to fill out. After that, take the kid and go."

Chapter 36

GINNY WALKED across the road toward Jake's barn. Beth and Jorge were getting ready to hose off Hero's Echo, who galloped for the first time since returning. Jake was down on his haunches, cupping the left front knee in his hands for signs of heat. When he spotted Ginny, he stood and pointed toward his office. Ginny altered course and moved toward Jake's office.

"What do you think?" Jake said to Beth, as if testing her.

She crouched and cupped the colt's knee. "Seems fine to me," she said. "Been off a while."

Jake nodded and seemed pleased. "Yeah, he's fine. We'll watch him for the next few days. Put some heat on and wrap him. He'll be okay. We just need to bring him along slower."

Beth nodded.

Jake slapped the horse on the hind quarter, turning to Jorge. "Rinse him off. Walk him out."

"You got it, boss."

Ginny was leaning against the wall of Jake's office, studying the condition book.

"Ginny."

"Jake."

Jake settled behind his desk and leaned forward on his elbows.

"Ginny." He paused for a second. "I need some time."

Ginny looked at Jake and nodded. Not a nod of agreement, a nod that said, *is that so?*

The silence caused Jake to continue. "I'm a little tight right now—"

"You were tight when you called me. Nothing's changed."

"Bastard tried to kill my filly, so I got to pay protection money. Will run me dry for about a week."

Ginny returned his gaze to the condition book. "What about the juice?"

"I need a week, Ginny. That's what I'm saying."

"So you don't even got the juice?"

"Ginny, I just need a little breathing room here. Got three horses in the next two days—"

"You'll be lucky to hit the board with one," said Ginny. He stood and moved directly across from Jake, only the desk separated them.

"Purse money will be available next week," Jake said. "Got a few owners with checks in the mail."

Ginny looked at him sideways. "Checks in the mail? Is that what we've come to?"

"Give me a week. I can get current."

"Not good enough."

Desperation in Jake required him to keep making offers.

"You know my filly can win that stake. That'll clean everything."

"*If* she can win it. She's good, but she's no lock." Ginny tapped the condition book against his open hand. "You know, a guy starts missing payments, even for the juice, it's liable to make a guy nervous."

"Ginny, you know I'm good for it. I'm gonna drop Gentleman Tim down to a nickel. Gotta race next week."

Ginny whistled long and low.

"He's worth twice that—three times," said Jake. "I own him outright. I'll get the purse and the claim price. Between that, the filly stake, and a few owners' checks, we're good."

"We're not good, Jake," he said, tossing the condition book onto Jake's desk. "But here's what I'm willing to do. How many horses you got outright?" Ginny leaned forward, pressing his hands against the desktop, getting in Jake's face.

"Me alone?" Jake asked, pulling back away from Ginny.

"Yeah. How many?"

"Three. On the grounds anyway. Gentleman Tim, Pristine Fiend, and Doxter.

"What about Devil's Harp?"

"I only own half. Along with Chip Dallas."

"Okay," said Ginny. "I want a half interest in all three, plus your half interest in Devil's Harp."

Jake's mouth dropped open.

"Hey, you're the one who can't pay the juice. Pay my juice, and we don't need a new deal. But?" Ginny said shrugging. "Guy starts missing payments, a solid lender's got to secure some collateral. Just business, Jake."

"What do you mean, half interest?"

"Kinda simple, Jake. I get half the purse money, and if you sell or have one claimed, I get half."

"On top of the juice?"

Ginny nodded.

"Are you insane?"

"There's juice on top of the juice you're already not paying me today. Purse money is on top of that."

"That's crazy."

"Well, Jake, here's the deal." A smirk slowly spread across Ginny's face. "You go out and get a loan from somebody else, pay me off, or—"

"You know I'm tapped out on my credit line."

"Not my problem, Jake. I'm just here with a solution. I sure wouldn't want the stews to learn you're insolvent. They might just rule you off, put a financially secure stable in your place. Those guys are kind of funny that way."

"Fuck. Ginny?" Jake leaned back in his chair, rubbing the side of his face.

"Hey, you came to me. Then you can't make the juice. I'm just trying to help you out. You're going the wrong direction. I need collateral. Simple as that."

"I win that filly stake, we're clear."

"You pay me the number and the juice, we're clear."

"And I get my half interest in the stock back?"

"You get your half interest back."

"It's bullshit, Ginny."

"Get a better deal and pay me off."

Jake looked Ginny in the eyes. "Filly's gonna win that stake."

"Want me to give her shoes a little tug?" Meaning did he want Ginny to apply turn downs on Aly Dancer's shoes.

"No, she wins straight up."

"Better hope so." He pointed a stout finger at Jake and walked out of the office.

She damn well better win.

Chapter 37

"GOODFELLA'S ON the Backside," the sports section of *The Washington Post* screamed. Jason Cregg broke the story of the extortion scheme carried out at Fairfax Park. The 30-point bold type headline and feature-length article appeared above the fold and dominated the Thursday edition.

Cregg had anonymous quotes from horsemen who blamed track management for failing to protect them. Owners shared stories about the horses they had lost and their waning interest in further investment without assurances or remuneration.

Dan folded the paper and pushed it into the wastebasket under his desk. He'd been able to keep AJ's name out of the article and that had been his sole objective when Cregg contacted him two days prior. The absence of an arrest and a refresher course on defamation carried the day. "A shooter" had been detained was all the article stated.

Biggs was quoted on the track's increased funding for security. Belker said they were committed to capturing those involved, but the spin of the article made management appear hapless.

The shooting had sent a shockwave through the community. No one was safe. Although Jake had come current with the extortionist, Dan still worried. Somebody trying to make a statement would take out a brilliant young filly rather than a tired claimer.

An individual as depraved as one that would fire a rifle at a penned-up horse could not be trusted and could not be left to his honor. It didn't make sense. Dan searched for motives, opportunity, and points of access. All seemed improbable. He could sit back and hope that everything went as planned, that his stock was safe.

Then again, he was never one to sit back and hope.

◆ ◆ ◆

AJ WAS always ready when Dan pulled up to the owner/trainer parking lot just inside the guard shack. Dan could tell that AJ hated to be away from his horses through the night, but it was a condition of his ability to keep his license on the backside.

Regardless of the decision made by the local sheriff's office, the stewards could rule someone off the property with little evidence. AJ was able to keep his job because Latimer had vouched for him, and Dan had agreed to house him off the property pending the investigation, which looked like it could be for the duration of the meet.

AJ was reluctant to move into Dan's condo. It was a two-bedroom condo, one bedroom of which was a home office, or as his mom called it, "the Oklahoma room," because it looked like a tornado had blown through it. AJ was content to sleep on the couch.

Dan learned quickly that AJ wasn't accustomed to air conditioning after living on the backside during the hot, humid summers. He would find him asleep, though shivering under three blankets. Dan wasn't about to go without the air con himself, but he did ratchet up the thermostat several degrees to make the home more tolerable for AJ.

He also learned that AJ had a narrow food window. It centered around French fries and grilled meat—the greater the fat content in the meat, the better. It had to have become an acquired taste living on the backside and eating at places like Crok's constantly. He and Milt would make a real dining pair, Dan thought.

Dan tried taking him to his favorite seafood restaurant and his friend's Italian place. Both times they ended up at the drive-thru on the way home. He simply wouldn't eat anything outside his familiar diet.

Dan even invited Beth to have dinner with them. Aside from just enjoying her company, Dan thought her personality might draw AJ out. Despite a pleasant dinner, Beth's brilliant smile, and a cooperative French chef—AJ had a burger and fries—the boy remained focused on his own world. Direct questions from Beth established that AJ knew the horse business, as well as ailments and treatments. He just didn't have any desire to interact, regardless of her tender prodding.

Little had been learned in the past week, and the list of "unprotected trainers" had grown shorter. Now it looked like about two in three trainers was paying the "safety fee."

AJ turned out of the shedrow and began walking toward Dan's car. Dan hopped out and quickly moved in his direction. "I need you to do something, AJ." He stopped and waited for Dan to reach him, then turned and followed him back toward the barn area.

"How was your day today?"

"Fine."

"Anything unusual happen?

"No."

He was a nice kid, but not a conversationalist.

They walked in silence, AJ about two feet behind him. They reached Jake's barn. "I want you to touch Aly Dancer." Dan didn't have to tell him which stall. He moved directly toward the third stall on the near side of the barn. Beth gave Dan a suspicious glance and stepped in front of the stall, blocking AJ's way. Having dinner was one thing. Getting close to her horses was quite another. "It's okay, Beth. Just want him to meet Aly Dancer."

"Might want to talk with Jake first," she said.

"Beth, it's okay. Last time I saw the training bills, she was my horse."

Beth hesitated, then stepped aside, and AJ slipped under the webbing. Beth quickly followed. She grabbed Aly Dancer's bridle and patted her on the nose. Dan walked up so he could see into the stall over the webbing. Aly Dancer shimmied nervously; she wasn't accustomed to having a stranger in her stall. Beth held her close and made cooing sounds to calm her.

AJ reached up and placed both hands on Aly Dancer's side. The filly suddenly became still. A humming sound started to come out of AJ. His eyes were closed, and he slowly leaned in and settled the side of his face on the horse's chest. Beth looked over at Dan like *what the heck is that?*

AJ hummed more loudly and began intermittently mumbling. The mumbling was indecipherable. The horse stood motionless. After several minutes AJ stood back and let go of the horse. Aly Dancer shook all over like she was shedding mosquitoes. Her breathing became heavier, but she remained calm and relaxed. AJ slipped under the webbing and stood next to Dan.

"How is she?"

AJ considered this for a long time, then looked at Dan. "In her mind, she's the best there's ever been."

"What do you mean?" Beth said. "Best there's ever been. I know that."

Dan gestured for Beth to stop and looked at AJ.

"What does that mean?" he asked.

"That filly is a special one," said AJ. "She got heart. She wants to compete, and she gets angry if anyone runs ahead of her. She won't back down. She won't back down for nothing."

"Have you seen that before? I mean sensed that, with another horse?"

"I've seen that before in good horses, but nothing like this. She got more will to win than anything I ever seen. She's a champion every minute of her life. Some horses, they just want to run fast. She wants to run fast, but more than anything, she wants to win."

Beth looked out over the webbing. "I coulda told you that."

"Thanks, Beth. You're a huge part of her success. It's not just her; it's you and her together, and I really appreciate it. You keep doing whatever you're doing with her."

Dan moved back away from the stall and began walking toward the parking area. "Let's go get some dinner. What do you say, AJ? How about a burger and fries?"

No laughter, no smiles. "Okay."

AJ walked along in silence behind him. Dan would slow down, trying to get him to walk alongside, but AJ would slow down and stay just behind him. Dan finally gave up and moved toward his vehicle.

"AJ, what do you do with those horses?"

"I dunno."

"No, really. What's the deal? How do you communicate with them?"

"I just touch them, and they tell me what they feel."

Dan didn't want to believe it, but he'd seen it too many times. "Any chance you can do that with people?" He chuckled to signal that it was a joke, but only half joking. Dan could quickly think of several witnesses in his pending cases that he'd like to have AJ lay his hands on. AJ could be his own personal truth squad, conveniently packaged in the shape of a young boy.

"Nope. Don't work with people."

"Why not?"

"'Cause people lie."

"So?"

"Horses don't lie."

"How do you know the horses aren't lying to you?" Dan asked.

"'Cause they can't. They only communicate one way. They always tell the truth. That's why horses are better than people."

"Not all people lie."

"No, but all people can."

They walked in silence, then AJ continued. "Best you can do with people is watch what they do. Have to ignore what they say—just watch what they do."

"AJ, let me ask you something. Do you know who's hurting the horses? Have you seen something?"

"I don't know who's doing it. But it don't make sense."

"What specifically?"

"Couple things. Can't steal a horse from a racetrack."

"Lots of horses have been kidnapped over the years, AJ. Even some famous ones. Held for ransom. It happens."

"They get taken from a farm, not a racetrack." He was right. To get a horse off a racetrack, you had to have papers and a trailer and pull it off with dozens of people watching. "What else bothers you?"

"Whoever's doing this is known by everyone."

"How do you know that?"

They walked for about a hundred yards. "'Cause we can see things that are different. Can't see things that are the same."

"So it's definitely someone working on the backside?

He shrugged, looking at the ground as he walked. "We can't see him, so he's the same as us."

"How do we catch him?"

AJ shrugged. "Know the difference between what we're told and what we see."

"So if we ignore what we've been told and only focus on what we've seen, we'll catch him?"

"Not sure if you'll catch him, but it's the only chance."

Chapter 38

TUESDAY AFTERNOONS were the slow time. No racing scheduled that day, so after morning works, it was time to relax, catch up on overdue projects, or just find a shady spot to rest. By two P.M. the backside was a ghost town. There were plenty of people around, but none were walking outside the shedrows. Many had left the property to play golf, do laundry, catch up on sleep, or just get away for a few hours.

AJ cut a solitary figure as he ventured from Latimer's barn toward Crok's. He struggled with understanding why he couldn't be with his horses around the clock, but he eventually fell into the routine of spending the night at Dan's house. It was all right but not as good as being on the backside.

A groom from Dellingham's barn came running around the far side of the barn toward AJ. He waved his arms and urged AJ toward him. Breathlessly, he pleaded for help with a downed horse in the adjoining barn.

The groom shot off toward the barn. AJ hop-skipped behind him, moving as fast as he could. Surprisingly, AJ was catching up as they rounded the side of the barn.

"Third stall," the groom said, pointing a weary arm.

AJ swung around the pole holding up the extended roof of the shedrow and stooped under the webbing, into the stall.

There was no downed animal.

There was no animal at all in the stall.

There were two stable hands standing in the stall, and the groom from Dellingham's barn quickly stepped in place, blocking any exit through the stall door.

"Well, if it isn't Mr. Superhero," said the tallest one. This was the same one Dan had dubbed Romeo.

AJ moved backward to get away from the men. Dellingham's groom shoved him forward into the middle of the stall. AJ looked down and tried to ignore them.

"Yeah," said the short one. "You think you're so special. You can take care of everyone's horses, like you did with the loose horse the other day. My loose horse. Didn't need your help, punk." He stepped forward and pushed AJ toward the front corner of the stall.

AJ didn't sense it coming, and he flew backward, landing on his butt with his head slamming into the corner of the stall. His backside landed in fresh manure, and he fell onto his side. His hat flew off, landing in his lap.

"Keep your hands off our horses. We don't need your help. You understand?" said Romeo.

AJ didn't respond. He was shaking and waiting for them to leave so he could get up.

"You understand?" He yelled this time, kicking the back of AJ's thigh. "Seems like we need to teach this guy a lesson. Don't we, Luke?" said Romeo.

"Sure as hell do," said Luke. He bent down, grabbed AJ's cap, and threw it onto the slick of horse manure. Then he stepped on it and ground the hat with the heel of his boot.

"Get up," yelled Romeo.

AJ didn't move; he was waiting for it to be over. He would wait them out.

"I said, get up." Romeo planted another kick to the boy's backside.

AJ slowly crawled to his feet and cowered in the corner, not looking at the men. Luke reached forward and slapped the boy. AJ kept staring at the matted straw. He made no effort to defend himself other than backing into the corner and moving his hands to cover his ears.

"Put your hat on," Luke said. The other men laughed. Luke kicked the hat, and it landed on one of AJ's tennis shoes. "Put it on, shithead."

AJ bent down and shook his cap holding the bill. Chunks of manure dropped off, but the right side was virtually painted in horse excrement. He tugged it onto his head, continuing to look down at the straw.

"You're gonna learn a lesson all right," said Romeo. "Time for a little blanket party." He reached behind him and tossed a horse blanket over AJ's head.

Luke grabbed him, pinning his arms to his side. All was darkness. AJ yelled, but under the blanket his plea was muted.

"Looks like we got us a screamer," said Dellingham's groom.

"Yep," said Luke. "We'll take care of that." He ripped the blanket off AJ's head. AJ stumbled back into the wall, blinking his eyes. Romeo yanked the boy toward him, then pinned AJ's arms. Luke stepped forward with a cloth wrap and tightly tied it around AJ's mouth. Then the blanket went back over his head.

They spun him around several times, then picked him up like a roll of carpeting.

AJ couldn't scream. No sound came out. He wanted it to be over. He couldn't control his shaking. He wanted them to stop and just leave him alone. They were carrying him out of the stall. He could only hear their laughter. He tried to focus on his horses, what he needed to do for them this afternoon. AJ tried to imagine it away. He tried to ignore it away.

Then, beneath the blanket, he started to cry.

This time, he realized, it was not going away.

Chapter 39

DAN WHEELED into the owner/trainer parking lot at the regular time. AJ was usually sitting on the white fence, waiting for his ride. Today, no AJ.

Little movement stirred on the backside today. Horses had all been exercised, fed, washed, wrapped, and penned back in their stalls. Two guys were shooting hoops in the stifling heat, and a few lonely souls were visible resting in the growing shade of the barns.

Dan walked toward Latimer's barn. AJ must be working on something last-minute, Dan thought. There was no movement around Latimer's barn as he approached. The door to the trainer's office was open, and a two-foot fan had been propped into the doorway. It hummed like a reluctant servant, pushing air but cooling little.

Inside, Dick Latimer was scanning the condition book, flipping pages, looking for opportunity.

"Hey," said Dan. "Was looking for AJ. He here?"

Latimer dropped the book on the desk and leaned forward. "He's around. Haven't seen him for a while. Check the stalls; he's here somewhere. Kid will be with a horse somewhere."

Dan started down the shedrow, looking in each stall. Sleepy horses stared back at him, shifting their weight and shivering to keep flies off them.

"AJ," Latimer yelled.

A dark face poked out of the room adjoining Latimer's office.

"Paulo," Latimer shouted. "You seen AJ?"

"No. Not for a while," said Paulo.

Dan spun around the corner. "He's not in the stalls." Then looking at Paulo, "When did you see him last?"

"I don't know—two, three hours ago."

"Shit," said Latimer.

"Got that right," said Dan, scanning the backside. He moved out of the barn area, looking left and right.

"Not like the kid to be gone five minutes. Where the hell—? Paulo, run up to Crok's and see if he's there," said Latimer. "Ask if anyone's seen him."

Dan ran toward the main track. "AJ. Hey, AJ," he shouted.

Two women sat in the shade of an adjoining barn. "You guys seen AJ? The kid who works for Latimer."

Both shook their heads, not evoking any emotion, apparently in an attempt to avoid expending any energy.

"Damn it," Dan muttered. Sweat beaded on his forehead and upper lip. He swiped it away and thought, *Where would he go? Test barn? No, no races today, so it would be empty. Grandstand? Nothing over there on dark days.* He saw Paulo running back from Crok's. He didn't need any words. Paulo hadn't found him and had no clues.

Dan ran east along the barns. "AJ," he yelled.

He came to the end of the barns. Two other stable hands were quizzed; neither had any information about AJ's whereabouts. Dan turned left away from the track and back toward Manassas State Park. *Would AJ have gone into the park? What the heck for?*

After crossing five rows of barns, he was near the spot where the loose horse was captured. *AJ had to be with a horse somewhere. He wouldn't be away from his barn unless he was helping some animal.*

Latimer was several barns to his left, inquiring, then jogging to the next barn. Dan saw him stop suddenly, questioning someone. Dan ran toward them. His shirt was soaked in sweat and clung to him like a body cast. Latimer took off running, Dan followed, slowly gaining ground.

"What is it?" Dan asked between breaths.

"Sons a bitches."

"What? Where is he?"

Neither was setting any land speed record as they moved westward. Latimer was hindered by age and cowboy boots. Dan made better time, but he didn't know where they were going.

Latimer huffed, "Dung heap."

Dan shot him a quizzical look, then realized what he meant. He raced forward toward the far end of the backside. Each day's straw and manure was mucked from the stalls, collected in piles, and carted to the far end of the backside. Every few days the mountain was loaded on trucks and hauled away.

In the distance he could see a mountain of mucked residue, but no AJ. The stench from the urine and manure hit him like a sledgehammer as he approached. His eyes filled with water, and flies darkened the area.

His vision was drawn to something on the back side of shit mountain. It had to be AJ. Someone was tied to a post with a blanket over his head. Dan sprinted the final fifty yards. "AJ? You okay?" The blanket moved slightly. Dan knelt down and untied the rope binding his hands to the post. Latimer rushed up and pulled the blanket off AJ. His mouth was gagged, and Dan quickly unbound him.

It had to be 120 degrees under that blanket, Dan thought. AJ was soaked from head to toe. Dan looked at a large wet spot on the ground near AJ's feet. The poor kid had peed himself.

AJ coughed and rubbed his mouth. His eyes were glassy and he bent over to take some deep breaths.

"AJ, who did this?" asked Latimer.

AJ just kept inhaling and wheezing.

"AJ?" Latimer said, grabbing the boy by the shoulders.

The boy looked up at him. "Don't matter," he said.

"What do you mean, it doesn't matter?" said Dan. "You coulda died under there." He shuddered to think that if AJ had vomited from the smell, he would have drowned in his own puke. "Who did this?"

"Couple guys." AJ said. "M-M-mad about me helping some horse."

"What the hell?" Dan said.

AJ started to move away. "Gotta go finish some wraps." He staggered sideways and nearly collapsed. Latimer caught him.

"Dick, get some water in him," said Dan. "He's got to be dehydrated. Get him someplace cool or air conditioned, and I'll find you. Motherfuckers." He looked at Latimer. "Where's Kimbrough's barn?"

Latimer had his arm around AJ and was walking him back toward the barn. "Trackside, third barn from the entrance," said Latimer. "Why?"

Dan turned and moved that direction. "I made a promise, and I'm going to make good on it."

Chapter 40

IN HIS search for AJ, Dan had nearly circled the entire backside by the time he made it to Kimbrough's barn. Anger surged through him as he thought about AJ. Red-faced and dripping with sweat, Dan strode into the grassy area outside Kimbrough's barn.

"Hey, Romeo," Dan yelled to the man and girl talking under the eve of the shedrow. "Get your ass over here."

Romeo pushed away from the wall and casually moved toward Dan. "Name's Paul."

"Get over here now," Dan said.

He walked out into the grass and stopped about eight feet from Dan. He stood with arms crossed and a smile on his face.

"What the hell's the matter with you?" said Dan.

"What."

"You nearly killed that boy," Dan said.

"What boy?" Romeo asked.

"You know damn well what I'm talking about," Dan said. "I told you anything happens to that boy and I'm coming after you."

"Just playing a game. We're just playing with him."

"He was assaulted and battered. He was tied to a post. That's not a game. That's criminal."

"We were just messing with him. Nobody, like, hit him or anything."

"I don't give a shit. I'm holding you accountable," Dan said, stepping forward. Romeo stepped back and raised his arms, to block a punch. "I'm not going to hit you. I'm going to get you ruled off. I'm going to get you thrown off the property."

As much as he wanted to smack the kid, Dan knew that he would lose all leverage with the stewards. Although AJ got hurt, if one of the guys who did it also got hurt, the stew's would rule it a dog fall.

Dan wanted to pummel him, but he had to be smart. It took all his resolve. Be calm. Be smart. Dan could give him physical pain that would last a few hours or he could give him economic pain—take his job away. That would last much longer.

Romeo smiled. "Stew's won't do nothing. There are fights all the time on the backside."

"This wasn't a fight. This was an ambush. A calculated attack. You're a predator."

"So, what are you gonna do?"

"I'm going to have you taken care of. You won't be messing with anybody from now on. I ought to knock the crap out of you right here, but I'm not going to hit you. I'm not going to give you the satisfaction." Dan moved in close. They stood eye to eye. "Why pick on that boy? What did he ever do to you?"

"Kid's a show off."

"How?"

"Like, like how he caught that loose horse. Like he has some kind of power to talk to these damn horses. Like he's better than us. He ain't nothing. We don't need him showing us up."

"He is better than you," Dan said. "You and all your little Nazi pals. But rather than watch and learn something from the kid, you've got to tear him down. He'll always be better than you."

Romeo shrugged and shifted his weight side to side. The slightest smirk appeared on his face. As if he realized he had won a stalemate in a game he should have lost.

Dan knew the kid was right. The stewards wouldn't do much, especially given the tension around the extortion plot and dead horses. A civil case was possible, but AJ, though compelling, wasn't exactly going to be a star witness.

"You and I aren't done. Far from it," Dan said.

"See ya round," said Romeo.

Dan turned to leave, then the thought of AJ under that blanket, combined with Romeo's smirk, got the best of him. He spun on his heel with balled fist. Romeo threw his hands up to block a punch to his face. Dan had no intention of hitting him in the face. He went low and buried his fist into Romeo's stomach.

As a lawyer, Dan knew evidence. A broken nose, a bloody lip, a swollen eye, those were direct evidence of an assault. The vision, even in photographs, screamed evidence of a crime. The blow to his unprotected midsection was as satisfying for Dan as any blow to the jaw. It also left little visual evidence. Romeo can to go the stews. Like he said, fights happened all the time. An owner striking a stable hand was unusual, but the claim would go nowhere.

The air flew out of Romeo like a balloon at a child's party. He doubled over gasping for breath.

Dan jammed his foot into Romeo's hip and pushed him sideways. Romeo stumbled for two steps, then fell to the ground.

Dan leaned down over Romeo. He was curled into a ball and struggling to draw oxygen. "That's an appetizer," said Dan. "You don't want me to serve the fucking entrée."

Dan turned and planted a kicked to Romeo's backside as a parting shot. "Leave the kid alone. This is the last time I'm going to say it."

Chapter 41

SUNDAY MORNINGS caused no change in the routine of the backside. More people were hung over and fewer horses worked on the track, but the routine and activity was the same. Dan had just dropped AJ off at Latimer's barn and stopped by to see Beth and Aly Dancer. The fact that Jake was paying the protection money was some small comfort to Dan. But the fact that someone had targeted his filly made it personal. He also kept an eye peeled for Romeo. He didn't need to get jumped by some punks as he walked the backside.

The My Lassie Stakes was Saturday, and he didn't think it would ever get here. Dan had learned that, with an improving two-year-old, the time between races seemed to stand still. When an owner had a common horse, the time flew by, accompanied by frequent training and vet bills.

Beth had been around some good horses, but her connection with Aly Dancer was something he'd never seen before. She spent all her free time with the horse and, according to Jake, had started sleeping at the barn to be around her. If the guy attacking the horses had any honor at all, Aly

Dancer should be safe, since Jake was now off the list, but Beth wasn't taking any chances. All the better for Dan.

Aly Dancer was eating well, and her coat shone like stained glass. Jake was going to work her on Wednesday to blow her out in preparation for the stake. Beth was finishing the last of the wraps on her hind legs. Two-year-olds were so brittle and still growing, so all the tender touches and special attention would add to her chances to become a stronger horse when she matured and grew up a little. Dan held a couple of peppermints in his extended hand, and Aly Dancer gratefully chomped them up. She crunched and threw her head around, apparently pleased.

"Don't spoil her," Beth said, laughing. "She has a job to do. We don't want her getting soft on us."

"You're the one spoiling her," Dan said. "And I really appreciate it. She does, too. You take care of our girl here. We have to be in some pictures come Saturday."

"We'll be there," she said.

As he rounded the back of his car, his eye caught something shiny on the ground. It was a cell phone. There was no vehicle parked next to him. Whoever had parked beside his car had dropped a cell phone on the way out.

Dan picked it up and examined it. After scanning the contact list, he realized this phone didn't have a hi-tech owner. No names in the contact list. He turned the phone off and turned it back on. If it was the same as his phone, the cell number would appear as it logged on.

Dan got into his vehicle as the phone was logging on. Sure enough, the number appeared. He pulled out his cell phone and dialed the number. It was odd to be dialing a number in one hand and holding the ringing phone in the other, but he wanted to see whether he could identify the owner from the voice mail message.

After five rings a voice came on. "This is Hank Skelton. Leave a message."

Dan opened Skelton's phone and clicked open the page for received, placed, and missed calls. He was hoping to find a clue in the received calls about who had placed the extortion calls to identify the drop.

There were several 312 numbers—could be friends in Chicago or owners. Hank had raced there. Dan also noticed a few 410 numbers—Pennsylvania, another state where Skelton raced and probably had owners. Some 703 numbers, but that was local and didn't tell him much. He clicked over to placed calls, again a smattering of 312, 403, and 703 numbers.

There was one 703 number that came up repeatedly. He checked the received calls again. There it was. Seven of the last ten calls received were from 703-544-8180.

He opened the missed calls. The 703 number was there as well. Three times. Could be his vet or could be a local owner. Dan dialed the number, this time using Hank's phone.

It rang three times, then a voice came on the line. "Belker. What's up, Hank?"

Dan snapped the phone shut, disconnecting the call. He flipped the phone back open and powered down the phone. Belker would be calling back. Why so many calls with Belker? Skelton was all over Belker and his staff over the kidnapped mare.

Belker's response was unusual as well. "What's up?" It could be just a common greeting. Dan didn't know Belker well enough to know whether he said that all the time. If Belker knew it was Hank, he wouldn't ask "What's up." He'd know he was going to be questioned about the kidnapped horse, maybe be asked for an update on the investigation. "What's up" seemed too casual.

Dan dialed the number again, this time with his cell phone. After two rings, the same voice came on the line. "Tim Belker, Fairfax Security."

"Hey, Tim, this is Dan Morgan. You know, the guy keeping the kid AJ at nights."

Belker grunted. "Oh yeah, you."

"Anyway, the reason I'm calling is, if I can be of any assistance in the investigation or provide any contacts, whatever, just want you to know I'd be willing to help."

"Well, uh, thank you. Dan, was it?"

"Right, Dan Morgan."

"Look, I appreciate the offer, but we've got a full team locally as well as investigations ongoing with the local sheriff's office and the FBI."

"Okay, just wanted to make the offer. Anything to help out. But I do have one question. I heard that Hank Skelton gets a call about where to drop the money. Is that a local number or any luck on a trace?"

"That's part of an ongoing investigation, so I can't discuss that."

"I understand. Just seems strange that we can't get a hit on the phone being used."

"The call is coming through some switchboard in the Caribbean. It's being bounced and coming through a Skype account, but it changes each time. It's become kind of a wild goose chase."

"Okay, let me know if there's anything I can do." Dan snapped off the call. He sat and thought for a few minutes, then powered up Belker's phone. He clicked on the received call page and deleted the history. Then he clicked over to the placed call menu and deleted those calls.

He got out of his car and walked toward Crok's. He could have simply walked to Skelton's barn and handed someone the phone but opted to be an anonymous Good Samaritan and just turn it in to Crok's and let them find its owner.

On his way back to the car, he pulled out his phone again and dialed a familiar number. "Mom? I need a big favor."

Chapter 42

THE HORSES flew past the finish line, and Milt shouted, "Yeah, baby. I got the exacta ten times."

"Not bad," said Lennie. "With the top two favorites, you'll be lucky if it pays twenty bucks."

"I'll take two bills," said Milt. "That race was like stealing."

Lennie had passed the race, as had TP and Dan.

"A little too chalky for my tastes," TP said. Chalk referred to the betting favorite. Astute horseplayers perceived the odds of a favorite winning were less than the potential return on a winning bet. Such that even if handicapping said a horse would win, they wouldn't bet on it because over time the gambler would lose money. In that situation it was better just to watch.

"Can't win if you don't play," said Milt. "I'm gonna roll 'em today. I can just feel it."

Lennie smiled to himself and turned his pages to the next contest. He looked over at Dan and said, "Hey, when you gonna run Hero's Echo?"

"May not find a race until the last month of the meet. Jake said he didn't lose that much conditioning as a result of the surgery, but we'll need a few weeks to get him on top of his game."

"Going to run in allowance company?"

"Yeah, he's still eligible for 'non-two other than,' and they have a pretty fair purse for those here." *Non-two other than* referred to an allowance, or non-claiming, race where the horses haven't won two races lifetime other than maiden or claiming races. Horse racing was based around grouping horses of similar experience and success through "conditions." Once a horse ran through its conditions, it would only run in open stakes, allowance or claiming events, where the competition was much stiffer.

"A lot of horses come back from that throat surgery and tear up the track," said TP.

"I guess before the surgery it's like running the hundred yard dash while holding your breath," Dan said.

"Emilio would fit your horse perfect," said TP.

Lennie shot back, "Teep, you'd say your boy could fit a lamppost perfectly if it could get him a mount."

"Kid can ride the hair off a goat," TP said.

"I leave all that to Jake, Teep. Talk to him."

"Wouldn't kill you to put in a good word."

"I will, but you know Jake," Dan said, laughing. "He does only what Jake wants. I just keep my mouth shut and pay the bills. It's worked well for me so far."

"Pardon me, boys," said Milt as he got up to move out of the box. "But I've got a date with the cashier's window."

"You mean you've got a date with a funnel cake and a corn dog," said TP.

Undeterred, he moved past them with the excitement of cashing a handful of tickets. Lennie studied his pages, and TP focused on the program in front of him, calculating jockey percentages and thinking of pitches and strategies to get his guys more rides.

"Lennie, you know anything about Skype?"

He looked up at the tote board to check some odds. "Yeah, I have a couple of pals from the U.K. and Australia who call me on their Skype accounts. We keep an eye on large carryover pools—pick sixes, twin tris, you know. If we see one getting really large, we go in on tickets together."

"You're a real global enterprise," said TP.

"I do what I can. These damn tracks conspire against the everyday gambler. If there's an overlay out there, we gang up to take advantage of it, from anywhere in the world."

"What kind of caller ID information do you get?" Dan asked.

"You mean the ID on the phone?" Dan nodded. Lennie fished his cell phone from his pocket and clicked a few buttons, then handed the phone to him. "Here's Graham, my virtual track buddy from Edinborough."

The caller ID was a series of numbers but didn't resemble a U.S. area code and number.

"So, do they ever appear like a U.S. phone number?"

"I think they can, but my calls come from overseas, so they usually appear that way."

"Can you dial them back?"

"Sure, just hit call when the number is up, and it dials right back. Why? You trying to move into the twentieth century? Upgrade your technology?"

"Yeah, something like that."

"Can you trace the number?"

"I suppose. The number links to an account or a computer, so it has to tie to something or someone."

Dan handed the phone to him, and Lennie went back to his sheets.

"How's the filly doing?" TP asked.

"Doing great," Dan said. "Can't wait for Saturday. Don't think it'll ever get here. Excited and scared shitless at the same time."

Chapter 43

"MOM, I really appreciate it." Dan leaned back in his office chair with his feet up on the desk. It was just after noon on Monday, and she was filling him in on what he had asked about after finding the cell phone.

"You know, things were supposed to have improved in the aftermath of 9/11, but the agencies don't share more now than they did then. I had Frank Matthews make a few inquiries since he's been on some interagency task forces and knows people well at the FBI. I don't like doing this."

"I know, Mom, I'm just trying to piece some things together, and I need to buy a clue about the investigation going on at Fairfax Park."

"Frank said there's no investigation on file with the FBI. Now, he said that could mean a file is being created or that they're seeking more information to decide whether to bring an investigation—but for now there's no formal action."

"How quickly do they typically move?"

"Well, if it's like here, pretty fast. The speed of criminal enterprise doesn't wait for bureaucrats to catch up. If they had valid information, they'd move on it in a heartbeat," she said.

Dan sat upright, elbows on his desk. "What about the local sheriff?"

"Now, they do have a file, but they aren't actively investigating," she said.

"What do you mean, they aren't actively investigating?"

"What Frank told me is that where jurisdiction overlaps the related agencies can make one primary and the other secondary. It appears that the private security has taken primary responsibility, so the sheriff's office is standing down. Providing resources when asked but not leading the investigation."

"How can that be?" Dan stood, pacing behind his desk, unknowingly testing the strength of the telephone cord. "Why would the local sheriff's office defer authority to a private company?"

"Well, they're a private company, but they have jurisdiction over park security. Fairfax Park is legally part of Manassas Park, which is federal property."

"I still don't get it," he said.

"Think about going to the airport. The security is provided by a private company, hired by the government. Even though they're private, they have jurisdiction over security in the airport. Now the fibbies or sheriff don't take over the responsibilities at the airport, even though I suppose they could. In deference, they wait to be asked to help. Otherwise, they stand down."

"But if an ongoing criminal enterprise was underway, wouldn't they get involved?"

"They certainly could. I suppose it depends upon the information provided by the agency with jurisdiction and how much support the local agency requests."

"Okay." His mind raced through the possibilities. "Thanks a lot, Mom. I've got to go."

"Dan, have you talked to Vickie?"

"Mom."

"I just think if you—"

"Mom."

"—talked to her, you know—"

"Mom."

"You might—"

"Mom. Enough." He softened his tone. She couldn't understand the divorce, he thought. Her marriage ended with an Arlington police officer standing on her doorstep. The idea of ending a marriage by agreement must appear unfathomable.

"I just think you need to talk to her, Dan. She's such a sweet girl, and you can work things out," she said.

Should I tell her about Beth? What's to tell? The idea of another woman in his life might suspend this line of questioning or at least divert it, but what did he have to tell? *I met a girl? That would set her off in a whole new direction. No, can't go there.*

"Mom, we talk. It isn't going to work. I've told you that. We're both okay with it." He stood and turned his back to the phone, twirling the cord with his fingers.

"But have you tried? Really tried? It's not too late."

"Mom, we've been all through this. I know you care about her."

"I care about *you*. She was so good for you."

"She's a great gal." *Gal? Wow, where did that come from?* "Mom, she's great. We're still friends."

"Friends? Danny, honestly."

"She really likes you, Mom, and you guys can still be friends." He wanted to say "No one died here" but bit his tongue. "Heck, maybe better friends. You can compare notes on me like usual." He chuckled, but the humor didn't translate. "I still love her, but it's not right. She'll be happier, and so will I."

"I just think—"

"Mom, I've got to go. Really. I'm kinda busy here. I'll see you Thursday for dinner. Thanks for all the help. Love you."

Chapter 44

AJ WAS waiting at his regular spot when Dan pulled up. With the exception of the run-in with Romeo and his bandits, Dan and AJ had fallen into a steady routine at the end of the work day. Tonight would be different.

"AJ, we're going on a little mission tonight."

"What for?"

"We're going to do what you suggested. We're going to watch what they do, not listen to what they say. But first, we're going to get something to eat—then we'll come back here."

After eating, they parked just outside the main drive of Fairfax Park. They waited for Skelton's white pickup truck. At ten minutes after eight, the pickup rolled out of the parking lot and headed north. Dan pulled in behind.

He'd never tailed anyone before, so his knowledge base was what he had learned in movies and on TV. Dan put two cars between his and Skelton's truck and hoped he wouldn't get left behind by a changing traffic signal.

Luckily, Skelton merged onto Interstate 66, headed toward D.C. Dan stayed well back from him in an adjoining lane. After about fifteen minutes he moved to the right-hand lane and got off at Highway 7100, headed north. Dan followed at a safe distance until Skelton's truck reached a red light.

As they approached, Dan had AJ duck down in the passenger seat. Skelton might not even look back in the rearview mirror, but if he did, there was a better chance he'd recognize AJ than Dan. They waited for the green light.

Skelton pulled away and traveled about three miles before turning right off the highway. They followed as he entered an apartment complex. Skelton drove around to the backside of the complex, parked, got out of the vehicle, and entered the apartment building. Dan backed into a parking stall, and they waited.

Dan wasn't sure what they were going to do next. Skelton probably lived here, but one thing was for sure; he hadn't made a drop with the money. Things were starting to come together.

Just then Skelton came out of the building. He had changed clothes and was wearing a blue baseball cap. He walked over to his pickup but didn't get in. Instead, he got into a dark colored Camry and drove off. Maybe he was going to make a drop, but why change clothes and cars?

Skelton got back onto 7100 and continued north. He merged onto the toll road toward Dulles Airport. He stopped to pay the toll, and rather than taking the chance of flying by him by using his easy pass, Dan stopped and paid the toll.

The toll taker gave him a confused look, apparently wondering why the guy would pay cash for the toll with an easy pass device on the windshield. Just past Dulles Airport they encountered another toll station. Skelton continued westward.

After a few more miles he exited onto Route 7 past Leesburg, Virginia, and into the countryside. Dan was becoming concerned because the farther they went, the fewer cars there were on the roads. It would become easier to notice Dan was tailing him, especially as he headed west on this two-lane highway.

Dan gave him some extra distance; in fact, he stayed back far enough that he could barely see Skelton's tail lights as he continued west into rural Virginia.

Several miles past Leesburg, Skelton turned right onto a two-lane highway, proudly proclaimed to be the Berlin Turnpike. Despite the austere name, it was a pitted asphalt road that veered left and right through dark and heavily forested woods. They crept along at a top speed of maybe twenty miles per hour.

If he was making the drop, they wouldn't see it. Then again, if Skelton made the drop, he would head back toward his apartment. Dan had come to believe there was no drop or at least none currently. They were watching what he was doing, not listening to what he said.

They continued north through the towns of Hampton Bridge and Wheatland. The scenery had changed from high-rise apartments and eight-lane roads to small subdivisions and four-lane highways to complete rural stretches along this two-lane blacktop road, with an occasional small town along the way. Homes or farmhouses were tucked back into the woods, barely discernable from the roadway as they crept along.

The twists and turns in the road diminished their speed further, and visibility was limited. After about two miles Dan lost the tail lights of Skelton's vehicle.

He slowed down and looked for any sign of light. As they curved left around a bend, he spotted two tail lights moving away from the highway. Dan pulled past the intersection where Skelton had turned and drove up about another quarter mile. He executed a perfect boot leg turn on the roadway and headed back to the intersection.

It appeared to be a driveway rather than a road. Five mailboxes along the roadside indicated it was probably a shared driveway for several parcels of land. Dan pulled up about one hundred yards past the intersection and entered a side road. He stopped the vehicle and turned off the lights. AJ looked at him curiously.

"I'm going back to take a look. Here's my cell phone. If I'm not back in thirty minutes, I want you to call Jake and tell him where you are."

"I don't know where I am."

"You're on the Berlin Turnpike about two miles north of Wheatland," Dan said. AJ nodded. Dan showed him Jake's number on the cell phone, so he could press a button to dial, if needed.

"And here's the most important thing," Dan continued. "Do not get out of this car. I don't care what happens—you don't get out of this car unless I'm here or Jake is here. Don't trust anyone. Do you understand?"

The boy nodded again.

Chapter 45

SKELTON DROVE past the barn on the left and pulled the car up on the far side of the house. A faint light came from the small clapboard cottage. Tucked away under two massive oak trees, the structure showed the wear that came with a decade of forgotten maintenance. Curled paint chips were visible hugging the window frames. The fencing around the front porch was a mouth missing several teeth. A woman's touch had not been present for ages. It was a guy's cabin, a hangout, not a home.

Skelton grabbed the package on the passenger seat and walked up on the wooden front landing. He glanced through the window and saw the man in the cowboy hat standing near the back of the main room. He turned the copper knob on the front door and entered the house.

"What was the take?" said Belker.

"Almost twenty grand." He threw the package on the kitchen table. Belker picked it up and began sorting through the bills.

"Who'd we get new?"

"Creighton, Keating, and Price, finally," Hank said as he opened the refrigerator and pulled out one of the beers remaining from the twelve pack.

"I knew Creighton would see the light."

"Yeah, I guess it helped when you blew the brains out of his best horse. What's up with that?"

Belker laughed. "Some people just need to see the light."

Skelton didn't join him in the laughter. "That was stupid. We don't need that kind of violence. For Christ sakes, you could have killed someone. Ever think of that?"

"What, you're getting all soft on me? You have no problem plugging a horse with poison, but you get all weepy about shooting one? Don't get all righteous on me."

"We were making good progress with what we'd done. Didn't need to escalate it like that," Skelton said.

"Nearly pinned it on that stupid kid," Belker said, chuckling to himself. "Actually glad they let him go. It could have cost us a bunch of money if we had to stop before the end of the meet."

"It's gotta stop, Tim. No need to hurt more animals. We've made our point, and the money is rolling in each week. I think we need to lay low for a while."

"Damn, you are going soft on me. We've got half a dozen barns holding out on us. Now's the time to ramp up, not slow down. Those punks owe us a bunch of money from the start of the meet. I've got a plan for this week. You leave it to me now."

"This is getting crazy. We were just supposed to get the money flowing and—" Belker held his hand up at Skelton and rushed over to the window.

"Anybody follow you?"

"No way."

Belker pulled back the tattered red, checkerboard drape and looked outside. "Sure as hell did." He ran to the back door, pulled his gun off the kitchen counter, and disappeared outside.

◆ ◆ ◆

DAN SLID the heavy barn door open and peered inside. Four stalls lined the right side of the barn. The left side was open, containing feed, implements, and a rusted wheelbarrow. The barn felt cavernous, with hay bales strewn in one corner. A frail wooden stairway led up to several pieces of plywood laid on top of 2″ by 8″ rafters, a makeshift second story.

A horse's head poked out the stall door and looked at him as it rustled the straw in the bedding. It had to be Exigent Lady. He pulled the door to close it and crept along the side of the barn to get a view of the house.

The Camry was parked on the side behind a Jeep Wrangler. Lights were on inside the house, and Dan could see a man with a baseball cap with his back to him. He couldn't tell whether it was Skelton, but it had to be. He stayed in the shadow of the barn and moved to his right to get a better look. He was going to have to get closer to the house.

Dan moved to the right to get out of view of the window and snuck up near the back of the Camry. If he could ID the man as Skelton, he could call the cops and get them out here before they could move the horse. That better be Exigent Lady in the barn, he thought, or he'd look like an imbecile bringing the authorities out. All he could prove is that Skelton went for a drive, hardly enough for the cavalry to be brought in. Dan had to get a look in the front window. Dan stepped from behind the Camry to get onto the porch.

"Hold it right there."

Dan looked in the direction of the voice, and Tim Belker had a gun trained on him.

"Who the fuck are you?" he said. Then he caught a better view from the light coming through the front window. "You're that lawyer who bailed out that kid. Get inside." He waved the gun, indicating Dan should move onto the porch.

He followed Dan onto the landing and into the house. Skelton spun around and recognized him. "What the—"

"Yeah, nobody followed you," said Belker. "Sit down over there."

"That's one of Gilmore's owners," Skelton said.

"Let's have your wallet," Belker said. He grabbed it from him and pulled out his driver's license.

"Daniel Morgan," Belker said. He threw the wallet on the table. "Dan and I are pals, aren't we, Dan?"

Dan ignored him as he studied the interior of the house for escape routes. Scarred wood framed furniture adorned the living room, with a solid dining room table and six chairs. Clearly, early trailer court was the motif the designer sought. On the right a darkened hallway led to what presumably was a bedroom and bathroom. A solitary beer can was perched on the dining room table alongside what appeared to be a stack of cash.

"Dan called me a couple of days ago," Belker said. "Wanted to know how he could help out with the investigation. Well, Dan, you're going to be more helpful in closing this investigation than you ever imagined." He turned toward Skelton. "Find something and tie him up."

Skelton started rummaging through the kitchen drawers.

"You're not going to get away with this. I've got people on the way," Dan said.

Belker stared at Dan, as though pondering his next move. He wagged the gun at him with a steady beat. "Well, they'll get here just in time."

Dan heard the tear and recognized the sound as Skelton turned with a roll of duct tape.

"Nice work, Skelton," Dan said. "Kidnap your own horse. May have fooled some people with that." Hank pushed him forward and started taping his wrists together. "You make me sick, Skelton. Killing horses. I can understand him." Dan nodded toward Belker. "What the hell's the matter with you?" Skelton didn't say anything, just kept taping.

"You know, I'm getting a little tired of you," Belker said. "But it doesn't matter. They're going to find you with a dead horse, and this investigation will all be tied up." He laughed. "So to speak."

"Whaddya mean, dead horse?" said Skelton. Belker just looked at him. "That's not the plan. The plan is for me to get my mare back." He threw the roll of tape onto the table and stepped in front of Dan.

"Plans change," said Belker. "If you hadn't been so stupid and let this guy follow you, we might have other options."

"You're not killing that horse!" Skelton screamed. His upper body lurched as though he was going to confront Belker, then thought better of it.

"I'm getting a little tired of your weak ass, Hank."

"That isn't the plan," said Skelton, waving his arms but not moving toward Belker. "I need that horse. After this break, she can run out a bunch of money for me. I'm supposed to get her back."

"Looks like you've been taken, Hank," Dan said. He wanted to keep the argument going. It seemed like the only chance he had. "But I'm sure Belker will pay you for the value of the horse. What is she, a quarter claimer?"

"Guy's right," said Skelton. "Mare's worth twenty-five thousand. You can't just kill her."

"Looks like he owes you twenty-five large, Hank," said Dan.

"Tape his mouth shut. I've had it with him," said Belker, moving toward the kitchen.

"No," said Hank, stepping toward him. "Not 'til we figure this out."

Belker calmly aimed the gun at Hank's chest. "Nothing to figure out. Now, do as I say."

Hank recoiled and took a step back. "No, this is over. We didn't need to hurt that many horses, and we sure as hell don't need to kill my mare."

Belker stared at Skelton, keeping the gun pointed squarely at the man's chest. The stare turned into a cruel smile. He re-gripped the pistol, showing his command over the situation.

"Well, Hank, you leave me no choice. Looks like Dan's accomplice will be found with him. Makes it even tidier."

Hank lunged toward Belker just as the shot went off. The sound was deafening, followed by a sickening thud as Hank's body hit the floor. He writhed on the floor making a raspy sound as he gasped for air.

"Holy shit!" Dan yelled. "Are you insane?"

Belker stepped around the boots that skittered and shook on the floor, leaned down, put the gun to the base of Skelton's head, and fired again. The boots stopped moving, and the raspy sound ceased.

"Stupid fuck," said Belker.

"What the hell are you doing?" The gunshots pounded and reverberated in his head like he was inside a church bell tower. He wasn't sure the words leaving his mouth made any sound at all. "Extortion wasn't enough for you? Now you're gonna go down for murder."

"I'm not going down for murder, Slick." He cocked his head sideways slightly. "You are."

"I'm going to enjoy watching them put the needle in you over in Jarratt, you bastard."

"I thought I told you to shut up a long time ago." He stepped away from Hank's body and walked behind Dan's chair. Dan cocked his head around to look at him as the gun swung down toward Dan's head. He snapped his head back around and tried to duck, then a stab of pain—and all became darkness.

Chapter 46

BELKER TIED Dan's arms to the chair. He rushed over to where Skelton lay and quickly rolled him up in the throw rug on which the body landed. He hoisted the rolled carpet onto his shoulder and shrugged it through the front door. He carried it across the roadway to the barn. While balancing the weight on his shoulders, Belker slid the barn door open, took two steps inside, and tossed the body down. He grabbed his knee and rubbed it, knowing his heavy lifting was nearly half done. Panting deeply, he ran back across the road to the cabin.

He placed two fingers on Morgan's neck to check for a pulse. Finding one, he unwound the arms from the chair and hoisted Dan over his shoulder as well. He grabbed the billfold off the counter and carried Dan to the barn. He stepped past the body and walked to the stall holding Exigent Lady. Belker quickly unlatched the stall door, and it slid sideways on its overhead rails. The door only opened enough to throw the body in. Morgan landed on his side and flopped facedown in the straw.

Exigent Lady's eyes were wide, and she danced sideways, fearful of whatever had just landed in her stall. Belker tossed the billfold next to Morgan, closed the stall door, and stared at Morgan's body.

Would a medical examiner know his hands were bound in duct tape? Not likely, after what Belker had planned. He drew his gun from the back of his pants, where he had tucked it after shooting Skelton. He threw it into the stall on the far side from where Morgan lay. It disappeared beneath the bedding of straw.

Next, he quickly unrolled Skelton from the carpet and tossed the material into an adjoining stall. Skelton lay face-down, likely the way he would have landed had he been shot in the back of the head while running away. Belker was breathing hard as he surveyed the scene.

What would the sheriff conclude? Would they be able to tell Skelton had been shot in the chest first, then in the back of the head? Stupid shits in these po-dunk towns—Belker could convince them of anything. He just needed to make sure the investigation stayed local. But even if they brought in forensic experts, the scene would work, and the local guys would screw up the scene anyway. The story would be good enough for rural Virginia.

Belker spun around and ran to the barn door. He pulled the door closed. The fifteen-foot-high doors slid haltingly on the overhead rails. Once secured, he fastened the latch, pulled a padlock off the hook nearby, and fastened it secure. Then he ran to the other side of the barn and confirmed that the padlock was in place on that side.

He wiped sweat off his face and raced to the cabin. He made a quick scan of the interior. Belker grabbed the two bulky packages with the cash and ran outside, tossing them into the passenger side of his Jeep. Back inside, he decided to leave the half-empty beer on the counter. He studied the spot where Skelton hit the floor.

A large knick appeared in the floor where the bullet through Skelton's head was lodged in the floor. Belker grabbed a knife, got down on one knee, and dug the slug of lead out of the wooden floor. Not much blood or brain matter had gotten through the carpet onto the wood floor. He scuffed the area with his boot.

After scoping the cabin one more time, he ran to the front door and secured it open with a brick, then shot across the cabin and exited through the back door, securing it open as well. It might be helpful for the story and at the same time would allow the gunshot residue to air out.

Belker was tired and dripping in sweat, but he had to keep moving. On the off chance that Morgan was telling the truth, he had to get out of there fast. He ran to the gas generator on the side of the cabin. About three feet from the generator was a beaten and rusted garbage can. Belker lifted the lid, reached inside, and pulled out a five-gallon can of gasoline.

With one hand weighed down by the gas can, Belker rushed as quickly as he could to the barn. He began sloshing the accelerant onto the walls of the barn and around the base. He did his little dance with the gas can all the way around the barn and poured the remaining gallon or so on the wall just outside Exigent Lady's stall. Belker ran to the end of the barn and threw the gas can as far as he could into the trees and brush.

He took some deep breaths and walked back to the spot outside Exigent Lady's stall. He reached in his pocket and drew out a Bic lighter. He knelt and touched the flame near the base of the barn. The flame popped and rapidly ignited the gasoline. Fire shot out in both directions around the barn. The aged, dried wood from the barn instantly absorbed the energy of the fire, and flames licked up the side of the barn. Belker ran to his Wrangler, fired it up, drove around the cabin, spitting gravel as he raced away from the burning barn.

Chapter 47

SHUFFLING, CRACKLING sounds.

A horse whinnied. The whinny turned to fright. More shuffling. A hoof cracked against wood. The taste of straw in his mouth.

Dan blinked and spit out a handful of straw sheaths. The pounding in his head wouldn't stop. It hurt to open his eyes. A horse shrieked, nearby. A hoof cracked against solid wood again. *Can't move my arms.* Head was pounding. *Now it's coming back.*

He rolled onto his side and saw a terrified horse on its hind legs, the front legs clawing in the air. The horse shrieked, eyes wild. The legs were going to come down right on him. Dan slid backward as the hooves hit the ground, inches from his face. Then he smelled the smoke and saw the flames rising up.

He had to get to his feet before the horse stomped him into the ground. He slid up on his side and leaned against the corner of the stall for balance, then jumped to his feet.

The horse, which had to be Exigent Lady, shrieked and lunged toward him. She slammed Dan into the siding, knocking the wind out of him. She reared up, and Dan dodged to the left, toward the front of the stall.

He could see flames all around the barn, and, given the way the fire was moving up the far wall, the place would be tinder in a few minutes. Dan turned his back to the stall door and faced Exigent Lady. He grabbed the iron railing above the wooden door and tugged to pull the door open. It wouldn't move.

The horse reared again and lashed out at him with her hooves. Dan ducked and moved left just as one hoof slammed the wooden door where he'd been standing. The noise from the fire was deafening enough to drown out the frightened noises made by the mare.

Dan slid back over to the stall door and leaned forward to get his bound hands high enough to make it through the railing. If he could get his hands out there, he could find the latch and open the stall door. After that, he had no idea. His bound hands wouldn't fit through the opening.

The flames had ignited the straw bedding in the stall. He moved to the back of the stall and began stomping on the flames. At best, it would only buy a few seconds. He dodged the mare, got a running start, and slammed his shoulder into the barn siding. It didn't give.

The mare spun around, and, as Dan was gathering himself to ram the wall again, her hind legs shot out at him. It hit him thigh high and buckled him back into the corner of the stall. Dan's head slammed against the wall. He shook his head to gather his senses. He had to move. She was going to kick again, and now she had a target. Smoke was filling the barn. Dan could barely see the horse in the same stall with him.

He saw the hind legs wind up again and tried to move, but he was jammed in the corner of the stall. His leg was killing him. It might be broken. The horse cried out and snorted. Dan ducked down as low as he could go. The hooves hit the wall just above his head. He started to think which way he wanted to die, being kicked to death by a horse or burned alive. They seemed equally inevitable at the time.

The mare backed closer. She wouldn't miss this time. All her primal fear was focused on one thing, killing this person in the stall. All had been fine in the horse's world until Dan entered. The fear, flames, and smoke were all bound together in one purpose—attack this thing in the stall with you. The horse spun around, going in and out of Dan's vision through the smoke. Their eyes locked briefly; then, she spotted where Dan was and turned her hind legs toward him.

He slid as far as he could toward the ground. Although his legs and body were completely exposed, he was doing all he could to prevent a blow to the head. The mare panted and cried out in continuous fright. The left hind leg went up ready to bash his brains out. Dan closed his eyes and braced for the blow.

Chapter 48

DAN WAITED for the kick. It never came. He blinked quickly. Smoke and dust quickly filled his eyes. He squeezed them shut and tried to get as low as possible. Nothing happened.

Dan opened his eyes, and the mare was standing perfectly still. He could only see the back half of her, but she was just standing there. Dan scrambled to his feet. The pain in his leg was excruciating, but he was able to stand by putting most of his weight on his good leg. The stall door was open, and someone was standing next to the horse. Dan stepped closer.

"AJ, let's get out of here." The flames had reached the ceiling, and the whole barn was going to collapse in a matter of moments. Fire was rolling up the sides of the barn, and pockets of straw scattered around the barn were adding to the inferno. AJ didn't move. He just held the horse. His body was shaking, and he was crying. Tears ran down his face. "AJ, come on. We gotta get out of here."

He turned and looked at Dan. He had a blank stare in his eyes, and he trembled and cried. It was like he had no recognition of him or the surroundings. He was somehow locked into the emotions of the animal. Dan bounded forward and bounced into him. "AJ, let's go." The jostling caused AJ to lose balance, and he fell. The mare's fright came back, and AJ stared at him. "Let's go. We gotta get out of here."

AJ jumped up, grabbed the mare's bridle, and began to pull her out of the stall.

"Hey. Untie me." AJ quickly unwound the duct tape while keeping one hand on the bridle. When freed, Dan rubbed his hands together to bring back the circulation.

AJ trotted the mare out of the stall and to the barn door on the left side. He tugged on it. It wouldn't open. "AJ, how'd you get in?"

"Came in through that window." He pointed to a window covered with a piece of plywood that had been pushed open. The flames had almost completely covered it.

"What about the other side?" Dan said, pointing toward the opposite door.

"Locked."

Dan saw a body lying on the ground alongside one of the stall doors. He was still a little dazed, but the shooting in the house came back to him. The smoke was heavy, but it was Skelton. Had to be.

Parts of the roof were beginning to fall in flame balls from the pitched ceiling. A beam came down in a fiery blast like a blazing tree falling. The barn creaked and listed to the side. The whole thing was going to cave in. Dan covered his head and limped over to where AJ was standing.

"Get on," AJ said, motioning to the mare.

"What?" Dan looked across the barn. Smoke filled the inside, and flames were running up the inside of the barn.

AJ had his hands back on the mare, calming her. "Get on."

Dan went around the side of the mare and put his leg up. AJ grabbed his ankle and hoisted him on the mare's back. The pain in his leg caused him to cry out, but that was the least of his worries now. AJ reached up with his right arm, and Dan pulled him up in front of him on the mare. Dan didn't know what he had in mind, but the barn was beginning to collapse.

AJ leaned down, gripping the mare's bridle on either side of her head. He whispered something to her, then shouted. The horse took off and was at full speed in two strides. Dan nearly flew off the back but had AJ around the waist. What the hell was he doing?

They flew across the barn. AJ half turned and said, "Get low." Dan closed his eyes. They were going to run right into the barn door on the other side. He leaned forward over AJ, getting as low as he could, and braced himself.

The trio hit the barn door like a head-on car collision. They veered to the right slightly. Wood splintered. The mare cried out. Despite the explosive force, they nearly came to a stop, then the remaining momentum carried them through the wall of wood and flames. They spilled out on the other side.

A splintered part of the barn door swept Dan from the horse's back. He landed and rolled just outside the barn door. AJ stayed on, but the horse stumbled forward and fell.

A loud creaking sound rose from behind Dan. He rolled away from the barn just as the roof collapsed, and two sides of the structure crumpled. The wash from the falling building sent flames skyward and blew ash, straw, and splintered wood outward, covering Dan.

He scrambled to get the burning embers away from him. A mushroom cloud of smoke erupted into the night sky. The remaining sides of the barn slumped inward as if giving up—too tired to actually fall. The flames kept eating the building.

Dan rolled over and got up, limping toward the mare. They had fallen several yards beyond where Dan went down. AJ was standing and had his hands on the horse. She was trying to get up. The mare lunged, couldn't get her feet under her, and fell again. AJ moved to her side. She lunged again and this time got her bearings. Who could blame her? Hitting that wall would knock anyone silly.

Blood was running down the side of AJ's face from a laceration over his eye. His head had to have slammed into the barn siding when they burst through. The blood oozed and mixed with soot that covered his face, making a twisted watercolor of black and red. He was oblivious to it. He shivered and mumbled, keeping his hands on the mare.

"AJ, we better get out of here." He had his head against the mare's chest and was breathing heavily. Dan reached out and touched him. "AJ?" He flinched from his touch, then pulled his head away from the horse and looked at Dan. "She's okay." Tears mixed with the blood and soot covering his face. He patted the mare. "This one's got the heart of a champion."

"I know, okay?" Dan said, looking around. He wasn't sure if Belker was nearby, perhaps drawing a bead on them as they spoke. "Let's get out of here."

Chapter 49

DAN FORCEFULLY pulled open the door to the racing office. Allan Biggs and Detective Darrell Manning followed, with two deputy officers in tow. He limped down the hallway. A picturesque multi-colored bruise adorned his upper thigh. He was lucky the mare hadn't broken anything. The plump gray-haired secretary outside the office looked up. "He in?" Dan said.

"Let me—" She stood and her eyes shot back to the procession behind Dan.

He pointed a finger at the woman as he passed by. "Don't do anything."

He entered Belker's office, but it was vacant. The secretary scampered from behind her cubicle to the office.

"Where is he, Gail?" asked Biggs.

"Oh, Mr. Biggs," she said, nodding as though in the presence of a deity. "He was in early this morning but then got a call that his aunt had passed away. He's flying down to Sarasota to be with the family."

Dan and Detective Manning eyed one another. Dan whispered, "Sure as hell, about the time he learned that the mare had been moved back onto the grounds."

"What time did he leave?" Biggs asked Gail.

"You just missed him." She scurried back to her desk. "I'll bet I can get him on his cell phone."

"No, don't bother," said Manning. "No need to disturb him." He motioned for Biggs and Dan to enter the office, and a nod told the deputies to stand outside. He closed the door.

"He got a jump on us," said Manning.

"Think he's really leaving?" Dan said.

"He's leaving. But you can be sure he ain't going to Florida. I'm going to put an APB out for him." He turned to Biggs. "You got a vehicle description for him?"

"Yes, detective, all full-time staff have assigned parking, so we've got what he reported to be driving at the time."

Manning thought for a moment. "We'll put a man outside his residence, but he's probably cleared out of there already—or damn sure is in the process." He turned to Dan. "You better watch your back."

"Hell, he's gonna be a thousand miles away from this place as fast as he can," said Dan.

"Better hope you're right," said Manning. "You're the only link we got to nailing this guy. Well, you and that kid. I'm gonna assign someone to keep an eye, and I'm going to put a man on the backside just to make sure he doesn't slip back over there."

"Whatever you need, sheriff," Biggs said, shaking his head. "No idea. We had absolutely no idea. Right under our noses, too."

Manning turned to Dan and continued. "I'm going to need you to come down for more questioning as we work to put a ribbon and bow on this for the DA."

"I'll give you a call this afternoon, Darrell." Dan patted him on the shoulder as he moved past him. "Now I've got to visit a filly."

He walked outside and was racked with a fit of coughing as the fresh air hit him. Despite the coughing, a bruised pelvis, assorted contusions, and a lump the size of New Hampshire on the back of his head, he felt perfect. Painful as it was, he enjoyed the walk to the backside. Dan had an undefeated filly heading into a graded stakes race on Saturday.

He had other business on the backside, too. If he could keep his courage up, he was going to try something he hadn't done for a long, long time.

He was going to ask a girl on a date.

Chapter 50

DAN TOOK a long pull on his coffee. Saturday had arrived, stakes day. For the past three days he'd focused on client matters, along with healing his beaten body. He'd hoped that his redirected attention would cause the time up to race day to go faster. He was wrong.

A quiet dinner with Beth on Thursday night was a positive diversion. She was quick-witted and carefree in all the ways Vickie wasn't. It wasn't an official date—or at least he didn't present it as one. But he definitely enjoyed spending time with her.

He'd rolled around in bed last night and didn't get more than a couple of winks. The My Lassie Stakes was the ninth race on today's card. He was one of the first patrons to walk through the turnstile when the track opened. He even had to wait for the first pot of coffee to be brewed.

"Nice suit, mister," the long-haired teenager said as he handed Dan his change.

Dan never wore a suit coat and tie at the track. Even when he came from the office, he stripped the tie and coat and left them in the car. Dan had owned horses for four years and had enough starts that he couldn't remember most of them. But this was different. This was the biggest race of his life. This was his Kentucky Derby. Abandoning his usual custom, he decided to dress for the occasion.

After five days of healing, he still had a purple bruise in the shape of a horseshoe on his upper thigh. He'd learned to walk without appearing to be too much of a sissy.

Lennie's box was empty; heck, the whole grandstand was empty as Dan sat down and poured through the racing form, studying the entrants. There was nothing Dan could do. He wasn't looking for another horse to bet, and all of his handicapping would make no difference to the outcome or to his rooting interest. Kyle, Jake, and Aly Dancer would either make or break it.

Arestie was back for this race, and rumor was she'd been working well. Dagens got the mount, which would be an improvement. Three shippers were in the field, two from New York and one from Kentucky. One of the New Yorkers, Shazzy Time, had run a 101 Beyer in her first out. The other two had also won their first outs. The Kentucky horse, Jillite, going wire to wire and the other New York horse, Built In, won with a burst down the lane against a good field at Saratoga.

The other entries came out of other maiden races at Fairfax Park, none as impressive as Aly Dancer and Arestie. The form had Aly Dancer at 4-1, with Shazzy Time and Jillite favored ahead of her, 2-1 and 5/2 respectively.

At one hour to the first post time he was still alone in the box, but people were starting to stream into the grandstand seats.

"I see they flew Barrilla in to ride Shazzy Time." Dan turned and saw Lennie making his way toward the box. "Kyle's going to have his hands full today."

Oscar Barrilla was the second leading jockey in the country by purse money won. He was the leading jockey on the New York circuit. The connections to Shazzy Time weren't taking any chances. They wanted the best. Barrilla wouldn't have come down if he didn't think he could win. He had to give up a day of mounts in New York at substantially higher purse structures to come ride at Fairfax Park.

Dan stood and let Lennie into his usual seat. "Unless Barrilla is going to pick up the horse and carry her across the line, it don't matter to me. Horses still got to run their race."

"I like your shot today, Danny boy." Lennie was unpacking his pages of racing data from his backpack. "You didn't get a clean shot last time, but she threw a huge late pace fig despite the trouble she was in. A clear path—and I figure she's right with the girls they shipped in. I also think Arestie's got more topside. She should be a good price today. Heck, you both will. By the time these knuckleheads empty their wallets, they'll have Shazzy Time down to even money; you just watch."

Magic Milt got to the track in time to hit the exacta in the first. No cash bonanza, but he was ahead and on a roll. "You know what they say, don't you?" said Milt.

Lennie didn't even flinch or look up. "You can't win them all if you don't win the first."

"Yep, that's what they say. I think I'm going to run the card today," said Milt.

Lennie glanced over the glasses on his nose at the tote board. "I'll alert security that you'll need an armed escort to your car tonight."

TP showed up after the third race. "Let's get the big money today, Dan."

"How's Kyle doing today?" Dan asked.

"Ice water, Danny. Kid's got ice water in his veins." He pulled the day's program from his back pocket and sat down. "Damn Barrilla flies in here and shakes up the place. Emelio lost three mounts. One he had a real shot on. Where's the sense of loyalty these days? These trainers get all big-time on you when one of the leading jocks wanders in."

"You'd do the same thing if you could put Barrilla up on one of your horses," Lennie said.

"I know," said TP. "Still pisses me off. Guy's got a right to get pissed off every now and then." He quickly turned to Dan. "We got a shot here, Dan-o. Kyle says she's tearing a hole in the track every time they lead her over. He won't get her in trouble like last time. If he does, I'll kick his ass before you get a chance."

"I just want a clean trip," Dan said. "I don't know if she's like the horses they shipped in. She can take any of the locals, but today we find out how she stacks up."

It seemed like time was standing still. The ninth race would never get here. Dan bounced his legs and tapped his form against the side railing.

Lennie looked over from his computer printouts. "You okay?"

"I think I'm going to burst right out of my skin." Dan shot upright and started to slide out of the box. "I'm gonna walk around a little."

"Danny, make sure you take the time to enjoy this. Hell of a lot of owners never get to this position, not with the real deal like your filly. This will be a day you'll never forget."

Chapter 51

DAN WANDERED the grandstand, trying to take some deep breaths. There was a strong crowd today. Good for the track and good for folks on the backside. He called Uncle Van and chatted up the race. Van had seen Shazzy Time's maiden win, and he was cautious. It was an impressive win. Today his money would ride on Aly Dancer. He wished Dan good luck.

Uncle Van and Frannie had retired and moved to Fort Lauderdale. Uncle Van made his way to Gulfstream Park on occasion—certainly more occasions than Frannie knew about. There was no way he'd miss the simulcast of today's race. No way in the world.

Vickie called just as he'd hung up with Uncle Van. She didn't understand the significance of the race, but she knew it was something that mattered to him. She said she'd read about it in the newspaper, which meant that someone told her about it because she never read the sports page. She just wanted to call and wish him good luck. It was the proper thing to do, and she always did the proper thing.

Dan slapped the phone shut and tucked it into his pocket. Two steps later it was ringing again.

"Dan, it's Darrell Manning."

"Detective, how are you?"

"Fine, fine. Hey, wanted to let you know—we got a hit on Belker's phone this afternoon."

"What are you, tracing his calls?"

"With the APB on him, we've got the bloodhounds out looking for ATM activity, phone calls, anything. Anyway, he's still in the area. Placed a call about an hour ago."

"Go pick him up."

"Wish it were that easy. He's on the move—wasn't on the call long enough to triangulate an exact position, but from the cell tower hits, he's in northern Virginia, not Florida. Or at least his phone is calling people from northern Virginia. Thought you'd want to know. Watch your back, Dan."

"Hey, who did he call? Can you tell me that?"

Dan could hear paper rustling on the other end. He did a quick 360-degree look around, holding the phone to his ear. "Called a number registered to somebody named Ginny Perino."

◆　◆　◆

SOME DAYS Dan would travel to the backside before a race and make the walk over with his horses, but today he was too nervous and in some way fearing that his nerves might affect the horse. Time was standing still as he moved from one end of the grandstand to the other. He walked down to the paddock and watched the field for the sixth race head toward the racetrack. Up on the fence, like a gargoyle guarding the entry to the track, was AJ.

Dan slapped him on the leg with his form. "You okay?"

"Yep."

"You guys got anything in today?"

He looked down at Dan. "Ran second in the first race and fourth in the third, but we're done for the day."

"You make it over to the test barn?" The test barn was where shippers were housed in the days leading up to the race. Dan knew he had been.

"Yep."

"What do you think of those fillies?" Dan asked.

"I think your filly can beat them. They got talent, but they got no heart. That Jillite don't like bein' here." He paused and watched the horses moving toward the track. "They been kid-gloved. Today they see a filly that can run. We'll see how they measure."

"I hope you're right, AJ. You take care of yourself, all right?"

He nodded.

Dan walked about six feet, stopped, and spun around. "You s'pose it'd be okay with Latimer if you got your picture taken—you know, just in case we win?"

"We got nothin' running against you. He won't see no harm," said AJ.

Dan pointed the form at him. "See you in the winner's circle." He got a smile out of him. Dan didn't think it was possible. A few weeks ago he couldn't even get him to look at him. Now he smiled. Dan tapped the racing form against his leg and walked away.

Lennie was right. Dan was lucky to be in this position, to have this horse, to have this shot. Dan smiled. Win or lose, this will be a day not soon forgotten. Winning would be better, though.

◆　◆　◆

KYLE LEANED back against his locker and rested. The strain and stress of race riding took a toll on even the best athletes. In thirty minutes he would ride in the biggest race of his life, on a filly with a big chance. He had his headphones on, and Lenny Kravitz cranked up on the I-Pod. He closed his eyes and tried to relax. As he'd done many times before, he tried to visualize the race.

He'd never ridden against Barrilla, and he desperately wanted to beat him, but he had to put that out of his mind and ride his race. Do the right thing for the horse. He had to win with her best run and not worry about the competition. As he nodded to the music, he felt a tap on the arm. Jim Dagens was standing above him. Kyle jumped slightly when he spotted Dagens. A crafty smile came across Dagens' lips, and he extended his arm downward with a closed fist. Kyle tugged his headphones down and returned the fist bump to Dagens.

"I'm gonna win this thing," Dagens said, "but I hope you beat Barrilla, too."

"You'll have to settle for second," Kyle said, with a laugh. "But I'll get you a picture of me in the winner's circle for your photo album." Dagens gave him a dismissive wave and walked off.

Since their scrum a few weeks prior, they had developed a mutual respect for one another. The race was shaping up as hometown against shippers. The hometown jocks always wanted to win, but if they couldn't, they wanted another hometown guy to win. It was more about knowing the guys they raced against each day were as talented as the guys they watched on national TV. It was about local pride. It was about dignity. It was about protecting turf.

◆ ◆ ◆

AS SOON as the eighth race was over, Dan headed toward the paddock. The paddock judge recognized him and looked a little stunned that someone was so early getting to the paddock. There was no one else there yet. He smiled, lifted the rope, and let him pass into the open air of the paddock. "Good luck today."

"Thank you. It's a great day."

They'd drawn the four post for the race, so he waited near the entrance to that stall. Eventually a few other trainers and owners made their way into the paddock. They nodded as they walked past. Finally, Jake came over, and they shook hands. "What do you think?" Dan said.

"She's got a ton of talent; we know that." Jake took a deep breath and exhaled loudly.

"Just don't know how much game those shippers got."

The grooms were starting to lead the horses to the paddock. Small tags attached to the bridles matched up with the assigned posts.

Keith Kimbrough, Arestie's trainer, stopped briefly and shook Jake's hand. No words. None were needed. Romeo led Arestie past them toward the assigned stall. Dan gave him a look, but Romeo didn't reciprocate.

A murmur shot through the crowd, and they turned to look. Beth was leading Aly Dancer into the paddock. Red roses were braided in the filly's mane. "Good lord, what's that?" Dan asked.

"She loves that horse, Dan. She's so damn proud. Spent her own money on the flowers."

Sensing Dan's unease, Jake continued, "Won't hurt her at all. Hell, she'll look great in the picture when were done."

As Beth approached, Dan said, "She looks great, Beth."

"She's a champion," Beth said. "She should look like one."

Beth led her into the stall and circled her, facing out. She patted the horse on the nose and talked quietly to her as Jake cinched the girth and saddle on her.

Shazzy Time was in the one post. She was huge. The filly had to be nearly sixteen hands high as a two-year-old. Her coat shone in the sunlight. She looked like a champion, too, Dan said to himself.

Built In was in the five post and wasn't happy. She reared and balked as they tried to get the saddle on. A groom struggled with the rope clipped to her bridle. She was having none of it.

Aly Dancer stood almost motionless as Beth scratched her behind the ears. She was acting more like a puppy dog than a race horse. That's okay—save your energy for the race, Dan thought. The paddock judge came by and lifted Aly Dancer's lip, comparing the tattoo to the list on his clipboard. "Good luck, Jake."

A bell gonged, and the jockeys came down the walkway into the paddock. Barrilla was getting plenty of attention from the onlookers. He twirled his whip like he was bored to death even to be present. Kyle was adorned in the blue and white silks Dan had designed for his stable. He walked past Barrilla without looking at either him or his horse. He reached the area by stall four, and they stood on the grassy area inside the large walking ring. The horses began circling on the walking ring in numerical order.

Jake put a hand on Kyle's shoulder. "Give her a confident ride. This filly's ready to rock. Don't get crazy if the one or five want to go fast, but don't be afraid of them neither. If she breaks on top, she can win from there. Give her a smart ride. She's got the ability."

Kyle nodded. Saying nothing was the best thing a jockey could do in this situation. Jake didn't say anything about the prior ride, but he was making himself clear—don't get in behind horses unless the pace was crazy.

The paddock judge called, "Riders up."

The horses circled past them one last time. Kyle bent his outside knee and lifted his foot. Jake grabbed Kyle's ankle and hoisted him up onto the saddle in one easy motion. "Get the money," said Jake as he slapped Aly Dancer on the hind quarter.

Dan made his way out to the apron of the grandstand as the track announcer was introducing the field for the My Lassie Stakes. In a typical race day he would never notice the introductions unless they interrupted a conversation. But today he could hear nothing else.

"Number 4 is Aly Dancer, owned by Dan Morgan, trained by Jake Gilmore, and ridden today by Kyle Jonas."

Dan looked up at the grandstand and saw Lennie, Milt, and TP cheering and thrusting their fists in the air. He'd never seen them do that. Not once in his life. They were making damned fools of themselves. Dan waved at them and motioned for them to sit down. It was embarrassing.

He took a deep breath and walked up the grandstand steps. Dan couldn't sit with the gang. He needed to watch the race alone, and he had to be standing. He might actually combust if he stopped moving for ten seconds.

His heart felt like it was going to break through his rib-cage and fall on the floor in front of him. *Won't be long now.* Dan got in line to make a bet. They trudged slowly toward the cashier. The lines were eight to ten people long, with lots of money being laid down. More than the wager, he knew the process of waiting in line would make the time move faster.

He put $500 to win on Aly Dancer and, following Lennie's advice, bought a fifty dollar exacta with his horse over Arestie. He didn't box them, putting Arestie on top. That would be bad luck.

A quick glance at the TV screen showed Aly Dancer at 5-1. Shazzy Time had been bet down to 6/5. Lennie was right. In things equine, Lennie was always right. Jillite was 7/2. Built In was 6-1, and Arestie was 9-1. The other five entries were all over 18-1.

Dan walked to an open area at the top of the first landing of the grandstand, where he could watch the race. Kyle was trotting Aly Dancer alongside the lead pony. She looked majestic and confident, and Dan was shaking noticeably. "Okay, girl. Let's see what you got."

Chapter 52

KYLE CIRCLED slowly on Aly Dancer. She had warmed up nicely, head down and tugging on the bridle. Just one race under her belt—but she knew what this was all about. The rider on the lead pony leaned slightly backward and said, "You gonna get 'em?"

"Damn straight."

"Good luck."

They were double loading the nine horse field, which meant the one and five were loaded into the gate together, then the two and six, and so on. Being in the four hole, Aly Dancer would be last to load before Arestie, the nine horse, completed the field. She wouldn't have to stand long. That was good. He watched as the three horse, Pleasure Is Mine, moved forward into the gate. The lead pony rider unclipped his rope as one of the gate crew slipped a leather strap through the bridle and led Aly Dancer forward. Kyle pulled his knees up and in, and Aly Dancer smoothly walked into the gate.

"One out."

◆ ◆ ◆

FROM THE grandstand Dan was not sure he was even able to breathe. *Get away clean. Just get away clean.*

"They're all in line...."

Dan leaned forward and grabbed the railing. Just get a clean break.

"And they're off...."

◆ ◆ ◆

KYLE HAD braced for the break and balanced forward on his toes perfectly. The gates flew open.

Aly Dancer came out like a shot.

"Aly Dancer breaks on top and takes the lead...Shazzy Time on the inside...Arestie in the middle of the track."

◆ ◆ ◆

DAN JUMPED and pounded his form on the rail in front of him. My God, she broke like her tail was on fire, but Shazzy Time was right there with her.

"Down the backside they go...Aly Dancer leads three parts of a length.... Shazzy Time is second on the inside...one back to Arestie...Jillite and Pan Magic inside her...Built In a length back on the rail...two back to Pleasure Is Mine and Millet Alley...Smoke Force trails."

◆ ◆ ◆

KYLE HAD a snug grip on Aly Dancer. She was tugging at the reins. She wanted her head free. She wanted to run. Kyle had to balance frustrating his filly by restraint or risk letting her burn up all her energy and have nothing left at the end of the race. He tipped his head down and looked to each side to see where horses were around him. He tried to judge the pace. He didn't want to go too fast early, but he also didn't want another horse in his filly's face.

"Aly Dancer continues to lead…Shazzy Time right there on the inside half a length back and Arestie creeps closer… opening quarter in twenty-two and three."

◆ ◆ ◆

DAN BANGED on the railing. His form was starting to shred from the beating. *What the hell is he doing?* Dan thought. *Twenty-two and three? Is he insane?* Jake had said to ride with confidence, but good lord. Shazzy Time and Arestie were cutting the same fractions, so they were all in the same boat. *I'll just die if she gets beat at the wire by a deep closer.*

◆ ◆ ◆

KYLE SAW Shazzy Time move closer on the inside. They were approaching the turn, and Kyle had kept Aly Dancer in rhythm and under a slight restraint. Shazzy Time had stayed close enough that Kyle couldn't drop Aly Dancer down onto the rail. If Barrilla wanted to move into that pace, that was more energy he had to use. Arestie was moving closer on the outside but still half a length back.

◆ ◆ ◆

"ALY DANCER leads entering the turn.... Shazzy Time now moves up to engage the leader. Arestie is next on the outside... two back to Built In on the rail."

Oh please, please, Dan thought. *Don't let that horse get by you. Don't give it up. Stay in there.* "Come on Aly. Come on, Kyle, God damn it."

◆ ◆ ◆

KYLE LOOKED to his left and saw Barrilla grinning. He was pushing on his horse—not all out, but he was being aggressive. Kyle waited. Barrilla looked over and yelled, "See you bay—bee."

When Shazzy Time pulled alongside, Aly Dancer saw her for the first time. She tugged on the reins, throwing her head forward. She'd pinned her ears back. She was angry. She didn't want that horse to get by her. Kyle waited. He couldn't wait too long, but he could wait some.

◆ ◆ ◆

"SHAZZY TIME puts a head in front.... Aly Dancer is next... Arestie moving up strongly on the outside...Built In tracking those three along the rail."

The crowd roared when the announcer called Shazzy Time ahead. At that moment Dan's natural hatred for chalk bettors escalated. *Damn it, we were the home team,* he thought. *Come on, Kyle, let her go.* Maybe they'd hit the board, hang on for third. He wanted to win so badly, but stakes placed in her second race would be nothing to be ashamed of. *She's still a damn nice filly.*

Just then he saw it.

Suddenly the race was in slow motion. Dan had been around racing long enough. He could see it. Many people unfamiliar with the sport would never see it, or, if they did, they wouldn't understand the significance. Years of watching horses and riders had taught Dan to spot the things that mattered.

Barrilla was urging Shazzy Time with vigor. They hadn't pulled their whips yet, but he was riding hard. Arestie was moving well, but the rider was pushing her as well.

Kyle was sitting chilly. He was just riding. "God, please be right," Dan muttered. Kyle wasn't asking her for run yet. *He's got a ton of horse left.*

"Shazzy Time leads by a neck...Aly Dancer right there... Arestie challenging those two on the outside...half mile in 44 and 4."

◆ ◆ ◆

KYLE CAME out of the turn, threw a cross, and yelled, "Haaaah." He gave Aly Dancer her head, and she responded. Kyle pulled even with Barrilla.

Without looking over, Kyle shouted, "See you, asshole."

Aly Dancer accelerated powerfully. Kyle shifted his weight slightly, and she changed leads, digging for home. This was what she wanted. She opened up and extended her long stride.

She covered ground like a Ferrari coming out of a turn and screaming into the straightaway.

She steadily moved past Shazzy Time and was soon clear on the inside, but Arestie was right there on her outside like she was glued to her hip.

DAN WAS holding a string of tattered newspaper. He threw it on the ground and pounded on the rail with the palm of his hand. "Come on. Yes. Come on, baby. Show them you got heart. Show 'em what you got."

"Aly Dancer moving powerfully—she retakes the lead... Arestie on the outside.... Shazzy Time is losing pace...Built In making a move toward the inside."

KYLE WAS pushing and scrubbing on her neck with his knuckles. He could hear the whip crack, as Dagens hit Arestie. Was it possible? Arestie was gaining on the outside. Stride by stride Arestie was eating into their lead. *How could we go those fractions and she's been outside me? How can she have anything left?* Kyle kept urging, "Come on, come on, baby." He flashed the whip along the right side of Aly Dancer's head. *Give me a little more; let's put this other one away.*

"*Arestie moves up alongside Aly Dancer…these two down the stretch.… Built In is third, two back.*"

Kyle couldn't wait much longer. He had to go to his whip. She was tiring, but he knew she was giving everything she had. Arestie had to be tiring as well. She'd been in an extended drive since the three-sixteenths pole.

If Kyle could create a little space between them, he could hold Arestie off. Just one surge, just a little space—they could break Arestie's heart.

Kyle raised his whip and cracked Aly Dancer; she lunged and dug in. He switched hands with the whip like he'd done thousands of times and smacked her twice on the left side. She responded. She ducked her head slightly and looked right toward Arestie as if to taunt her. Two jumps later she had her head in front of Arestie.

That's when Kyle heard the snap.

PART FOUR

DOWN THE STRETCH

◆   ◆   ◆

FILLIES WERE SIMPLY DIFFERENT
from their male counterparts—and not merely in
matters of reproduction.

Fillies exhibited pain thresholds significantly
higher than colts. Maybe it was a genetic
inheritance that prepared the female species for
the pain of birthing. Maybe it was a kind of focus
and determination the male equines don't possess.

Great fillies would occasionally beat
great colts, but more often than not a comparable
male could beat a comparable female. That's why
they rarely raced against one another.

Genetics made males bigger and stronger, but
it gave females the will to win in spite of the pain.

That's how AJ could convince a frightened mare to run through a burning wall. For the desired outcome, a female race horse would run through all levels of pain, would run beyond the load supported by tender bones, would push ligaments to the point they snapped like a taut rubber band.

The heart of great fillies should never be questioned. Down through the ages they have come—Ruffian, Go For Wand, Eight Belles.

From all corners of the racing world they waited impatiently for that special one. When she appeared, they watched, breathlessly, awestruck by the brilliance, the speed, the beauty.

Deep inside they knew they were watching something magical, something that stopped time, and they never wanted it to end—something beyond skin, and bones, and muscle. They were watching a symphony in motion. They were watching Picasso at an easel. In that moment they were peering over God's shoulder.

Fillies of this caliber were never beaten; they succumbed, reluctantly, only to their own hearts.

That kind of filly became a selfless victim of her desire to win, her desire to please, her desire to compete, her desire to run fast despite conditions.

For that kind of filly, the heart pushed her to a place the body was simply incapable of following.

Chapter 53

KYLE RECOGNIZED the sound. He had heard it before, and it made his stomach quiver. Arestie was trying to get past his horse, but Kyle's filly was running her guts out to stay in front. The next instant, they were alone. Kyle turned to look, even though he didn't need to. He knew what he would see.

"Arestie and Aly Dancer...strongly toward the wire... three back to...Arestie's down...Arestie's fallen on the track. Aly Dancer alone to the wire.... Built In will run second with Smoke Force third."

The groan from the grandstand was seismic. Arestie fell forward, catapulting Dagens onto the track. Arestie crashed into the racing surface and flipped tail over head. Dagens hit the track face-first. He bounced and pin wheeled down the track, his arms and legs flailing like a rag doll thrown out of a speeding automobile. Arestie crashed in one final gut-wrenching collision with the track. She landed no more than four feet from where Dagens lay motionless, facedown on the track.

The jockeys went into emergency control and attempted to guide their mounts around the injured horse and jockey.

Some were still trying to get in contention for a check; others were just trying to avoid another pileup by veering clear. They knew the horse, they knew the silks, and they knew the jockey. But most of all they knew it could be them down on the track.

A slip here, a shift there, a young horse, an unpredicted injury, someone moving the wrong way at the wrong time and they could be the one on the track. They rode without fear, but they knew what fear was. Now it was a jumble of bones and flesh down on the track.

The grooms for each horse stood near the finish line so they could put a cinch on their horse when they returned to the unsaddling area near the winner's circle. They were the first to respond. Arestie and Dagens lay about sixty yards from the finish line. Half a dozen men raced toward them.

Kyle rode Aly Dancer to and through the finish line. He stood in the stirrups, bent over at the waist, and eased Aly Dancer. He had just won the largest stakes races of his career. It would be one of his biggest paydays. He had first call on an undefeated two-year-old filly. He knew she had more potential and natural talent than any horse he'd ever climbed on, but now fear gripped him. He looked down and swallowed hard as Aly Dancer galloped out. He had to lean off to the right side so the vomit wouldn't land on Aly Dancer.

◆ ◆ ◆

LIKE THE rest of the crowd, Dan cringed visibly when Arestie fell. He didn't even watch his horse cross the finish line. His eyes were glued on the horse and rider tumbling onto the track. From the first landing of the grandstand, he watched several grooms race toward the fallen competitors. Dagens wasn't moving. He was facedown on the track. One of the grooms was down on his hands and knees, trying to talk to Dagens. The groom quickly sat upright and motioned for assistance. Dagens didn't move.

Arestie was trying to get up, and she screamed out in pain. Dan could see that her front legs were broken. She tried to get her front legs under her, but she would collapse, only to try again.

These were proud animals. They lived on their feet; they slept on their feet. They did everything on their feet. Not being able to stand made no sense in a horse's world. The pain mixed with the fear caused Arestie to try even harder to get to her feet. Her genetic code was firing off a singular message to her brain. Get on your feet.

The grooms had reached her and were trying to keep her down. She was fighting them with everything she had. They were trying to prevent more damage and to calm her. It was a fight that was unwinnable.

The ambulance sped onto the track and rapidly approached the scene. In the distance Dan could see the vet trailer being brought onto the track from the backside. The vet trailer was a state-of-the-art equine medical vehicle. It provided the means for injured horses to get transported off the track and be surrounded by medical care to aid and care for the animal.

In the corner of his eye Dan witnessed a vision he'd seen before, a hop and run, a hop and run. AJ had jumped the fence and was moving as quickly as he could toward the horse.

Emotions were running raw. It was the frustration of trying to help the horse while knowing the situation was dire. Keith Kimbrough had run over to the spot where Arestie was being held. He knelt next to her and tried to hold her neck down so she wouldn't have the leverage to attempt to get up again.

AJ was moving as quickly as he could. He looked to his right and saw the ambulance go past him. The ambulance would park nearer the finish line to allow them to treat Dagens but also to provide room for the emergency vet van to get near Arestie.

AJ never saw it coming. He hopped and ran in his unique way until he was about ten feet from the horse. Kimbrough's groom, the one Dan called Romeo, threw a roundhouse punch that completely cold-cocked AJ. Dan ran down the stairs toward the apron. He had to get to AJ.

The impact of the punch nearly lifted AJ off the ground. He spun with the motion of the right cross and flew backward, landing face first on the track. The blindsided punch should have rendered him unconscious. It should have broken his neck.

Amazingly, he scrambled to his hands and knees and continued toward the horse. The groom tried to knee AJ to keep him away, but the boy kept crawling. There were several men standing near the horse, including Vic Dancett, who was talking to Kimbrough. AJ crawled between the legs of the standing men and reached forward to place his hands on the horse.

Arestie suddenly went quiet. She continued to breathe powerfully but didn't struggle to move or get up. AJ was shaking and convulsing. Blood was pouring from his mouth and nose, covering the horse and the dirt track. AJ was crying out something unintelligible, and several men stepped away. The boy's entire body was in a tremor, sweat was streaming off him, and tears ran down his face, mixing with the blood.

When Dan got to the track and moved toward the scene, he could see Dancett and Kimbrough talking. The vet van had been parked to block the view of the grandstand. Kimbrough put his hands to his face, pushing his cowboy hat back on his head. He was shaking his head side to side slightly. Dancett stared at him directly and put a hand on his shoulder. Kimbrough brought his hands down and nodded.

Dancett moved quickly to the vet van and rummaged through a side panel. He quickly drew out two long, slender boxes and cracked the casings to remove the hypodermic needles. Dancett skillfully pierced the small medicine bottle with one of the needles and drew in the fluid. He handed the hypo to a man standing near him and filled the second needle with the same liquid.

In the trade it was called "the pink" because of the tinged color to the substance. In the lab it was called sodium pentobarbitol. For this filly it would simply be the end of suffering.

AJ was kicking out wildly with his legs and was on his belly, shaking and convulsing. He wouldn't remove his hands from the horse. All stood back a step as Dancett approached.

AJ was oblivious to all that was around him. Arestie was still. That made Dancett's job easier. He wouldn't need to administer a tranquilizer.

Dancett knelt next to the horse and found a bulging vein in Arestie's neck. He deftly injected the barbiturate from the first needle, then threw that one aside and held his hand out to the man holding the other needle. Each injection was 60 ccs of the pink and would depress the respiratory system until death quickly ensued.

All was quiet with the exception of the engines of the vet van and ambulance and the sounds coming from AJ. Dancett leaned forward.

Dan suddenly had a sickening feeling. He couldn't define it. He rushed forward. "AJ, get away!" Dancett plunged the second needle to the hilt. "Get the boy's hands off the horse," Dan screamed. "AJ, let go!"

Dan ran forward, trying to get through the group of men standing near the horse. "Get his hands off." Dancett's needle was empty, and he withdrew it. Dan dove toward AJ and tried to pull him off the horse.

AJ had collapsed onto the horse. Dan pulled and tried to roll his small, sweaty body near him. AJ flopped over and was unresponsive. Dan put his hand on his chest and could feel no heartbeat. He wasn't breathing.

"Get a doctor over here," Dan shouted. He put his fingers on AJ's neck as he'd seen done in television programs. He couldn't feel a pulse. "God damn it, get a doctor over here."

Dancett stared at him. He was on his knees, still holding the needle, and looked at Dan like *I didn't do that.* Dancett jumped up and came to where Dan was, on the other side of the horse. "We need to give him CPR."

Vic cleared AJ's mouth and smeared blood away from his nose. He pressed the nostrils closed and put his mouth on AJ's. Dan waited for three breaths, then compressed AJ's chest for five beats. Vic repeated, then Dan repeated. Vic repeated; Dan repeated. They checked for a pulse. They repeated and repeated and checked for a pulse, for a breath, anything.

"Don't stop," Dan said, wheezing from the exertion.

Vic repeated; Dan repeated. The men, who moments before had formed a fortress around them, sagged and shuffled away, heads hanging. Finally, Vic looked across and shook his head. Dan kept going, exhausted, breathless, but relentless. He gave CPR and pressed on the boy's chest. His motions were ragged and choppy. Vic sat silent. There were no right words. Dan looked pleadingly at Vic. Blood covered Dan's chin and ran down the side of his face. Vic's eyes told all.

Dan collapsed back on his haunches. Vic slowly got to his feet and walked past Dan, pausing to squeeze his shoulder lightly.

Somewhere, sixty yards away from Dan, they were taking the picture of Aly Dancer in the winner's circle—his baby, the winner of the My Lassie Stakes, his undefeated two-year-old filly. The picture would show only Jake, Beth, and Jorge standing in the winner's circle. When the photo was snapped, Kyle was sitting, looking up the track toward the commotion. No one was smiling. A tear could be seen glistening on Beth's cheek.

Dan put one arm underneath AJ's neck and one under his knees. He carried him to the ambulance. They had Dagens on a bed inside the ambulance, and there was a flurry of medical activity around him.

One of the EMTs met Dan outside the back door of the ambulance. He reached forward, took AJ from him, and lifted the boy into the ambulance.

Dan collapsed backward onto the seat of his pants. He put his elbows on his knees and his face in his hands.

And he cried.

Chapter 54

THE DRIVE home was interminable. The stop lights seemed to last hours—so long one's life could flash before his eyes while waiting for a green light. He slogged forward through the traffic like rancid water through a plugged pipe.

All thoughts turned to what he should have done. Why he failed to act? How he could have changed the outcome?

He visualized himself lunging for AJ and pulling his hands free from Arestie. The boy was dazed, sobbing, and resistant but still alive. Then reality would crack him between the eyes like an axe handle.

He just stood there and watched his friend die. How could he have known? He knew. Yes, he knew. He had just failed to act.

Why do people leave me? he thought. His dad, Vickie, now Ananias. What caused these people to turn from him, to desert him? Or did he desert them?

Maybe that's why his relationship with horses was better. No emotional baggage—just property, just an investment. The emotional baggage was there all the same; it was just temporary. And if he controlled how long "temporary" was, everything was fine. Horses were better. You owned them for three years, maybe four, then they moved on. Or maybe Dan moved on—he wasn't sure.

He eased forward and stopped at the intersection as the light flashed from yellow to red. Loud honking erupted behind him. Only in Virginia were drivers chastised for failing to run a red light. He shook his head and replayed the events again. Darkness had shrouded the highway, and pin oak trees adjoining the highway leaned forward like a jury eager to convict him of cowardice.

The honking returned as he failed to move the instant the light flashed green. He didn't go to the barn following the race. He didn't go anywhere. He sat in the middle of the racetrack as the ambulance pulled away with Dagens and his dead friend. After a while, Doc Dancett extended an arm and helped him to his feet. He said something, but Dan couldn't hear him and couldn't remember what it was.

He staggered back to the grandstand, turned, and looked back to where Arestie had lain on the track. Everything was gone, except for the ghosts that taunted him. After several minutes he made his way to the parking lot. The winning tickets in his pocket were un-cashed and long forgotten.

He sat in his car with his head on the steering wheel and his fingers laced behind his neck until he was the last car in the section. He'd driven home alone all his life. He never felt more alone than now. The weight in his chest pulled him farther down into the car seat as if he were going to fall through the bottom of the car onto the asphalt.

At last he turned into the parking complex by his building. He eased down to the last open parking space at the far end of the building. He opened the door and was awash in humidity and the smell of freshly cut grass. His suit coat that had been freshly pressed ten hours before was like a year-old dishrag as he pulled it from the backseat.

He cast it over his shoulder just as the body crushed into him from behind. He flew several steps forward and slammed onto the asphalt like a rookie quarterback blind-sided by a blitzing safety. His hands fell under him, and he slid forward on his chest and the backs of his hands. He couldn't gather his breath, facedown with a large body on his back. He tried to move but couldn't.

His arms were ripped behind his back despite his efforts to wedge his hands under him. He tried to look over his shoulder but could only see the cowboy boots and jeans of the man who knelt on his back. His hands were quickly secured with a plastic handcuff.

Dan tried to scream, but a calloused and powerful hand enveloped his mouth and nostrils.

"Don't yell."

He knew the voice. It was Ginny Perino.

Chapter 55

DAN TRIED to look out the sliver of window. It was all that was available from this angle. He tried to pick up any kind of landmark. He noticed a gas station sign and knew which direction they were headed. Then he realized that, from this angle, all gas station signs looked the same. They could be heading anywhere.

Several turns quickly made the process random. The left-hand turns were particularly noteworthy as they would throw his head into the side of the pickup, and he would crunch up into a ball as they rolled that direction. His hands were bleeding yet felt cool because of the loss of circulation.

Apparently believing that Dan would yell if given a chance, Ginny had fastened a silver piece of duct tape over Dan's mouth. Ginny swooped Dan off the ground like a man picking up a sack of jelly beans and tossed him into the back of the crew cap pickup. Once in the vehicle he became truly terrified.

Ginny pulled out his cell phone. The conversation was short. "Got him." Followed by "Where?" and "Thirty minutes." The phone slapped shut.

They drove in silence—no radio, no conversation, just the sound of rubber moving over the cement. Ginny's instructions to Dan were "Don't move." Even if he did move, there was nothing he could do. Ginny could lay a beating on Dan from his position and never be distracted in driving the vehicle.

After a long stint on a straight highway, Ginny made a right turn, a left turn, another quick right, and pulled up to a weathered red brick warehouse. Dan could see the blackened and pock-marked bricks along with the one boarded up window. It was a place that, unfortunately, would ensure extreme privacy. Ginny honked the horn, and the overhead door went up. After a few seconds the pickup pulled forward. The door came back down behind them.

"Dan Morgan—long time, no see," said Belker. Ginny pushed Dan forward and made it apparent that he was to sit on the lone chair in the middle of the warehouse. Belker was full of himself as he chuckled. "Nice win today. Too bad you'll never see her race again."

Dan winced as Ginny ripped the tape off his mouth. He spat and said, "You make me sick."

Ginny unfolded a knife, walked behind Dan, and in one motion sliced off the handcuffs.

Belker shot a puzzled look at Ginny. "Yeah, I guess we don't need a dead body in handcuffs," said Belker as he pulled the handgun tucked into his belt. Dan rubbed his wrists and shook his fingers. They were blue and cold.

"Appreciate the help, Ginny," Belker said.

Ginny just glared at Belker. The look made Belker step back and reach for a package on the stack of boxes behind him. "As agreed. Twenty Gs." He tossed the package to Ginny. It hit Ginny in the chest and fell to the ground. Ginny kept moving forward.

"What?" Belker pleaded. "That was our deal. What are you doing? What do you want?" He moved backward against a wall of boxes. Then apparently remembering that he was holding a gun, Belker shook it at Ginny as if to say, *Look, I have a gun.* Ginny kept moving.

"Don't make me do it, Ginny."

"You won't do it," said Ginny.

"Wha-what do you mean?"

"You won't shoot me."

Dan had seen him shoot a man already. He knew Belker could do it.

"How do you know?" said Belker.

"'Cause you're a coward."

Belker extended the gun just as Ginny leapt toward him. Ginny knocked Belker's arm to the side. The gun fired. Cement dust splashed up from the floor a foot in front of Dan. He lunged from the chair and dove behind the edge of Ginny's truck.

Ginny was on Belker. He grabbed the gun from Belker's hands like he was taking a rattle from a baby, except he crushed Belker's hand in the process.

"What are you doing?" Belker squealed. Ginny grabbed the front of Belker's shirt and slammed him against the boxes, then he slammed his fist into the side of Belker's face. The sound was like a bat hitting a melon. "What are you doing? We had a deal."

Ginny hit him again and again. Belker's legs went wobbly, and Ginny let him fall to the ground. Then he got down on one knee and hit him again and again.

Dan jumped up. "Ginny. Stop. You're going to kill him." He wanted to run but couldn't bring himself to move.

Belker was beyond providing resistance. Ginny hit him again, then gave him two downward shots to the ribs. "Ginny. That's enough," Dan yelled.

Ginny looked over, slipped another plastic cuff from his back pocket, and quickly bound Belker's limp arms together. Then he stood. He wasn't even breathing hard.

Dan raised his hands and backed away. "Ginny, come on now. I got no beef with you."

Ginny swept his hair back into place with his left hand. "Guy pissed me off." He walked past Dan without looking at him. He walked past the pickup and hit the button to open the garage door. Dan stammered for something to say. Nothing came out. "No need to hurt those horses," Ginny said. "Guy pissed me off."

"Ginny, I don't get it. Why'd you rough me up and tie my hands? I would have gone along."

"Needed you to be believable."

"Believable?"

"Hard to fake bein' scared." Ginny opened the pickup door and pointed at Dan. "You were scared."

"Jesus, I guess."

Ginny smirked as he started to get into the truck. The first expression of any emotion Dan had ever witnessed in Ginny. Dan pointed at the package on the floor. "What about the money? Ginny, take the money."

"Not my money. Didn't earn it."

Ginny backed out of the warehouse and into the street. He shifted into drive and pulled away without looking back.

Dan walked over to where Belker laid on the floor. He was moaning and wheezing, his cheek bone damaged and nose busted. Dan kicked the gun, and it skittered across the floor, hitting the far wall. Dan walked outside and dialed his cell phone.

"Detective Manning, this is Dan Morgan. I've got Belker. Come by and pick him up."

"Where are you?"

Dan looked up at the street signs at the intersection. "Warehouse at Collins and Simmons."

"Where's that?"

"Bring along medical assistance." Then he hung up.

Manning arrived by squad car twenty minutes later. The ambulance arrived a few minutes earlier. The EMTs stood outside despite the fact that Belker was again conscious. They didn't want to contaminate a crime scene.

"What do we got here?" said Manning as he approached.

"He grabbed me at my place, tied me up, and brought me here." Dan waved toward the chair where the cut hand-cuff and duct tape were. Manning motioned to the techs to assist Belker, who was rolling side to side on the floor. Dan continued, "He cut the cuffs off me, which was a mistake. He was going to shoot me, but I created a diversion. The weapon was fired. Nobody hit."

Manning looked down at Belker's battered and blood-ied face, then back at Dan. "You did this?"

Dan locked eyes with Belker. They'd had a little conver-sation about that before the EMTs arrived. Belker didn't do much talking. Dan wasn't sure Belker understood anything, the way his brain was rattled. With all he faced right now,

round two with Ginny Perino wasn't something Belker
would want any part of.

Dan glanced down to his bleeding hands and back
to Belker. "Yep." Belker nodded slightly, or maybe it was
just a twitch that Dan saw. "Guess I had a little surge of
adrenaline."

"No shit, you think?" Manning waved to the other officer and motioned him to bag up the gun, cuff, and tape.
"What's the package?"

"Cash. From the extortion scam."

"What? He brought it in from his jeep just to—what?
Brag about it?"

"Something like that," Dan said.

"You carry around spare sets of plasti-cuffs?" Manning
asked, looking around the warehouse, studying everything
but Dan.

"He had them in his pocket. I guess his failsafe."

"Damn convenient."

"Self-defense, detective," Dan said.

Manning stared straight at Dan. "Let's see. Guy nabs
you off the street, has you bound and gagged, drags you all
the way to Back Ass, Virginia, to kill you, then decides to
cut you free—you know, so it's a fair fight, I guess. Let's you
get close enough to jump him, misses you with a pistol shot;
you overpower him, beat the living crap out of him, and tie
his hands with the man's fail safe, spare set of plasti-cuffs.
Am I tracking you so far?"

Dan just stared back.

"It's either a crock of bull, or you're the luckiest son of a
bitch to walk the earth."

Dan didn't laugh or change expression. "It was self-defense."

Manning pinched the bridge of his nose and squeezed his eyes shut. "Unbelievable. This from the guy who rode a freaking horse through the wall of a burning barn. Jesus." He opened his eyes and watched as the techs rolled Belker toward the ambulance. "I suppose Belker will confirm all that. That is, after they pull the feeding tube out of the guy."

"He will, unless he decides to lie about it. He's done a little of that already."

Manning squinted at Dan, shook his head, and scratched the back of his neck. "Yeah, what the hell, looks like self-defense to me."

Chapter 56

THE PHONE rang early. It was John O'Kelly, the backside pastor. They were holding a memorial ceremony for AJ at Crok's following Monday's morning works. He wanted to know whether Dan would say a few words. Latimer mentioned to O'Kelly that he'd known the kid. Dan didn't know what he could say but agreed anyway.

Crok's was jammed with folks holding their hats in their hands. A makeshift podium was at the far end of the kitchen. All the seats were filled, and people were lined up against every wall. This wasn't a typical religious crowd. These were just people looking for some kind of answer and a way to reconcile what they had witnessed with what they knew. Dan had no idea what he would say to the group.

O'Kelly opened with a group prayer. Dan couldn't focus on anything he was saying. He only heard words being spoken. Several of the women were crying quietly. A few of the hard boots scratched the floor with their heels and looked down. When he'd finished, he asked Kyle to come forward.

Kyle stood behind the podium and couldn't look at the group. "I, uh, I went to the hospital this morning and got to see Jim." He coughed and cleared his throat. "He's a tough guy." People nodded in agreement. "Anyway, he's got a busted collar bone, punctured lung, and three broken ribs. Oh, and a concussion."

He paused as if reflecting upon the fortune, the fragments of bones and matter, and the pressure that would place him in that hospital bed rather than Dagens. "He wanted me to send a message to the jockey colony. He said he's going to keep track of everyone who takes any of his mounts, and he's going to kick their ass when he comes back."

The crowd laughed nervously. As if catching himself, Kyle looked at O'Kelly and said, "Sorry, Father, but that's what he said." O'Kelly nodded. Being around the racetrack, he'd heard every form of profanity, but this one had the potential to actually heal some people.

Kyle continued, "He wanted me to thank everyone for their prayers and good wishes. And he's coming back just as soon as they let him out. Thank you."

He nodded to the crowd and stepped away from the podium. O'Kelly moved to the podium and pointed at Dick Latimer. "Dick's going to say a few words."

Latimer stood behind the podium like he was paralyzed. There was no more sympathetic audience, but he struggled to come up with anything to say. He rubbed his hand over his face and scratched the stubble on his cheek. "He was a good kid," he said; then, he stopped.

Latimer looked like he knew he was going to cry if he kept going. He looked down and rolled his head slightly, searching for any kind of composure.

"He was a good kid. He was a quick learner." Latimer paused and cleared his throat. "He was never a problem." He looked out at the audience, and the fear was evident in his water-filled eyes. Then he froze. The audience's heart tried to will him to go on, but he could not. Caught between the courage to display emotion publicly and the pride of a hard boot, he opted for the pride. He couldn't go on. "I'm gonna miss that kid." Then he walked away.

O'Kelly stepped back up. "Thank you, Dick. Tough time for all of us. I know he meant a lot to you. Next, I'd like to have Dan Morgan come up and say a few words. Dan?" He pointed to him near the back of the room.

Dan walked forward and scooted between two tables to get to the front. Beth jumped up, pulling him forward and tightly wrapped her arms around his neck. She was as tough as they came, but tears streamed down his neck and into the fabric of his shirt.

She mumbled something that sounded like a mixture of "I'm sorry" and "don't get it." She pushed back and held a tissue up to her nose, sucking in and holding her breath. He stroked her hair, looking down at her, then inhaled deeply and moved toward the front of the room.

He rested his hands on the podium and leaned into it. He had given closing arguments; he had given speeches in grand conference rooms. He had even given eulogies at massive funerals. This was the only time in his life that he was preparing to speak and had no idea what he was going to say.

"I'm Dan Morgan. I own a few horses. Jake trains for me." He gestured over to where Gilmore was standing. "I didn't know AJ very well. Would like to have known him a whole lot better, but—"

Dan looked to the back of the room and noticed Romeo standing against the wall. Scenes flashed through his mind, from that first day in Crok's kitchen with the men hassling AJ to that satisfying gut punch to the haymaker that caught AJ unaware. Too much violence, he thought—too much hatred borne of fear.

Romeo was pale, disheveled, and confused. Rings under his eyes evidenced a combination of lack of sleep and hard-scrubbed tears. In a few tragic seconds he had lost a promising filly, and in his grief risked losing his liberty, but he was here.

Dan turned toward Latimer. "He was a good kid, Dick. He cared so much for those horses. Anyone's horses. We work in an industry that exists only for competition. We live to beat the other guy, to get the purse, to win the stake, to—" He shrugged. "To get there first."

He took a deep breath and leaned into the podium. "AJ came at life from a totally different angle. He cared singularly about the horse. Now, we all do, but he cared about them in a way we'll never comprehend. He had a gift. I don't understand it. I can't explain it. I saw it with my own eyes, and I still don't get it. But he could connect with horses."

"When he put his hands on a horse, they communicated. He gave them a voice. And in doing that, he gave them peace. He could calm a frightened animal, he could sense pain and discomfort, and—"

Dan shook his head. "And he could feel what they felt. I believe he could actually experience the emotion of the animal. No one will believe you when you say that. You had to see it, and even then—" He looked out and only saw faces of people trying to comprehend what they'd witnessed. Tears were flowing, and few looked at anything besides the floor.

"AJ and I had many things in common. First and foremost, we love these animals. We love the backside. We all have our personal problems and challenges, but we'd rather be right here than on any stretch of earth on this planet. Here, the horses are kings, and we're their servants. Sure, we have plans and dreams for them, but unless we treat them like royalty, they'll never achieve their potential. It occurred to me that we're all like that."

Dan took a deep breath and re-gripped the podium. "This would be a better place if everyone thought like that. When you meet strangers, you never know what to expect of them, nor what they expect from you. If we try to understand them and treat them with respect, maybe we both win. AJ was a—a boy of few words. He didn't have to say a lot. He spoke through his actions.

"I'm convinced that he knew what was going to happen when Arestie was put down. I think he knew the significance of having his hands on her when the needle hit the heart. He just couldn't let go. He couldn't let that horse down, not for one second. He'd committed to help a distressed animal. His commitment, though fatal, was one he couldn't bring himself to relinquish.

"He was a boy—he was a man of his word. We've all heard it, and we know it's true. These majestic animals give their lives for our pleasure. AJ gave his so that one of those creatures wouldn't endure one more second of pain."

He paused and gathered his breath. O'Kelly motioned to him like he was going to move to the podium. Dan waved him off.

"What we don't understand frightens us. That won't change after today. But I know that, whether I understand or not, I can always help. It's that simple, and it's all we need to take away from this."

He stepped back from the podium. A groom in the back of the cafeteria slowly pounded his hands together. A few more joined in, and soon the room exploded with applause. It wasn't for Dan, though. These people, these witnesses needed to express themselves somehow, and clapping was the most primal release.

Dan joined them in the applause. He needed it, too.

Chapter 57

DAN MADE his way through the crowd of people, who were milling about following the service. It was what people did: milling around. The trauma of the past several days, mixed with the emotion of the moment, caused people to freeze up. They would stay this way until something jarred their system, and then they would go back to their lives. But for now, they milled about.

He wanted to get over to Jake's barn so he could be alone.

His path intersected with Romeo. "Heard they're looking at you for AJ?"

Romeo nodded, trying to regain some of the toughness lost through the tears.

"Call me," Dan said, handing him a business card.

Romeo studied the lawyer's card. "Why? Why'd you help me?"

"Let me be straight about this. I don't like you. As a matter of fact, I'd like to repay the shot you gave AJ right here. But you didn't kill that boy. I'm likely the only guy with a legal degree within a hundred miles of this racetrack who can believe that."

"But you was friends with that kid. Wha—"

"Didn't you listen to a damn thing I just said up there?" Dan said, pointing over his shoulder to the podium.

"I'll—I'll think about it."

"You'll go down for assault. Hell, there were only about twenty thousand witnesses to that. You'll take that plea and whatever comes with it. But you got to worry about manslaughter. I'll help if you want. If you don't, that's fine, too." Dan turned and walked away.

An older woman in a bright red St. John's knit outfit reached out an arm toward him. "Dan? Do you have just a moment?"

Her hair was perfectly cropped as a blonde helmet, not a hair out of place. Streaks of mascara were the only things to disrupt an otherwise perfect picture of grace and composure. She held a wadded-up tissue under one eye to soak up a tear. A lanky, gray-haired man in a pin-striped blue suit accompanied her.

"I'm Madeline Kaine. AJ's mother. And this is—"

"Josh Kaine," Dan finished for her. He reached forward and shook the man's hand. Josh was the CEO of Kaine Enterprises, a Fortune 500 company in the retail industry. Dan had recently read a feature story on his acquisition of Bid-Mart in *Forbes* magazine.

"You're AJ's parents? I had no idea."

Madeline nodded. "Thank you for all you did for AJ. He told us about you when he would call. We were so glad he had someone to look out for him." She paused and swallowed hard. "A friend."

"I wish I could've done more. He was a nice young man, and I've never seen anyone with his level of care and skill around horses."

Josh put his arm around Madeline. "Dan, thank you. AJ had a difficult time making friends. He lived in a world of his own. Kids like AJ can become fixated on things. Some like trains or trucks—"

"Or horses," Dan added.

Josh nodded. "From the day he was born, he was all horses all the time. And as AJ learned more about them, it wasn't enough to read books or watch programs about horses. He had to be around real horses. All the time. I'm not proud of this, but AJ ran away from home several times. When we'd find him, he would always be with horses. He was happiest when he was around them."

"We had to do a lot of soul-searching and research. So, Madeline and I decided we had to do something, both for AJ and for our sanity. Dick Latimer is Madeline's cousin. We agreed to let him work for Latimer. We wanted to set AJ up with an apartment, but he wouldn't leave the barn. So we did what we could to make sure he was safe and in a somewhat controlled environment, where he could be with horses."

Madeline pushed the Kleenex under one eye and said, "We finally realized we had to let him do what he wanted, not what we wanted." She sniffed and put the Kleenex under the other eye. "He had to call us every day, and we checked in with Dick a couple of times per week," Madeline said. "Always made sure he had what he needed. I was so scared at first. Neither of us knows anything about horses or horse racing. And to send AJ off—" She extended her arms and looked around the cafeteria. "Into God knows what. I was a nervous wreck. But he called every day. That's one of the things about AJ; his routines didn't vary. I'm just glad that calling his parents was one of his habits. I think I would have gone crazy otherwise."

"AJ didn't have many friends," Josh said. Dan could see this was hard for Josh to talk about. He was starting to choke up. Dan needed to interrupt him.

"Mr. Kaine, I was proud to have been his friend. I wish I could've spent more time with him. Gotten to know him better," he said.

Josh cleared his throat and gathered himself. "Please, call me Josh. We were so excited when AJ told us about you. Of course, we had to have you checked out. I hope you understand. Dick said you were an all right guy. Not one to take advantage of AJ or get him into trouble. And I appreciate your efforts to help him when the police took him in."

"Not sure what I said, but we got him out on his own recognizance," Dan said. "Honestly, I couldn't explain why they changed their mind so quickly."

"I admire your candor. Probably had something to do with me being a close friend of the governor," Josh said. Dan thought his persuasive argument had carried the day. Turns out it was a phone call to the governor from Josh Kaine.

"Dan, I understand you're in private practice here in Virginia. I had our general counsel check out your practice and experience. Occasionally, we have a need for local counsel in Virginia. If it's okay, I'd like to have our GC set you up on our preferred list for legal services. No guarantees—but, Lord knows, we always seem to have plenty of work for our outside counsel." He smiled and handed him a business card.

"Thank you, sir. I'd love to help out any way I can."

Madeline reached forward and hugged Dan. It was like she didn't want to let go—like Dan was her last connection with AJ. "Thank you," she whispered. Then the tears came again.

They started to move away. "Mr. and Mrs. Kaine? I have one other thing I want to ask you. His name? Ananias Jacob. Where did that come from? Is it a family name?"

Madeline brushed away some tears and said, "We had always planned to name him AJ. Actually, it was going to be Andrew Jacob. He was born six weeks premature. He was sick and weak. We went through all the grief stages while he was in the neonatal intensive care unit."

She paused and seemed to reflect. "We had kind of an awakening. He was such a fighter. He wanted to live despite his size and the odds against him. Watching him struggle inspired us. He opened our eyes to what life was all about. I mentioned that phrase to our minister, and he shared the story of Ananias from the Bible, and we thought it fit. So he became Ananias Jacob."

"I'm sorry," Dan said. "Uhm, how does that tie in with the biblical story of Ananias and Sapphira? I don't get it."

"Oh, not that Ananias," she said. "The other Ananias.

"The other Ananias? What do you mean?"

"There are two Ananiases in the bible. The one you mention—but also Ananias of Damascus. Totally different people. Our Ananias was the one who touched Paul and helped him see." Dan gave her a puzzled look. She continued, "God asked Ananias to touch Paul and cure his blindness.

Whether that was allegorical or physical, who knows? But after Ananias touched him, it changed Paul's life." She took a deep breath and held it for half a second. "AJ changed our life. He changed the way we saw the world, so it made sense to us. He was our Ananias." Then the tears came freely.

Josh patted Dan on the shoulder, and they walked away. Dan simply stared as they moved through the thinning crowd.

Chapter 58

D AN WALKED the mezzanine inside the grandstand. It was an hour to the first post, and only the true die-hard handicappers were present. Of course, he spotted Lennie down below in his box, scribbling and examining his computer sheets. Dan stopped by the nearest vendor and ordered two large black coffees. He slowly descended the steps and handed one of the coffees to Lennie. He nodded and accepted it. Dan sat down and pulled the lid off the steaming liquid and stared out into the infield.

"Wasn't your fault," Lennie said. "Wasn't anything you could do."

"I don't know about that."

"Dan, if it wasn't this Saturday, it would have been another time when you weren't around. You couldn't protect him from himself."

"Protect him from himself? He had a gift. He shouldn't need to be protected from himself."

"That's the nature of the world, Dan-o. We all need to be protected from ourselves, but in the end, we're on our own, and the decisions we make are sometimes disastrous. That's the world we live in. Friends help friends, spouses help spouses, sometimes strangers even help strangers, but in the end we're on our own. We can't always be protected from ourselves. And you can't blame yourself for that. You didn't make the rules."

Dan blew on the coffee and took a sip. Neither said a word for a long time. The steam from the java swirled upward into Dan's eyes as he hunched forward, holding the cup with his hands between his knees.

Dan couldn't help himself. He thought of AJ.

He had a gift so big—why a life so short?

Dan couldn't change anything. He was sad, angry, depressed, and, maybe worst of all, just missed the kid. There was his simple innocence and his laser-like focus to serve these four-legged athletes. He didn't deserve this. He was taken while trying to relieve an animal from pain. It was a sacrifice he didn't have to make but at the same time one he was compelled to make. *Did he know it would kill him? Was that what he wanted?*

Dan could sense Lennie wasn't studying his sheets. He was looking at him. Finally, Dan turned his head and said, "I'm okay."

"Yes, you are, my friend."

"I just don't understand it."

"Well, join the club." Lennie stacked some pages on his lap and turned to Dan. "Thomas Edison was one of the brightest inventors in our nation's history. Hell, the world's history, for that matter. You know what he said, don't you?"

Dan looked at him, not saying anything. He knew Lennie would continue.

"He said, we don't understand one millionth of one percent about anything."

Dan smiled.

"And Dan-o, he was a smart guy, so if that's the way he looked at the world, what chance do you and I have?"

"Still bothers me."

"Means you're human," said Lennie. "And last time I checked that was a good thing."

They both sipped coffee and watched the grandstand start to fill.

"You like anyone today?" Dan said finally.

"Whaddaya think? I just come out here for my health? I like Gilbert's horse in the third. Our boy TP's got a shot with Emilio in the sixth. Should be at good odds, and the feature's got a vulnerable heavy favorite. It's a beautiful world. You know what else?"

"What?"

He stabbed Dan's shoulder with his index finger. "My best friend has an undefeated stakes-winning filly. You going to the Breeders' Cup?"

"I doubt it. She's eligible under the 'win and you're in,' but Jake wants to try her at a distance against softer company. Maybe Florida before the end of the year.

"The way she came back after being passed at the head of the stretch. That's special, my friend. Can't teach that. And she'll get a distance of ground. Bred to. Her daddy nearly wired the best three-year-olds in the country at a mile and a quarter. Little race run on the first Saturday in May—maybe you've heard of it. Momma broke her maiden in a route race. Oh, she'll get a distance of ground all right. Lots of money to be made with a good three-year-old filly. I smell Kentucky Oaks." He referred to the filly version of the Kentucky Derby, run the day before the Derby each year.

334 ♦ STEVE O'BRIEN

"But knowing your horse could be in the Breeders' Cup and passing. Wow, that takes nerves."

"Much as I'd love to, Jake's job is to make sure we do the best thing for the animal." Dan chuckled. "I guess he's supposed to protect the horse from my ego."

Dan looked up the racetrack. A line of grooms slowly walked horses from the backside toward the paddock for the first race.

Milt slapped him on the back as he slid past into the front row seats of the box. "Gonna roll 'em today, boys. I can just feel it."

Lennie didn't bother to look up from his sheets. He deadpanned, "I'll make sure they have plenty of large bills, so you don't hurt your back carrying home fives and tens, Milt."

"I'd appreciate it, Lennie. I would appreciate it."

With a hand on his forehead to shield the sun, Dan squinted hard as the line of horses approached. In his heart he searched for AJ. He strained to see that distinctive limp. Of course, he wasn't there. He never would be.

Dan would never get over the loss of Ananias Jacob Kaine. And right now, even though it hurt, he was okay with that.

Ten horses in single file, heads down as they lumbered along the track's outside railing. In a few short minutes they would run with all their hearts, bursting with adrenaline, striving to get to the wire.

Each appeared contemplative, like a solitary boxer in a deserted training room minutes before a championship bout.

Only one could win.

The rest went home defeated. That was the game. That was the life.

They existed simply and humbly. They waited for that one second. For that moment when they broke into the clear down the home stretch, and no one was going to catch them.

They lived for that one chance—the chance to get home first.

THE END

Author's Note

THERE IS no racetrack in Northern Virginia, but there should be. Fairfax Park is an imaginary combination of racetracks and backsides I have had the privilege to visit. Primary among them is Ak-sar-ben Racetrack in Omaha, Nebraska. It is gone now, a victim of fierce competition for wagering dollars. I hated to see it go, but it lives on in my fondest memories. Those were simple days. All we had to do was pick the winner, and they'd actually give us money for that.

I have taken certain literary liberties with Aly Dancer's preparation and training. Getting these athletes to peak performance takes time, care, and patience. When done right, it is a triumph of man and animal. Any errors or inconsistencies in protocols or procedures are solely mine. Hey, it's a novel.

Finally, some may feel that AJ's ability to communicate with horses is too extreme to be believable. Horse whispering was once thought to be an exaggeration also. Medical research has established that a small percentage of those afflicted with conditions on the autism spectrum have qualities of intellect that stagger the mind. AJ's condition is of my own making, but I refer you to studies of synesthesia, the theory of multiple intelligences, and research on brain-wave entrainment, particularly between autistic children and dolphins. Extreme? Perhaps. Impossible? Who's to say? It may well be too early to tell.

I have always believed that what God takes way in one dimension, he repays with gusto in another. The only question is can we, as simple humans, comprehend and appreciate where God has doubled down.

We all have a gift.

Life's challenge is to discover it, nurture it, and best of all, enjoy it.

Acknowledgements

FIRST AND foremost, I thank Becky who makes my world complete. So many people have provided encouragement for my writing. If I listed them all, it would double the length of the book. You know how much I value your support. My deepest appreciation to Mike Garrett for editorial direction and advice, to Dr. Noon Kampani, for insight and assistance with medical issues, to my favorite law enforcement personnel, P.B. and B.C., for help with protocols and procedures, to my single strongest advocate as a writer, Billie Caredis, to Don and Susan DeCarlo for the laughs, the friendship, and a great name for the protagonist's love interest, to Harrison for tirelessly working to keep me humble, and to the McLean Mafia, for…well, because I have to.

Finally, to Our Buckwheat, Darla's Charge, Pray, Oscar, and Fly Girl. You'll never know how you made my heart sing.

Recognition for

Elijah's Coin

By Steve O'Brien

BOOK OF THE YEAR, FICTION
Books and Authors

WINNER, NOVELLA
Next Generation Indie Book Awards

WINNER, TEEN-YOUNG ADULT FICTION
Reader Views Literary Awards

WINNER, FICTION AND LITERATURE, YOUNG ADULT FICTION
National Best Book Awards

SILVER MEDALIST, AUDIO BOOK AND SPOKEN WORD
Nautilus Book Awards

SILVER MEDALIST, MEN'S FICTION
Living Now Book Awards

SILVER MEDALIST, MID-ATLANTIC BEST REGIONAL FICTION
Independent Publisher Book Awards

FINALIST, BEST NEW FICTION
National Indie Excellence Awards

FINALIST, AUDIO BOOK OF THE YEAR
ForeWord magazine

Also by A&N Publishing

ELIJAH'S COIN

By
Steve O'Brien

So I chided the old man
'bout the truth that I had heard.
He just smiled and said—
"Reality is only just a word."

—Harry Chapin, "Corey's Coming"

Chapter 1

ONE HOUR from now I am going to change my life forever.

I am lying on my back with my fingers intertwined behind my head. I wait.

One hour from now I am going to be in charge of my life.

I glance to my left and my digital clock clicks from 12:59 to 1:00 A.M. I smile.

One hour from now I am going to do something I've never done before.

I'm going to take what I want, when I want it. I'm going to enrich myself. I'm going to set myself on the path to instant riches. The future will be mine. I will be in control.

You see, one hour from now I will be a criminal.

I am not one of those down-on-my-luck, need-a-break career criminals. No, I am more of a freelancer or hobbyist criminal. I'm a college freshman at Tech in Blacksburg, Virginia, with no real need to commit crimes. It is very simple: I am doing this because I can. That's the only reason I need.

On the way to my prospective crime scene, I am dressed all in black. It is kind of an "in" thing for us criminal types. Adrenaline is surging through me as I contemplate going through with this or not. When the time comes, will I do it? Will I chicken out? I'm sure all criminals go through this self-doubt just before their first big job.

I had "cased the joint" as they say. I had done my home-work. Cashion's Sporting Goods was going to be my first mark. It was about a mile and a half from my dorm, so about fifteen minutes by bike. No need to take my car as the bike will give me more options and be easier to hide. The drive-thru bank on the corner will be the perfect spot to stash my bike during the break-in. I had been in the store and viewed the exits. I had been outside during the day and at night. I knew how to get in and how to get out and, most impor-tantly, there were no dogs, no watchmen, and no alarms.

I am on this mission alone. Come to think of it, every-thing I've done the last few years of my life has been alone. I'm not much of a joiner. For the most part, I've learned if you trust someone you'll be disappointed. Anything I do, I do by myself. Anything I want, I get for myself. I'm my own rock. I can count on me; I can't count on anyone else.

My dad called my cell phone earlier in the evening. I let the phone ring. He didn't leave a message. He was finally getting the point.

Being away at college was the break I needed. Class-es were mostly lame, filled with freshman overachievers. Many were so avid to make an impression on professors that it was embarrassing to watch. Some were actually pret-ty smart; others should avoid the expense and just move home to work in gas stations and beauty parlors. Home-work was easy. Much of the assigned work was easier than high school. Humanities and writing? Boring. Accounting? Nearly indecipherable as the TA was Japanese or Chinese or something like that. Calculus? A re-run of senior year.

The only course that held my attention at all was something called "The Theory of Knowledge." It was taught by an aged elf of a man named Dr. Summerlin. He started teaching here about the time the Appalachian Mountains were forming. The class was more about logic, thought, and debate than the title let on. He would state a problem. Half the class would write a short article to defend the stated position; the other half would attack the position. His classes were less like lectures and more like Socratic discussions. He would never answer a question or give evidence that he supported any particular opinion; he would only pose more questions.

Many of the "sheep freshmen" in my class were terrified. There was no textbook; there were only assigned readings, sometimes an op-ed piece in *The New York Times*, sometimes an article in the latest *Rolling Stone*. You couldn't really take notes because it was a meandering conversation, not a lecture. One of the more courageous sheep asked how the class was going to be graded and whether there was a final exam or a term paper. Dr. Summerlin only smiled and said, "I will grade you on what you learn and how you apply yourself. This is 'The Theory of Knowledge,' not some mundane collection of facts that you can memorize and spew back on a test. This class is about learning to learn and understanding to understand." About a quarter of the class bailed after that little announcement and dropped the class in favor of art appreciation or geography or some other "safe A."

I really didn't care what grade I got from him. I enjoyed the way he thought and the way he could move a discussion. He would listen to one student ardently defending a position and with a wave of his hand ask a question that so stumped and repudiated the advocate that it left others breathless. It was never done in an intimidating or threatening fashion. The counter was quick, efficient, and intellectually deadly. It was like a jujitsu move on a street thug. It was over before the thug knew what had happened, and there was no reason to think it would go differently if repeated. He would also praise original thought. In an odd way I think he enjoyed being surprised by random ideas and probing and pondering the extension of the ideas. This wasn't a class with a lesson plan or a series of tidy lectures. It was free-form intelligence flowing through the room. Were it not for Dr. Summerlin's class, I could have skipped the whole semester and never left my dorm room.

Speaking of my dorm room, I'm more than happy to have it to myself. It took me about six weeks to get my assigned roommate to move out. He was a nice enough guy, but I chose not to talk to him. Ever. I think it kind of freaked him out. I ignored him totally. He tried to build a relationship with me, even invited other guys on the floor to our room to try to get me to open up, but I would have none of it. I had my world; he had his. They didn't need to intersect.

Eventually he couldn't take it anymore. He went to the resident assistant and asked to be moved. The resident assistant asked me about our relationship, and I told him I thought there was something wrong with the guy. The guy was obviously laboring under some form of latent "attachment issues." Moving him might be a good thing. The next day my roommate was moved to another floor. I think his name was Brandon or Brent—something like that. Doesn't matter. It works out much better this way. I don't need people asking me questions about classes, and I certainly don't need someone nosing into what I will bring home from my burglaries. No, alone is the way I want it.

It hadn't always been like this. Only since two years ago—September 28. My life had been a picture of normalcy. Junior year—on the varsity football team, not a starter, but, heck, I had a jersey with my name on it. Girlfriend—not the most attractive girl in school mind you, but she was smart, athletic, and well-liked. Classes were easy. College visits were on the horizon.

All that ended September 28. Coming home that crisp and clean fall evening, I coasted my bike up the driveway, slid to a stop, and headed toward the back door, like I'd done a thousand times before.

The back door was open, which was odd. That became a minor detail as I entered the kitchen. I knew something was wrong immediately. No sound. It was like entering a mausoleum. Then I knew instantly. We had been robbed. Everything disheveled in a random grope for valuables. It was hard to avoid the blood splatter in the hallway. I raced to the living room and found my mother curled into a ball on the floor. I guess the shape your body makes when it is resigned to death. A pool of blood surrounded her head. One arm was extended as if she were reaching out for something. Then I spotted it. Her arm was stretched out because the killer had stolen the wedding ring off her finger. I started to gag and raced to the kitchen, where the remains of my lunch hit the sink and counter.

A madman dialed 911 and screamed into the phone. Then I realized it was me. It took six minutes for the unit to respond. It seemed like seven years.

She wasn't breathing. Her skin was cold and clammy. What should I have done? Hug her? Move her? Stay inside? I paced the floor. Where were they? It had been four seconds since I had hung up the phone.

I don't remember crying. I'm sure I did. I know I did later. Doctors called it shock or traumatic stress disorder. I don't care what it is; I just want to know when it ends.

The Washington Post called it a brutal killing. When you're seventeen, and it involves the murder of your mother in your own home, is there another kind?

Blunt force trauma, the ME said. "Probably been dead since early afternoon." Signs of B and E the policeman said.

My dad drove up. No one had to say a word. He collapsed on the front porch. The sight of that probably hurt me the most. He would never recover.

They say only children grow up fast. Only children whose mothers are killed in their homes on September 28 become adults instantly. Innocence, trust, kindness, and love are all stripped away and crushed under foot. You go from a devil-may-care adolescent to a hollow, emotionless human in a series of rapid heartbeats.

Never found the killer. Never found the ring or anything else for that matter. Never made an arrest. Why is it that the perfect crime is the one involving the murder of my mother on September 28?

People pulled back from me at that point, or maybe I pulled away from them. No more sports. Former friends didn't know what to say or how to deal with this. They started avoiding me in the hallway. Who could blame them?

No girlfriend. She tried to weather it, but I couldn't talk. It was a one-way relationship with her. She finally gave up. Who could blame her?

Dad starting drinking heavily. We had nothing to talk about. We sold the home and moved into a two-bedroom apartment. Grades slipped. Visions of UVA or Ivy League educations turned sour. I was lucky that Tech took a chance on me. One of my dad's friends pulled some strings, told them the story, and somehow got me an acceptance letter.

I couldn't wait to move away to college. Not like the others who wanted the freedom, the partying, and the new life. I wanted to go away just so I could be alone. So people wouldn't stare at me with sad eyes or shake their heads like "damn shame." I just wanted to be anonymous. I wanted to disappear. So I didn't have to talk to anyone, especially my dad. We hadn't actually spoken in months. Who could blame us?

Maybe I'm bitter, maybe depressed, but I'm going to take what I want. Like the burglar who killed my mom in the process of stealing our stuff, I'm going to take what I want. I don't want pity; I just want people to leave me alone. Who could blame me?

About the Author

STEVE O'BRIEN is an attorney, author, and former thoroughbred owner. *Bullet Work* is his second novel. It follows the critically acclaimed *Elijah's Coin*, recipient of nine literary awards, including Best Young Adult Fiction, National Best Books Awards, and Best Novella, Next Generation Indie Book Awards. He lives in Washington, D.C.

Give the Gift of
BULLET WORK
to Your Friends and Colleagues

CHECK YOUR LEADING BOOKSTORE OR ORDER HERE

❑ **YES**, I want _____ copies of *Bullet Work* at $14.95 each, plus $4.95 shipping per book (District of Columbia residents please add $.89 sales tax per book).

❑ **YES**, I want _____ copies of *Elijah's Coin* at $21.95 each, plus $4.95 shipping per book (District of Columbia residents please add $1.32 sales tax per book).

Canadian orders must be accompanied by a postal money order in U.S. funds. Allow 15 days for delivery.

❑ **YES**, I am interested in having Steve O'Brien speak or give a seminar to my company, association, school, or organization. Please send information.

My check or money order for $_____ is enclosed.

Please charge my: ❑ Visa   ❑ MasterCard
                    ❑ Discover ❑ American Express

Name_____

Organization _____

Address _____

City/State/Zip _____

Phone_____Email_____

Card # _____

Security Code: _____Exp. Date_____ Signature_____

Please make your check payable and return to:
A & N Publishing
3150 South Street, NW Suite 2F • Washington, D.C. 20007

Call your credit card order to: 202-329-1412
www.AandNpublishing.com